ALSO BY TALIA HIBBERT

RAVENSWOOD

A Girl Like Her

Damaged Goods, a bonus novella

Untouchable

That Kind of Guy

THE BROWN SISTERS

Get a Life, Chloe Brown

Take a Hint, Dani Brown

Act Your Age, Eve Brown

JUST FOR HIM

Bad for the Boss

Undone by the Ex-Con

Sweet on the Greek

STANDALONE TITLES

Work for It

Guarding Temptation

Wrapped Up in You

Merry Inkmas

D1286802

THE PRINCESS TRAP

A ROYAL ROMANCE

TALIA HIBBERT

NIXON HOUSE

COPYRIGHT

THE PRINCESS TRAP: TALIA HIBBERT

CONTENT NOTE

Please be aware: This story contains scenes of domestic abuse that could trigger certain audiences.

To the princess-lovers who hoped for more than a frog.
No shade. But shade.

CHAPTER ONE

C herry Neita was not the type of woman to voluntarily use stairs.

As far as she was concerned, they were inconvenient, inappropriate, and a public nuisance. Unless she was firmly strapped into a sports bra, with a bottle of Lucozade in hand, Cherry avoided physical exertion like the plague.

Which was why she had perfected the art of pushing into the queue for the lift. And her colleagues here at the Academy made it so *easy*. Bless them.

"Excuse me, gentlemen, thank you!" Cherry wiggled her way through the gaggle of men loitering in front of the building's single lift.

Why the Academy's senior leadership team was housed with the lowly administrative staff—and *why* the tower they all shared had only one lift—Cherry didn't know. She avoided wondering about it, too, because poor organisation made her skin crawl. Honestly, if they'd only consulted her during the bloody planning stages...

"Morning, Cherry, darling," beamed Jeff, the Academy's rosy-cheeked Head of Key Stage 4. For a man who spent so much time working with teenagers, he was always remarkably cheerful. Cherry had to admire his fortitude.

"Morning, Jeff. How's—?" Her response was interrupted by a disgruntled muttering from somewhere behind her. Cherry turned to find Mike Cousins, Head of Geography, giving her a dark look. The sort of look that said, *I've been waiting here for ages. How did* she *get to the front of the queue?*

It was the arse-crack of bloody morning, so Cherry's mood was not the best. But cussing someone out at work for having the audacity to *look* at her would be a trifle unreasonable, so she collected the threads of her patience with great effort, and dragged her lips up from a demure smile to a full-on, charming grin. Mike blinked under the force of her dimples, then smiled back, all annoyance forgotten.

The men in this place responded to a pretty face like babies to a bottle. And she was supposed to respect them.

Sigh.

Turning back to Jeff, Cherry continued. "How's Sandra and the kids?"

"Not bad, not bad." The lift arrived with a *ding*, and Jeff stepped aside to let her walk in first. What a gentleman. "Little one's teething," he went on, "but otherwise well."

"Wonderful!"

A handful of staff members forced themselves into the lift behind Jeff and Cherry. They faced front like good little soldiers. Cherry, unembarrassed, studied her reflection in the lift's mirrored back wall. Life was too short to pretend you didn't want to check your lipstick.

"And how are you, Cherry?"

"Oh, you know." She fluffed at her hair, as though the mass of dark coils weren't springy enough already. "Same as usual."

Ding.

"Well!" Cherry turned away from her reflection with a smile. Just a small one, no dimples. She tried not to unleash them in enclosed spaces. "I'll see you later, Jeff."

"Cheerio, love." He smiled back, genuine as always. Jeff was probably the only senior member of staff who didn't make her want to be sick. He was sweet, he was honest, and he cared about the kids, so Cherry always had a kind word for him.

The rest of them could get fucked.

She stepped out of the lift and into the safety of the admin floor with relief. It was the only place at Rosewood Academy that felt like something other than a greedy, corporate pipeline.

See, once upon a time, Rosewood had been an actual school. Until a mate of the Prime Minister's with a background in private education had taken over and 'academised'—AKA *monetised*—the place. Now the kids were pumped through the system like battery hens, and woe betide anyone who fell below industry standard.

Cherry wound her way through the rows of desks and occasional offices that filled the floor, greeting colleagues as she went. She didn't bother with exaggerated wiggles and dimpled smiles up here. No-one was silly enough to fall for it, or dangerous enough to warrant her Darling Doll performance, anyway. She reached the HR office and paused, reading the sign blu-tacked to the door with a frown.

CHERRY NEITA, KEEP OUT!

With a shrug, she swept into the room.

"Oh! Cherry! What are you doing here?" Inside the office, two women huddled protectively around Cherry's desk. She struggled to place them. They were in finance, she thought... and the little, dark-haired one *might* be called Julie.

3

The taller of the two women looked at Cherry as if she were a rampaging bull. "Didn't you see the sign?"

"No," Cherry said blithely. "What are you doing at my desk, girls?"

Across the room, seated neatly at her own desk, Rose McCall snorted. She raised one pale, wrinkled hand to her spectacles, peering at Cherry over their half-moon lenses. "What do you *think*, darling?"

Cherry held back a sigh. It took great effort, but she managed.

"Sorry, Cherry," the tall one wheedled. "It's just that Julie and I were talking, and she—"

Cherry held up a hand. "You don't have to explain. Have I ruined the surprise?"

"A little bit," Julie admitted. "I don't know *how* you missed the sign."

"It's a mystery for the ages," murmured Rose. Cherry gave the older woman *A Look.*

"Well, anyway," Julie said. She tried for a grin, but it looked more like a wince. "Surprise!" The pair sprang apart like show girls, waving their hands towards Cherry's desk. Or rather, towards the monstrous mess they'd made of it.

Her neat and tidy workspace was covered in glitter and confetti. In the centre of the desk sat a huge, ceramic number '30' in a screaming shade of pink. As if she didn't know precisely how old she was.

God, Cherry hated birthdays. They were so... unnecessary. All that attention, and none of it under her control.

"Oh, you two," she said, pasting a coy smile onto her face. "You shouldn't have."

"Really," Rose echoed. "You shouldn't have."

The woman was a bloody nuisance. A brilliant bloody nuisance, but a nuisance all the same.

Julie's hopeful face fell. "I know you hate a fuss, but—"

"No!" Cherry said firmly. "This is lovely. I very much appreciate it. I—" she broke off as she caught sight of a little box beside the ornament. "Is that *Hotel Chocolat*?"

"Yes!" Julie said proudly.

Rose sat up straight in her chair. "Where?" she demanded, squinting across the room.

"Never you mind." Cherry stepped forward and swept up the box with a smile. "Really, ladies, thank you so much. What a lucky girl I am."

The admin staff persisted in sucking up to her purely because Rose, the Head of HR and mistress of all she surveyed, was impossible to suck up to. Usually it was rather annoying, but in this case, Cherry couldn't pretend to mind. As the girls left, looking rather pleased with themselves, she ripped open her box of chocolates.

"Don't be greedy, love." Rose stood and sauntered over, her fluid movements as deceptive as her plump, rosy cheeks. Rose McCall was, Cherry knew, sixty-seven. She appeared no older than fifty, despite her lavender-grey chignon.

"Says you," Cherry mumbled, her mouth full. But she held out the box, and didn't even complain when Rose took two truffles at once.

"I *am* sorry," Rose said conspiratorially. She perched herself on the edge of Cherry's desk. "I had no idea they were going to surprise you. Truthfully, I didn't realise anyone knew your birthday."

"Facebook," Cherry said glumly.

"Oh, yes." Rose popped a truffle into her mouth. "Well, you know I don't hold with that nonsense myself."

"I don't know," Cherry mused. "It can be annoying. But there are a lot of cat videos."

Before Rose could reply, the door to their office burst open. *Again.* Really, all this human contact was a bit much for one morning.

It was Louise, one of the receptionists, all pink-cheeked and wide-eyed. "Rose!" she gasped. "Cherry! Oh, you won't believe what's happened!"

"Calm down," Rose frowned. "Are you alright?"

"No!" Louise shrieked. "I'm as likely to pass out as—" she broke off, her eyes narrowing. "Is that *Hotel Chocolat*?"

Cherry slapped the lid back onto the box. "All gone. Sorry."

"Bugger. Anyway, listen to this!"

Cherry listened. Rose listened. Louise paused dramatically.

"Come on, then," Rose finally snapped. She wasn't known for her patience.

Louise relented, her tone hushed. "There's a *man.*"

Cherry looked at Rose. Rose looked at Cherry. They might work in a school—sorry, *educational academy*—but men *did* appear from time to time. True, they tended to belong to senior management rather than, say, the admin team. But they were hardly a rare sighting.

"A *man*?" Rose prompted.

"Yes." Louise nodded like a bobble-head. "A *new* man. A visitor. And he's absolutely bloody gorgeous."

Cherry leaned forward. "*Is* he, now?"

"His backside is unbelievable," Louise breathed. Her voice was reverent. Her eyes were slightly unfocused. Cherry's interest was most firmly piqued.

"And who is this man?" Rose demanded. "What's he doing here?"

Louise hesitated.

"Oh, for Christ's sake. That's all the gossip you have?"

"I'm afraid so, Rose. He's just come in, you see, and Chris fairly whisked him away…"

"Well," Rose sniffed. "You'd best get back to reception, before you miss anything else."

"You're right," the younger woman murmured, almost to herself. "He might come out again. There might be *more* of them!" She disappeared without bothering to say goodbye. As the door swung shut, Cherry wondered just *how* handsome this man could possibly be. Perhaps she could…

Don't even think about it. You're a sensible adult who does not make a fool of herself at work. You are a mature woman entering the prime of her life, not to be distracted by —

"Go and investigate, will you, darling?"

Cherry stood. "If you insist."

CHAPTER TWO

His Royal Highness Prince Magnus Ruben Ambjørn Octavian Gyldenstierne of Helgmøre—widely known as Ruben—was trying his best not to look bored. After all, contrary to popular belief, he did have *some* manners.

But he was almost certainly failing.

Still, he supposed it didn't really matter. Chris Tabary, the source of Ruben's current boredom, was so far up his own arse that he probably wouldn't notice if Ruben whipped off his trousers and threw them out the bloody window.

"After lunch," the older man droned, "we'll begin touring the new build—soon to be the *elite* branch of the Academy, for our particularly promising pupils…"

Ruben's mind, which had been in the middle of deciding how soon was too soon to leave, pounced on the word *elite* like a cat with a mouse.

"What does that mean?" he demanded, leaning forward. He could almost feel the eyes of his close guard and best friend, Hans, boring into the back of his head. Could almost hear the other man's voice: *Don't let your mouth run away with you. Again.*

Clearing his throat, Ruben attempted to sound polite. "I mean—when you say 'elite', you are referring to...?"

Tabary blinked. Clearly, he was not used to being interrupted. But he collected himself in record time, clasping his slender hands together and offering what he probably thought of as a charming smile. It was a little too wide, a little too plastic, and showed far too many teeth.

"By 'elite', Your Highness—"

Ruben sighed. "Please. No titles. I assume Demetria sent you the materials?" It was a rhetorical question. Demetria *always* sent the materials.

"Ah, yes." Tabary appeared slightly unsettled by his mistake. He winced a little, his smile wavering before he dragged it back into place. "My apologies. I should say, *Mr. Ambjørn*. Here at the Academy, we pay special attention to those students identified as elite via our stratified testing system. Students are monitored throughout the term, and tested once per year—"

"Aside from the national tests, you mean?"

"Precisely. Every September, we undertake school-wide testing to ensure that our most elite intellectuals are separated from the other students."

Ruben's alarm bells were not simply ringing; they were screaming. "By testing," he said carefully, "you refer to... ah... examination? In a room?" At Tabary's slight frown, he added, "My English. You understand."

Ruben's English was perfect, courtesy of three years studying at the University of Edinburgh. But surely he must be misunderstanding here? Surely Tabary did not insist on extra testing just to create some kind of intelligence-based class system in his school?

Tabary offered a benevolent smile. "Well, yes, examinations. The students are taken into a room and asked to complete a question

9

paper in silence. Then we mark the papers... *et voila!*" He chuckled.

Ruben nodded along politely. Mentally, he was planning the easiest way to extract himself from this situation.

Rosewood Academy was *not* an appropriate contender for the scholarship programme he planned to create. Excessive testing was something Ruben disapproved of anyway, but sending the children that his Trust catered to—children of disadvantaged backgrounds and unique needs—to a school that openly referred to better-testing students as *elite*...

Demetria would be so smug when she found out about this. Hadn't she told him to stop accepting applicants based on nothing but social networking?

Shifting in his seat, Ruben turned to catch his bodyguard's eye. Hans stood, as always, by the door, looking dour and dangerous as ever. Ruben would give the signal, and Hans would think up some sort of excuse—

The sound of voices floated in through Tabary's office door. It was muffled, but still clear enough to distract Ruben from his plan.

"Oh! Hello..." The voice softened, trailing off into a low murmur that he couldn't quite catch. Then came another voice in response, much lower than the first. *That* was one of his guards. Who were they talking to?

"Are you alright, Mr. Ambjørn?"

Ruben turned back towards Tabary, and found the man looking at him with a frown.

"Yes, yes," Ruben said. "Just... thought I heard something."

"Oh, there's often a racket along these corridors." Tabary waved a hand. "We share the tower with the administrative staff. They roam around clucking like hens, bless them. Our girls love a gossip."

Ruben's brows shot up. *Our girls love a gossip?* The patronising little shit.

Fuck manners. He was leaving.

But, before he could make a move, there came a sharp knock at the door. He had just enough time to wonder if there was some emergency—hadn't Tabary asked not to be disturbed?—before the door opened and a hurricane swept inside.

"Chris, darling!" She tottered in on high-heels, closing the door behind her with a bump of her hips. And good Lord, what hips. "I'm *so* sorry to disturb you, but this absolutely couldn't wait."

The hurricane was a woman. A woman with laughing eyes and a heart-shaped face and a figure that could kill a man. A woman whose dark, springy curls gleamed like midnight, who had incongruously chubby cheeks and brown-sugar skin.

She sailed past Hans as if he wasn't even there, and Ruben wondered what had happened to the men stationed outside. Then he watched her hips sway as she walked, and decided they'd probably passed out at the sight of her.

"Cherry," Tabary said, frowning at her. Ruben wondered why he was calling her Cherry—a pet name?—and why he was frowning at the most beautiful woman on earth. Had the man no fucking sense? "This is a very important meeting," Tabary continued.

"Oh, I'm *so* sorry," the woman said, her tone dripping with apology. But Ruben had the strangest impression that she wasn't sorry at all. Then, for the first time since she'd come in, her eyes flitted over to his.

And he realised that *beautiful* was an understatement.

Her face was almost unnaturally perfect. For one disturbing moment he was reminded of his sister—but Sophronia's beauty was cold. So fucking cold.

This woman might burst into flame at any moment.

She slapped a stack of papers on Tabary's desk and bent at the waist, leaning over his shoulder as she pointed at something on the first page. Her cleavage, already magnificent, swelled against the neckline of her dress. Ruben reminded himself to keep breathing.

"If you could just have a look at this," she said, her voice soft. "I can't quite get a handle on it…"

Tabary's frown disappeared, and he gave the woman a look of affection. That look made Ruben's fists clench, made him grind his teeth—which was both ridiculous and inevitable. He may not know this woman, but something about her triggered a single, disturbing thought.

I have to have her.

Confusing. Surprising. He'd seen plenty of beautiful people in his time, and he'd never reacted like this. But Ruben wasn't in the habit of ignoring his instincts.

"Oh, Cherry," Tabary tutted. "Silly girl. Look here; you've mucked up the sums. That's all."

The woman put her fingers to her lips. No—she brought them to hover just over her lips, which were painted scarlet. Her eyes widened like a doe's as she gasped. "Oh, Chris! You're right. What am I like?"

Tabary rolled his eyes dramatically, a grin bursting across his narrow face. The kind of grin that weak men released when offered the chance to correct a supposedly stupid woman. His annoyance forgotten, he handed the papers back with a fond smile. "Off you go, Cherry, dear. I *am* in the middle of something."

The woman straightened up, clutching the papers to her chest. Her eyes settled on Ruben with exaggerated surprise, as if she'd only just noticed his presence. And he knew instantly that she'd orchestrated this entire thing.

"Oh, gosh," she said. "How rude of me." And then, skirting around Tabary's desk, she stepped right up to him, held out a hand, and said: "Cherry Neita."

Cherry. Her *name* was Cherry.

Ruben stood and took her hand in his. Her skin was warm and soft, her fingers tipped with the most outrageous nails—long and pink and glittery, all studded with gems. Ridiculous. He adored them. Bowing over her hand, Ruben pressed the ghost of a kiss to her knuckles.

Then Hans, the fucker, cleared his throat. Loudly.

Oh. Right. Kissing women's hands wasn't the best way to *blend in.*

Trying not to wince, Ruben straightened up and gave her his handsomest smile. Prince Charming he was not—as the press loved to remind him—but for this woman, he'd do his best.

"Ruben Ambjørn," he replied. It wasn't a lie, he told himself. Not technically.

"Lovely to meet you," she murmured. And for a moment, her voice dipped from the light, airy tone she'd used with Chris to something low and earthy that suited her far better. Then she looked down at their hands, arching a brow—and he realised that he was still clutching her fingers like a lost child.

He should probably let go.

No, his newly animalistic mind whispered. *Never let her go.*

Hm. His mind was starting to sound like a stalker.

Ruben released her, trying not to make his reluctance obvious. "What is it you do here, Ms. Neita?" He imagined she'd make an excellent teacher. Her class wouldn't know what'd hit them.

But God, if he'd ever had a tutor like her…

"I'm in HR," she said, shattering his fantasies. "And I really should get back upstairs. *So* sorry to intrude." She turned to Tabary and flashed him a smile, wider this time—and Jesus fucking Christ, she had *dimples*. That simply wasn't fair. "See you later, Chris!"

With that, she disappeared, hips swaying beneath her tight skirt. The door swung shut behind her, and the office descended into a dazed sort of silence.

Cherry fucking Neita. Fancy that.

CHAPTER THREE

C herry wound her way through the clusters of teachers filling the staffroom, sticking to their cliques as firmly as the kids out in the playground. She found Rose waiting in prime position, of course, at the table right by the toaster. Beside her were Beth and Jasleen. It would be a full interrogation, then.

Cherry settled down into the last empty seat and gave them her breeziest smile. "Lunch already! Time flies."

At least, it does when you're loitering about the I.T. Department so you don't have to go back to your own floor.

Rose's only reply was an arched brow. Jas snorted, and Beth leant over the table, cradling her mug in both hands. "Don't be coy. Where've you been all morning? You've *seen* him, haven't you?"

Cherry met Rose's eye across the table. "I don't know what you mean."

"Spill the beans. Don't keep him all to yourself, you slut."

Cherry faked a gasp. "You're one to talk, Elizabeth Briggs. Weren't you caught with that mousy mathematics teacher at the Christmas party—"

"Shut up!" Beth hissed.

"—in the reprographics room, on the *photocopier*, no less!"

Beth sniffed. "You must be mistaking me for someone else."

"You dickhead," Jasleen smirked. "It was me that caught you."

"Alright! Enough about me! Tell us about the man, will you?"

Cherry rolled her eyes. She pretended to hesitate. In fact, she didn't really have to pretend.

Ruben Ambjørn. He was foreign, from his accent—Scandinavian or something. Only he didn't *look* Scandinavian, like they did on TV. He wasn't all blonde-haired and blue-eyed.

But he *was* singularly gorgeous. And deliciously broad. Cherry liked large men. Especially large men with crooked smiles and lazy confidence and dark eyes and...

Rose snapped her fingers in front of Cherry's face. "Have we lost you, darling?"

"Oh, bugger off," Cherry said, but there was no heat in it. "I'm sure half the teachers must have seen him by now, anyway. I heard he was getting the grand tour."

"Maybe they have," said Jasleen. "But they'd rather die than tell *us* anything."

There was a strict hierarchy at the Academy, you see. Well—less a hierarchy, more a clear boundary. Teaching staff on one side, and everyone else—admin, I.T., finance, cleaners and groundskeepers —on the other.

Which Cherry didn't mind. Their side of the line was, after all, much more fun.

"Fine," she sighed, Clearly, she wasn't getting out of this one. "He's..."

Rose filled the gap. "Tall, dark and handsome?"

"Well, yeah," Cherry admitted. "That about sums it up. Oh, and—"

"Incredibly well-dressed?" Jas supplied.

"Ye-e-e-s," Cherry said. Usually, she and Rose were the only ones who cared about a man's dress sense. "And—"

"Kind of sexily intimidating?" Beth murmured.

"Christ, have you seen him already?"

"Cherry," said a familiar voice. It was deep, and it was smoky, and it was coming from right behind her.

Oh. *Oh.*

Moving slowly—she had to maintain *some* sort of dignity—Cherry turned in her seat to face Ruben Ambjørn.

He towered over their little group like a looming angel. He certainly had the bone structure for it—like one of those terribly beautiful statues. Greek, or French, or whatever. She should probably stop thinking about nonsense and say something, but her mind appeared to have latched on to his eyebrows. They were almost black—a shade darker than the stubble at his jaw. She wasn't one for facial hair, but—

Rose kicked her under the table.

Oh, yes. Talking.

"Mr. Ambjørn," she said, to hide the fact that she didn't know what *else* to say. Speechlessness wasn't something Cherry experienced. Ever. Yet here she was, flapping about like a fish.

It was his fault. He'd surprised her.

He had the grace to step in and save the conversation from collapse. "Could I steal you for a second? I have a small question, and I know you're just the woman to answer it."

"Oh! Of course." Cherry turned back to the table, grabbing her handbag. Then she stood as gracefully as she could, pointedly avoiding Rose's gaze—and Jasleen's smirk, and Beth's gawp. Really, the woman had half a sandwich in her gob.

The staffroom's ever-present chatter quietened down as Cherry followed Ruben out. She supposed they made a conspicuous couple. She was tall, very tall in her heels.

And he, unusually, was taller.

He led her out of the staffroom's double doors and into an abandoned side corridor, one that led to the loos. She should've been more preoccupied with the smell of industrial bleach than with the way he looked at her. But she wasn't.

Oh dear.

"Cherry," he said again, his voice soft. People tended to say her name a lot—as if they couldn't quite believe that it was really her name. Which, to be fair, they probably couldn't.

The corner of his lips kicked up in a lazy sort of smirk, the kind that was self-assured enough to speed up her pulse. Confidence was another thing that Cherry loved. Not that it mattered.

She cleared her throat and assumed her most professional voice— not the childish trill she'd put on for Chris that morning, but something closer to her usual self. "How can I help you, Mr. Ambjørn?"

His lips twisted, part amusement and part discomfort. "Ruben. Just call me Ruben."

I'd rather not. It gives me ideas. "Alright. Ruben."

He ran a hand through his hair, pushing the dark, wavy strands off of his face. They sprang back into place immediately. "Listen," he said slowly. "I don't want to make you uncomfortable. Feel free to tell me to go fuck myself…"

Fuck yourself? *That would be an awful waste.*

"But I was wondering if we could have lunch together?"

Cherry blinked. "You mean... you'd like company in the cafeteria?"

He licked his lips, gave her that little smile again. "I mean I'd like *your* company. Anywhere."

"Oh." Cherry wasn't usually this slow on the uptake. She blamed the breadth of his shoulders beneath his deep blue suit. Jas had been right. He *was* incredibly well-dressed.

But he'd look far better naked.

He was staring at her like there was nothing else in the room. Nothing else in the *world*. But she shouldn't be flattered. He was that kind of guy, probably—focused. She wondered if he'd kiss like that, with all that burning intensity. If he did, she might faint.

No, she wouldn't faint. She'd be too busy ripping his clothes off.

"I don't know," she said finally. "I am the Deputy Head of HR, you know."

He rolled his eyes. "Head of this, Deputy of that. This school is ridiculous."

"Academy," she corrected.

He smirked. "Ah, yes. How could I forget?" Then he reached out and captured her hand in his. Just like that. Cherry used casual touches herself, often—they worked psychological wonders, after all—but this?

His skin was warm and slightly rough, his hand dwarfing hers. He ran his thumb over the back of her knuckles, and a spark of electricity trailed from the point where they touched to the tips of her tightening nipples. With every stroke of his thumb, the current pulsed harder. Fuck.

"Let me take you out," he said softly. It was less of a suggestion, more of a command. Everything he said possessed an edge of confidence, the kind that made it clear he was used to being obeyed. That shouldn't have added to Cherry's attraction, but she was a grown woman; she'd learned a while back that *should* and *shouldn't* had little bearing on reality.

"Is this how you usually do things?" she asked. "You find a woman, tell her what you want, and she just... goes along with it?"

He gave her a smile that was almost predatory. "Something like that."

Made sense. He had some kind of celebrity entourage and was being courted by Chris, so he was probably a prospective sponsor. Which meant he must be rich as hell and powerful to boot.

She opened her mouth to say "There's no fucking way I'm going out with you."

But what she actually said was, "Okay."

Oh, dear.

Before she could think of a polite way to retract her agreement, he smiled. *Really* smiled, a grin that was full and bright and utterly unstudied. He looked happy. Less like a ruthless seducer of not-so-innocent women and more like a kid who'd been allowed a treat.

And then, to make things even worse, he said, "Thank you."

Well, she told herself, she couldn't change her mind *now*. He might be sad. And she'd hate to make him sad.

Right. Because you always *put the needs of random men above your own.*

Cherry pushed that thought away. It was her birthday, for God's sake. She could take a day off from being sensible. Couldn't she?

"You're welcome," she managed to say. "Um…" Her voice trailed off, suddenly uncertain. "Did you mean now?"

"Oh, yes," he said. And beneath the sweetness of his smile, she caught something low and warm and intense that made her breath hitch. "I most definitely meant now."

CHAPTER FOUR

Ruben couldn't believe his fucking luck.

Even the knowledge that Hans was loitering along this street somewhere, dogging their every step, wasn't enough to wipe the smile from his face. He was walking into town with Cherry Neita. *Cherry Neita.* This morning, he hadn't even known that name. Now it held as much significance to him as Jan Amos Komensky's.

Although, he'd never wanted to fuck the father of modern education senseless. So maybe not quite the same.

She strutted beside him, her hips twitching within the confines of that tight, knee-length skirt—not that he could see much of it, thanks to the coat she wore. Bloody January weather.

But his imagination was filling in the gaps just fine.

"Are you sure you want to walk?" he asked. "It's cold."

She gave him an odd look. "The town centre's just around the corner."

True enough; he could hear the busy traffic already. But he didn't want her to walk a metre if it wasn't necessary. Ruben cast a worried glance down at her high heels. "Don't your feet hurt?"

"No," she smiled. Not enough for the dimples, but enough to make him feel slightly dizzy. "They aren't that high."

He raised his brows, sceptical.

"They *aren't*," she insisted with a laugh. "I'm just tall."

"How tall?"

"Five-eleven. How tall are you?"

At home, most women knew his exact height. It was part of his supposed eligibility, and one of the only positives about him. But here in England, no-one gave a fuck about the royal family of a tiny Scandinavian island—which was why he came here so often. No-one knew him until he knew them. That was how it should be.

"I'm six-four," he said. "I like that you're tall."

"Oh, well if *you* like it, I can rest easy."

He looked over to find her pursing her lips, her eyes crinkling at the corners. "Feel free to laugh at me," he grinned back. "I know I'm arrogant."

She chuckled. "As long as you know."

"What I meant," he said, "is that I like talking to people who are at eye level." They turned into the town centre, right onto the little high street. "Where do you want to eat, by the way?"

She shrugged. "I don't really mind. Somewhere with cake."

"You like cake?"

"I love cake. Plus, it's my birthday." The word ended quietly, her voice fading away, as if she wanted to snatch it back. Her eyes flew to his, and he had the distinct impression that she hadn't meant to tell him that.

Well. Too late now.

"Your birthday," he repeated slowly, coming to a stop. He caught her hand in his, swinging her around to face him. Every time he touched her, something inside him snapped to attention—as if, now they'd made physical contact, the party could really begin.

Right. Because women always went from hand-holding to the bedroom in a matter of minutes.

She looked up at him—but not *up* up. She really was tall, and he really did like it. A lot.

"We should do something to celebrate," he said.

She shook her head. Her hair bounced around her face. He had the strongest urge to sink his hand into the curls, but she'd probably slap him for it. Definitely, in fact.

"I don't celebrate," she said, her voice low.

"Ever?"

"Not birthdays."

"Why not?"

She shrugged. "*Well done, you continued to exist?* It's ridiculous. Birthdays are for children. I am not a child."

"But you want birthday cake," he murmured. Did she notice the fact that he was pulling her closer? He didn't think so. She came as if floating, half-dreaming, and now he imagined that he could feel the heat of her body, even through both their coats. There was barely a breath between them. He could kiss her. Did she notice? Or was she as mindless right now as he was?

"I always want cake," she replied, her voice absent. "Everyone wants cake." But her eyes were focused firmly on his lips. Maybe he *should* kiss her.

A bus barrelled past, its engine thundering and its heavy wheels splashing through the puddles left by last night's rain. In an instant, Cherry went from half-hypnotised to razor-sharp, twisting away from the road until she stood firmly behind him.

Ruben blinked, disarmed. "What are you—?"

"A bus splashed me once," she said. "*Ruined* my stockings. Anyway, shall we go? I've only got an hour, you know."

His heart fell. She no longer sounded hypnotised. But on the bright side, he now knew that she wore stockings rather than tights.

That was valuable information.

"You know," he said, "I'm sure Tabary wouldn't mind if I kept you out a little longer. It's not like you have a class schedule, right?"

She rolled her eyes. "Are you serious? Chris is all about punctuality. I'd have to be the Queen of bloody England to get away with that."

Ruben felt his lips twitch. "Fair enough." He turned his attention to the high street, scanning the rows of shops and cafes before them. "That place looks good."

"Copper?" She blessed him with a smile. "You have great taste. Let's go."

CHERRY WAS no stranger to flirting.

In fact, she counted it as a hobby. At least 60% of her daily social interaction consisted of flirting, and sometimes she even went wild and followed it up with dates and sex and... well, that was it, really. But the point was, when it came to flirting, Cherry was something of an expert.

Or she'd thought she was. But for the past thirty minutes, all she'd done was choke down her sandwich and avoid eye contact and try not to wring her hands. It was all very embarrassing.

Ruben sat across the table, looking irritatingly gorgeous and infuriatingly confident. He hadn't mentioned her sudden silence. He hadn't really tried to lure her out of it, either. There was a gleam in his eye that said he knew exactly what had her so quiet.

She believed that gleam. He seemed the kind of man who knew things. A capable kind of man, the sort with a hard-won and well-earned confidence that sent shivers down her spine and dangerous thoughts through her head. Which was why she suddenly couldn't flirt—or even speak.

Cherry sent shivers. *Cherry* inspired thoughts. *Cherry* drove people wild. Cherry did *not* forget herself in a public street over the curve of a man's lips or the incongruous length of his eyelashes.

Yes, it was all incredibly embarrassing. She might be infatuated.

She patted at her lips with a napkin, then rifled through her handbag, which she'd stashed on the seat next to her. At the time, she'd thought it best that he couldn't sit beside her. But now he was sitting in front of her, and she'd spent the whole meal trying not to drool over his hands. His *hands*, for Christ's sake!

She pulled out a tube of lipstick and a compact mirror—but he reached across the table, catching her wrist. It was the lightest touch of skin against skin, hardly a restraint, but it released a torrent of dark images in Cherry's mind. He *could* restrain her, if he wanted to. If she asked him to.

God, she was ridiculous.

"What?" she clipped out.

"Cake," he said simply. And despite herself, she softened. He'd remembered the cake.

Of course he did, her inner voice snapped. It sounded suspiciously like her mother. *Don't give him points for basic recollection.*

He plucked a dessert menu from the centre of the table and handed it to her with a flourish. It was odd—everything he did seemed so natural, so easy, yet he was constantly and completely charming. In Cherry's experience, charm took work. Perhaps he was especially good at faking it. The thought should have made her wary, but instead, she began to think of him as a kindred spirit.

A kindred spirit with deliciously broad shoulders and a beautiful smile. And very big hands.

"What would you like?" he asked.

"Um…" She studied the menu, as if she hadn't come here a thousand times. It was a touch upmarket for a weekday lunch, but his cufflinks were mother of pearl. There was no point taking him to bloody Greggs.

"Can't choose?"

"I might be struggling," she admitted, allowing herself a small smile. And then, before she could think better of it, Cherry slid the menu into the centre of the table and leant forward. "What do you think?"

He looked delighted. As if he'd been waiting for just this moment —for her to make a move, to come to him. Which she hadn't, she told herself firmly. She just wanted some advice. Cake was a serious business.

But clearly, Ruben didn't receive that message. He leant forward too, until their heads were perilously close, and he gave her another of those beautiful smiles. Fine lines fanned out from the corners of his brown eyes, and his scent—clean and fresh, like linen, with a hint of something spicy—enveloped her.

Moving towards him had been a very bad idea. But she couldn't take it back now. It would be rude. And she was rather enjoying the proximity.

"The obvious choice is chocolate," he said. "But then, you strike me as a woman with individual tastes." His gaze caught hers and held.

Beneath the table, Cherry crossed her legs, clenched her thighs. The heel of her shoe slipped free, dangling from her toes...

And then it disappeared, falling off completely. No—it had been *nudged*.

"Did you just knock off my shoe?" she demanded.

He shook his head. "Don't know what you mean. Oh, look; they have Cherry Bakewell."

"Very funny," she muttered, her stockinged foot gliding tentatively over the floor beneath the table. Where on earth was that shoe?

Instead of her patent leather heel, she came across... another foot. Also shoeless. But much bigger than hers.

Cherry's eyes flew to Ruben's. His gaze was steady as ever. "You don't like Cherry Bakewell?" he asked.

"Of course I do," she huffed. "Bakewell's only up the road. My parents took us there every summer."

"Us?" he asked, leaning closer. In fact, he was so close now, there might as well be no table between them at all. When had that happened? His hand meandered over to hers, which rested on the table top, and he stroked a finger over the gems on her nails. "You have siblings?"

"I have a sister," she said. Beneath the table, his foot rubbed against hers. It was a slow, rhythmic touch, almost soothing. But it was hard to feel soothed by a man who set your every nerve-ending alight.

"Older or younger?" he prompted.

"Um… Younger. Maggie. She's in America." Usually, Cherry loved bragging about her sister, even though it came with a twinge of worry. Always, she worried about Maggie. But today, her words were as muddled as her feelings. "I mean—she goes to Harvard. She's very clever."

"Takes after you, then?"

Cherry's brows shot up. "I'm not clever."

"Oh, that's right." He rolled his eyes, and then his voice flattened in a fair imitation of Chris Tabary's. "Cherry, you silly girl, you've mucked up the sums!" Returning to his usual deep tones, he grinned. "I know you did that on purpose."

Despite herself, she smiled. "Okay, yes. I was on a mission."

"And that mission was…?"

"To see you," she admitted. "Everyone was going on about the gorgeous man in Chris's office. I was sent to investigate."

"And did I meet your expectations?" he asked. The arrogant arch of his brow, that lazy smile, told her he already knew the answer.

But still, she only said, "Wouldn't you like to know?"

"Yes," he said simply. The look in his dark eyes became burning hot, its intensity completely at odds with the casual confidence he exuded. But then he looked away, and his easy smile returned. "I like your nails," he said. Apparently, they were changing the subject.

"Thanks. I got extra sparkles. You know, for my birthday."

He laughed. "For a woman who supposedly doesn't like birthdays—"

"I know," she admitted. "I just like to feel my best, starting a new year and all." It was only the 9th of January. She could attribute the nails—and the new lipstick, and the lace on her garters—to New Years' cheer rather than birthday extravagance.

"You need to choose your cake," he said. "Or you'll be late back."

"Oh, yes." He was right. She'd lost track of time. Which she never did.

But they *wouldn't* be late, because he had things under control. And, apparently, gave a shit about her schedule. How refreshing.

Cherry belatedly realised that her standards appeared to be rather low.

"Chocolate," she said firmly. "It'll save dithering. Just chocolate."

"Just chocolate it is," he murmured.

But when the cake arrived, it was a bigger slab than she'd ever seen in a middle-class cafe—places of notoriously stingy portions.

And it came with two forks.

CHERRY WAS LOOKING at the pair of cake forks like they'd hopped up from the table and started dancing the cancan. Ruben bit down a smile. He had a feeling she wouldn't appreciate being laughed at.

He wouldn't have thought, based on first impressions, that she'd be... like this. Direct in some ways, skittish in others. Verging on shy. Maybe she needed to get to know him. Maybe she found it easier to beat people into submission with those dimples and that cleavage than she did to just... talk.

Or maybe she was as blindsided by this attraction as he was, and had less experience following her instincts. All of those explanations felt right, but he'd like to know for sure. He'd like to know her.

Ruben picked up a fork—since she clearly wasn't going to—and said, "Do you mind?"

The words seemed to jerk her into action. If Cherry was a puzzle, manners were her key. "Oh, no. Of course not." She picked up her own fork and, after the slightest hesitation, dug in.

And here came the part he'd really been looking forward to. Watching Cherry eat cake.

She carved out a neat little piece with her fork, scooping up as much fudge icing as she could. He approved. She slid the mouthful between her lips, or rather, between her teeth. She appeared to have perfected the art of eating without messing up her lipstick. He didn't know why she'd bothered pulling out that little mirror. She must know that she still looked perfect.

He'd like to smudge that lipstick for her. Wondered if she'd let him. Of course, he was getting ahead of himself. The sight of her lashes fluttering in pleasure, of her tongue sliding out to trace her scarlet lower lip, would do that to a man.

She let out a satisfied sigh as she chewed. Then her eyes flitted to his and she raised her brows. Swallowed. Said, "Aren't you eating?"

He, of course, said the first thing that came into his head. "I was enjoying the view."

She rolled her eyes. "Predictable."

"I suppose you hear that kind of thing a lot."

"I certainly do." She speared another bite of cake. "Seriously, eat. I can't finish all this on my own."

"I had no idea you were such a delicate flower."

"Fuck off."

He laughed as he finally dug in. "If *Chris, darling,* could hear you now."

"God," she snorted. "He'd skin me alive. Swearing at important visitors."

"How do you know I'm important?"

She arched a brow. "Those men outside Chris's door this morning. What were they, bodyguards?"

Ruben choked on his cake. "What—why would you—?"

"My uncle on my mum's side, and all his kids, they're in the military. Mostly air force." She tapped her temple. "Plain clothes can't hide that training. I can see it in you too."

"Right," he said faintly. His throat felt slightly scratchy. He reached for some water.

"And you're rich as shit." She nodded towards his suit. "I know that's a Ricci."

Great. He'd gone from choking on his cake to choking on his drink. "*How* do you know it's a Ricci?" he spluttered.

"Mind your business," she sniffed.

"Mind *my* business?"

"Yes. Here's a tip: if you want to fly under the radar, try toning it down to Armani or something."

Ruben sighed. "Noted."

"So what's up with that? Are you sponsoring the Academy?" If he wasn't so attuned to the tone of her voice, to the tilt of her lips and the light in her dark eyes, he might have missed the tinge of disapproval in her words. But Ruben had spent their lunch watching her as closely as he'd watched her hips that morning. So he noticed. And he wanted to know why.

"If I weren't," he said carefully, "would you try to persuade me?"

"Persuade you?" She took another bite of cake. He watched her jaw work as she chewed. The sight should not be erotic, but apparently his libido was on the rampage today.

"Convince me to join the cause," he explained. "Enlist me. Whatever."

"Ah. Um… Why, would you listen?"

"To you?" Beneath the table, his ankle was hooked around hers. Almost absent-mindedly, her foot had started rubbing against him, silky and slow, like a cat. "You know I would."

"Oh I *know*, do I?" She grinned, and those damned dimples popped into view. "Because we're such good friends?"

He leaned in, his voice low. "We could be good friends." He shrugged. "Or something."

"Or something?" she repeated, her voice soft.

He reached out to capture her wrist. No reason, except he enjoyed the sight of his fingers holding her still, and she seemed to enjoy it too. Every time he did it, her eyes widened and her lips parted and he wondered if that was how she'd look when he—

"Oh crap," she said, twisting her head to read his watch. "I'm going to be late."

Well, shit. So much for his skills of seduction. "Don't worry. We've still got fifteen minutes."

"We should start walking now, then," she said. She retrieved the lipstick and mirror from her handbag, popping open the compact with an ease that spoke of practice. She arched a brow at him as she twisted up her lipstick. "Catch a waiter, darling, would you?"

Ruben requested the bill with just a look. Again: practice. Then he turned back to Cherry and said, "Don't *darling* me."

She paused, the lipstick partway through its journey round her mouth. She had a ridiculously defined cupid's bow. He wanted to trace it with his tongue. "I beg your pardon?"

"You don't need to manage me. I'm not Tabary."

Her lips pursed, one side bright, the other faded. "No man wants to think of himself as a Chris Tabary. But whether you are or not remains to be seen." Then she winked.

Winked.

This woman would be the death of him.

"Fair enough," he sighed, and she graced him with a smile. As if she was proud of him for being so reasonable. How would it feel, he wondered, for a woman like Cherry Neita to hand him all that glittering power of hers? To willingly submit?

If he asked, she'd probably say she'd rather die. But he wouldn't ask.

She would.

Ruben settled the bill as she slid on her coat, doing up the neat little buttons. He'd taken pity on her and pushed her shoe over, beneath the table. Neither of them mentioned the fact that he'd effectively stolen it in the first place.

As they left the cozy warmth of the cafe, Ruben reached out to catch Cherry's arm. She turned towards him, and she was so ridiculously beautiful, he almost forgot to breathe. His body screamed, *Kiss her.*

But, for once, he managed to ignore his baser instincts. Instead, he simply said, "Two questions."

"What?"

"First: you don't think I should sponsor the Academy." Of course, he hadn't intended to, but she didn't need to know that. "Why not?"

She rolled her lips inwards. Shifted from one heel to another. "I don't want to discuss that."

Fair enough. But she hadn't denied it—and that was all he needed to know. His suspicions were confirmed.

He would not be partnering with the Academy for his Trust's scholarship.

"Alright," he said. "Second question: if I wait for you, after work —will you come out with me again?

"No," she said immediately.

Fuck.

But then she continued. "I'd have to get changed first. I don't dress like this all the time, you know." She smiled. "Maybe you could come back to my flat. While I get ready."

Ruben shifted, trying to lessen the sudden pressure of his cock against his zip. It didn't help; not with the way she was looking at him, mischief and challenge and lust in her eyes. So he just said, "Yes. I will most definitely come with you."

"Good," she said softly. And then she turned on those high heels and headed up the street.

CHAPTER FIVE

For Cherry, Ruben put up with Tabary for a whole day. He smiled and nodded and feigned interest, and a couple of times he caught Hans giving him approving looks.

Of course, his friend's approval was revoked soon enough.

"Why are we hanging around in a school carpark?"

"Does it matter?" Ruben shifted lower in his seat, even though the Hummer's windows were tinted. Not as dark as he'd like, but there were national regulations to be followed. Of course, he could always travel with a royal congregation and be exempt from regulations. But that would amount to pissing all over his last bastion of privacy.

Children had begun pouring out of the Academy half an hour ago, but Ruben had waited. Next came a trickling of staff, and still he held off—because she'd asked him to. He'd like to go up to the admin floor of that monstrous tower and carry her down the damn stairs, but she'd insisted that he wait out here.

Which was fair enough, he thought grudgingly. But the animalistic side of him, the instinct that had caused him so much trouble throughout his life, wholeheartedly disagreed.

Fetch her. Now. It doesn't matter who sees.

He ignored the voice inside his head and sank deeper into his seat.

"Your Highness," Hans said.

Ruben sighed. Coming from anyone else, that title suggested respect. From Hans, who'd been calling him 'Ruben' forever, it signified an impending lecture.

"Don't start," Ruben said bluntly, slipping into their mother tongue. His eyes scanned the car park. He felt slightly unhinged. Was he really so eager to see this woman again?

Yes. Embarrassingly eager. Hurry up.

"Your Highness," Hans repeated, ignoring his prince's words. As usual. "You know as well as I do that the king—"

"Really, Hans? You think I want to hear about my brother right now?"

"Fine. I was going to remind you that the king will not bear another scandal, but that doesn't matter. *You* will not bear another scandal."

Ruben stiffened. "Who said anything about scandal?"

"Don't treat me like a fool. I know you're waiting for that woman."

A spark of anger flared in Ruben's gut at his friend's derisive tone. But he controlled his temper, because he knew where all this nagging came from.

Hans was worried about him.

And so he kept voice tone carefully even, almost teasing, when he said, "Why shouldn't I wait for her? She's quite brilliant. Don't you agree?"

"Oh, yes," Hans said. "I agree. Blindingly brilliant. A sentient trap—"

"Shut your mouth."

"You know she's just like your sister."

"If she were just like my sister, I wouldn't be waiting for her. So shut. Your fucking. Mouth."

Hans glared. "No. You didn't listen to me with Kathryn—"

"Jesus fucking Christ," Ruben snapped. "First Sophronia, now Kathryn—who will you compare her to next? My mother?"

"Of course not." Hans frowned. "You misunderstand me. The problem is not so much the woman herself as it is your eagerness to… to make yourself vulnerable."

"It's been eight months," Ruben reminded him.

"Yes, it's been eight months. Barely any time at all. I remember exactly how bad it was, even if you don't, and I am worried about the possibility of something similar happening."

Ruben snorted. "Something similar? I can't be exposed twice, Hans. That's the beauty of it. All of Helgmøre knows everything there is to know about me." His voice was as steady as always, but Ruben's heart thundered against his chest like a horse's hooves. For the first time in the last eight months, he'd been attracted to someone without thinking immediately of Kathryn. Of the mess she'd brought to his door. And Hans had to fucking ruin it.

The man had his safety in mind, of course. But Ruben's desire to know Cherry—know her in every way—had been so pure. Free of suspicion and distrust and anxiety and bad memories. Now it was coloured by past experiences. Now, when he thought of the power her beauty held, it felt less like something to admire and more like something to fear.

Fucking Hans. Fucking Kathryn. Fucking life.

"Ruben." Hans's voice was soft. "I don't mean to suggest that you shouldn't... return to normal. Pursue relationships. But you act without thinking."

Wrong. Ruben thought plenty. And then he followed his instincts regardless.

Look where that got you the last time.

He ground his teeth, meeting his friend's pale gaze for the first time. "I understand. But I cannot allow one bad experience to change who I am." That would go against everything he'd ever fought for. Everything he'd ever fought to become.

Hans nodded. "Fair enough. Just... be careful. I promised the king that there would be no more scandals."

Ruben's jaw tightened. "She doesn't even know who I am. This is England, for Christ's sake. They have their own royals."

"She seems a capable woman. I'm sure she'd figure it out on her own. And then—"

Ruben held up a hand in the universal sign for *stop*. Hans, of course, ignored that crystal-clear signal and continued his speech. But Ruben didn't hear another word.

She was here. She left the school gates with that familiar wiggling strut, her statuesque figure instantly recognisable. Ruben got out of the car and strode over to meet her.

"Your Hi—Ruben!" Hans called. He sounded irritated, but then, he usually did. Ruben didn't give a shit.

As soon as she saw him, Cherry smiled. Not the charming, dimpled grin she unleashed like a weapon, but something softer, almost involuntary. Her round cheeks plumped and her red lips curved, and Ruben allowed himself to imagine that she was as pleased to see him as he was her.

"You're here," she said. As if anything could've kept him away.

"Of course I'm here. Come on." He took her hand, trying to hide the way even that small touch affected him. Trying to act like it was normal, casual, when really he felt like cheering when she didn't pull away. "How was your day?"

She slid her eyes over to his. "Are you trying to be all thoughtful and charming and whatever?"

"I don't have to try. It just comes naturally."

"*Really*," she snorted. But he saw the laughter dancing in her eyes, even if she wouldn't let it pass her lips.

"Yes, really. I hope you're taking notes."

They came to a stop in front of his car. The door was now shut— Hans's doing, clearly. Hopefully he'd let himself out while he was at it. Cherry might have figured out the bodyguard thing, but he didn't know how she'd react to sharing the back seat with one.

She stared at the car. Then she frowned, pursed her lips, cocked her head and her hips to one side. "Is that a Hummer?" she finally asked—with the same tone she might use to say, *"Is that a cockroach?"*

Ruben raised his brows. "You don't like it?" Most women liked the Hummer. Why the fuck wouldn't she like the Hummer?

"It's very.... large," she said finally. "Are you compensating for something?"

He smiled. "I absolutely am not."

Cherry's eyes slid down his body, bold enough to make his balls tighten. "You would say that, though, wouldn't you?" she murmured.

"It's true. Get in the car, and I'll happily provide hard evidence."

Her dark eyes danced. But her voice was serious when she said, "What about *my* car?"

"I can have someone handle that for you."

Her brows shot up, and too late, he realised his mistake: she didn't know who he really was. And she certainly had no reason to trust any of his staff with her car.

But all she said was, "No, I don't think so." And then her face lit up. "Oh! I know what we'll do!"

"What?" *I'll do anything as long as it gets me where I need to be. Alone. With you.*

"We'll take my car," she said. "Someone can *handle* yours. Right?" There was challenge in her wry smile, in the soft kiss of those dimples.

And that was so fucking sexy to Ruben, he didn't even think before saying, "Whatever you want."

It was only when she led him to her old, rickety Corsa that he realised: Hans was definitely going to kill him for this.

CHAPTER SIX

The journey was fast and silent, a ten-minute drive thick with tension. The air between them swelled like ripe fruit: ready to burst, lush and gleaming—but beneath the sweet anticipation, the threat of something rotten. Something too far gone.

The rotten thing was Cherry's growing anxiety. As they pulled into the square of tarmac that served as her little flat's carpark, her arousal deflated like a balloon. She parked up and dropped her keys into her lap, staring straight ahead. Right at the bare brick wall of her little building. She probably looked like a zombie. Didn't matter. She was thinking.

Ruben sat beside her in silence. Maybe he was waiting patiently, maybe he was freaked the fuck out, or maybe he'd been abducted by aliens while she was trapped in an internal battle. She didn't know and she didn't care.

Was she really doing this?

The first voice in her head was, unsurprisingly, Rose's. Not an imagined response, but a memory of the words she'd said when Cherry casually mentioned that she'd be seeing Ruben again— that very night. *Don't do anything silly, darling.*

Bringing an almost-stranger to her flat meant that she was already doing something silly; Cherry knew that. Men who were delicious enough to make you lose your head should be imbibed sensibly. Like rosé or Lemsip. She was not imbibing sensibly.

The next voice in her head, her mother's, agreed. It screeched, *Are you trying to kill me, child? Or are you trying to kill yourself?* And then, because Dad was never far from Mum, she heard his voice too: *Be sensible, Cherry Pie.*

But the last voice was her little sister's. She knew exactly what Maggie would say right now.

Get yours, sis.

Her lips quirked. Maggie would already have him inside.

Of course, she didn't have to invite him in at all. He'd asked to take her out. *She* was the one who'd brought him here—all because something about the tone of his voice and the look in his eye and the way that he touched her made Cherry think he might…

She pressed her lips together. Then she turned to face him.

He hadn't been abducted by aliens; he was right there, where she'd left him, waiting patiently. The way he dominated the little space put her in mind of a caged beast, but his eyes, for once, were soft.

"You okay?" he asked.

She swallowed. "Yes."

"Do you want me to wait here?"

"No."

"Can I kiss you?"

Four words. His voice was as soft as his eyes. He was all folded up into the tiny car's front seat, his long legs bent, his powerful thighs straining at his suit trousers, and... oh. Something else strained at his suit trousers, too, hard and thick. She let her eyes rest on his erection for a second before looking back up at him. He met her gaze easily, making no move to hide his arousal, and Cherry's nerves disappeared. Anticipation was a red-hot weight in her chest, and desire thrummed through her pulse.

He raised a hand and grasped the back of her neck, pushing her hair aside. The warm weight of his palm rested against her skin, and then he leant over the centre console towards her. His forehead bumped gently against hers.

"You have to tell me," he whispered. "Yes or no. Can I kiss you?"

She sounded embarrassingly breathless when she said, "Yes."

He barely let her finish the word. In a heartbeat, his lips were on hers, soft and gentle. So, so gentle. But that hand on her neck was big and rough and demanding. His fingers sank into her hair, tightening slightly around the roots, and he pulled her head back, just a little. Just enough to make it clear that he was in charge. And still, his lips brushed against hers like a ghost's. She shivered at the contrast. She wanted more. Much more.

As if he'd read her mind, he gave it to her. His tongue slid out to trace its way across her lower lip, and then he groaned softly into her mouth, as if he liked the taste—oh, yes, he liked the taste, because now he was sucking her bottom lip into *his* mouth, each pull tugging at her tightening nipples, at her suddenly-sensitive clit. Cherry squeezed her thighs together, shifting in her seat, chasing the pressure she needed to relieve that delicious ache between her legs.

He broke the kiss and pulled her head right back, exposing her throat. She wanted to whimper at the loss of his mouth, but his expression made her swallow the protest.

He looked... hungry.

"Tell me what you want," he rasped. His breathing was loud in the quiet space, laboured. "You have to tell me."

"I... This," she whispered. "I like this." *Understatement.*

The hand in her hair tightened. He pressed a hot, open-mouthed kiss to her throat—then turned it, at the last minute, into a bite. Just firm enough to make her moan beneath him, to make her breath catch in her chest.

He pulled back. "Like that?"

"Yes," she gasped. "That. Anything you want."

His smile was slow, intense. "Careful, love. You have no idea what I want to do to you."

She met his eyes. "I think I do, actually. I'm quite looking forward to it."

He muttered something under his breath. It sounded a lot like *Fuck.* Then he said, "Get out of the car."

She'd thought she was wet already. But at the command in his voice, desire pooled hot and sticky between her thighs.

Oh, dear.

RUBEN HAD LOST HIS HEAD.

The minute he noticed his security detail *wasn't* following them out of the car park—and decided to do nothing about that fact—he knew he was losing it. They probably hadn't noticed him leaving, since he'd gone firmly against protocol and disappeared in someone else's car, but he should've stopped then. Only he hadn't, because touching Cherry felt more urgent than fucking protocol.

It felt more urgent than anything he'd ever done.

She led him across the car park through a little alleyway, their hands intertwined. "Shortcut," she said, tugging him along. Her heels clicked sharply against the concrete. She was rushing. She was precisely as desperate as he was, and the knowledge made him harder than ever.

The winter sun was low over the horizon, the sky was a clouded bruise, and the streetlights snapped on around them. In the walkway between two apartment blocks, light faded and shadows grew tall. Cherry's hips swayed in front of him, her hand tight around his, and the memories of her gasping little cries teased at his mind.

Ruben stopped walking.

She turned to face him, a furrow appearing between her brows. "What?"

Without a word, he pulled her closer. When she came towards him with a smile curving her lips, he wanted to roar in triumph. Even the slightest acquiescence from this woman felt like a prize. He slid his hands around her waist and pulled her into him, against him, her softness a balm to the ragged edge of his lust. But it wasn't enough.

Ruben backed her into the wall beside them, covering her body with his own. He captured both her wrists in one hand, bringing them up over her head, his grip firm. His eyes on hers. Searching for something indefinable.

He found it.

She arched into him and said, "Hurry up." So he kissed her, because he fucking had to.

He felt like he was on the edge of control, like something savage, but when their lips met his desperation calmed. He licked his way into her mouth, revelling in her taste. He must be covered in her damned lipstick by now. He liked that idea. Let her mark him. He traced a thumb along the line of her jaw, her skin velvety.

"Makeup," she muttered against his lips, pulling away—but he tightened his grip.

"If you don't want to mess up your makeup," he said softly, "you've brought the wrong man home."

"I don't want you to get it on your clothes."

"It's fine," he said. "They'll be gone soon, anyway."

"God, you're so fucking…" Apparently, she had no idea what he was, because with an adorable little growl she reached up and kissed him. Her tongue met his and she sighed, arching into him.

Fuck. He sucked on her plump bottom lip, imagined doing the same to the tits currently pressed against his chest—and then she released a whimper and wrapped a leg around his waist.

Ruben felt like he was drowning. Like every movement was slower and harder than it should be, than it needed to be, and he was desperate for things to speed up. He grabbed her thigh with his spare hand, pulled her leg higher, then shoved up the thick fabric of her coat because it was only getting in the fucking way. Next he shoved up her skirt, and then his fingers came into contact with the softness of her stockings. But even that wasn't enough.

He plundered her mouth as his hands crept higher, searching out heaven. Searching out her skin. Finally, he found it, soft and almost vulnerable. He snapped the elastic of her suspenders and dragged himself away from her lips. "You weren't kidding about the stockings."

She blinked at him, looking deliciously dazed. Her lipstick was indeed a mess. But she recovered in an instant, her eyes flashing as she smiled. "A figure like mine requires the proper foundation."

"Oh it does, hm?" He bit his lip, hoping the sharp edge of pain would control the flare of his arousal. It didn't. "Jesus. I wish I could fuck you right here."

"You know what they say about following your dreams."

He exhaled, clinging to the last of his control, feeling his grip slip. "You love to push, don't you?"

"Yes." She tilted her chin up as if she were the one in charge. Like his hand wasn't binding her wrists right now. "Do you want me to stop?"

"Fuck, no." His fingers abandoned her suspenders and travelled higher.

"So..." she breathed, the word shimmering in the air between them, white-hot.

"So don't stop," he repeated, and then his hand found the satin edge of her underwear, traced it until she moaned. "Push."

Their eyes met, and he saw his own need reflected in the shadows. He knew, in that second, that he would do anything she asked.

Then he heard the footsteps, fast and heavy, splashing through the alley's puddles.

And *then* he heard his worst fucking nightmare. "Your Highness!"

That voice didn't belong to Hans.

CHAPTER SEVEN

"**Y**our Highness!" A camera flashed bright white in the darkness, illuminating everything he'd ever wished to hide. "Who's this? Who is she? Can I get a smile, sweetheart?" The last sentence was in English, the first few, thank God, in Helgmøre's antiquated Danish.

Ruben turned, using his body to hide Cherry from view, dragging a hand across his jaw—which was probably covered in scarlet lipstick.

"For fuck's sake," he snarled, slipping into his mother tongue.

Another flash. "Come on, Your Highness. Where's the whips and chains?"

Ruben felt a growl rise in his chest, felt his pulse pound and saw the world around him turn red. Rage tinged with panic flooded his throat, the phantom taste of blood and imminent regret. His fists clenched.

But then he felt the lightest touch against his back, like a butterfly coming to rest. And he remembered. How could he forget?

Cherry.

"You can't take our picture," he said hoarsely, his sense returning, the alarm in his head fading away. He squinted into the darkness. "Niklaus?"

"Awww, you remember me!"

Of course he fucking did. Paparazzi dogged him often enough, but this particular photographer had been his own personal poltergeist over the past few months.

Until Demetria had forced Ruben's brother to cut a deal.

"You can't take our picture," he said again, louder now. More confident. "Or you'll lose the privileges my brother promised."

"Ah, ah. I can't take *your* picture." *Flash.* "So I'll blur you out. The king said nothing about your whores—"

"Have some fucking respect," Ruben snapped, "before I—"

"What, Your Highness? Careful." White teeth flashed in the shadows. "I'm recording."

Of course he was.

"So come on, who is she?"

Behind him, Cherry whispered, "What's going on? Why is he taking pictures?"

"Don't worry," Ruben whispered back in English. "It's nothing. I—"

"Your Highness! Who is she?" Another camera flash, and Ruben was thrown right back into the worst days of his adult life. The days when every aspect of his identity had been thrown to the wolves and torn apart for consumption, for analysis. Judged and found wanting. As always. He felt the visceral pain in his gut.

"She's my fiancée," he said. "And if you don't erase those photographs, you'll lose all access to the wedding and be in viola-

50

tion of your agreement with the Crown. Is that what you want, Niklaus?"

The flashes stopped. Ruben blinked as if emerging from a dream, phantom brightness still blooming over his vision.

Then came Niklaus's familiar voice, thready and whining as the buzz of a fly. "Fiancée?"

"That's right. Which makes her part of the family. You can't take our picture."

Before Niklaus could reply, more footsteps came. Faster and more familiar than the first, bringing a smile of relief to Ruben's lips.

Hans led the pack, cornering Niklaus with a grim smile, more intimidating than ever.

"Woah, woah!" The photographer held up his hands, one still clinging to his camera. "Let's not get overexcited, gentlemen! I was just speaking with the prince—"

"Hans," Ruben interrupted. "Niklaus has agreed to delete all photographs of *my fiancée*. Since they are in violation of his agreement with my brother's estate. Please see that he does so."

He waited with bated breath in the darkness, the silence deafening. But then Hans said, his voice monotonous as ever, "Of course, Your Highness."

Only a man who'd known Hans forever would detect the thread of disbelief hidden in those words. Or the undercurrent of fury.

But he'd deal with that later.

Satisfied, Ruben turned and put his arm around Cherry, switching to English. "I'm sorry. Come; we need to leave."

She walked quickly, barely hesitating. But her shoulders were stiff, and her jaw was set.

Ruben had the sinking realisation that she didn't want his touch.

CHERRY PACED her open-plan living room in stockinged feet, her mind churning.

Ruben was lounging on her sofa as if he owned the place, watching her with an infuriating smile on his face and an unsettling wariness in his eyes.

Finally, Cherry pulled herself together and turned to face him. "So you're... some kind of celebrity." She may not speak Swedish, or whatever language they'd used down there, but that much was obvious. "And you didn't see fit to tell me that before doing... *things*. With me. In a public place. Correct?"

He rested one hand casually against the back of the sofa and arched a brow. "I suppose."

"You suppose? You *suppose*?" She sounded like somebody's mother. Reigning in her unease and her anger, Cherry forced herself to relax. She fluffed out her hair—he'd probably squashed the curls at the back against that fucking wall—then remembered her makeup. Crap.

Snatching her bag from the coffee table, she rifled through for a mirror. There weren't any on the walls of her flat, except for the one in the bathroom. She didn't need to be beautiful when she was alone.

"Cherry," he sighed. "You look fine."

"Fuck off." Wait—she was supposed to be charming him. She flashed a smile to soften the words, then studied her reflection. Her hair was frizzy and her lipstick smudged beyond belief. Fine. She'd go with the 'just fucked' look and hope he liked it.

Snapping her mirror shut, Cherry sauntered over to the sofa and sank down beside him. She swung her legs onto his lap and took his hand in hers, toying with his long, thick fingers. But now was not the time to focus on that sort of thing. Beneath his usual confidence he seemed unsettled, almost panicked. And downstairs he'd been absolutely frantic.

Looking up from under her lashes, she studied his face. His features were drawn, his jaw hard. "Are you married?" She asked. "You can tell me, you know."

He smiled slightly. "Can I?"

Fuck. She nodded beguilingly.

"Yes," he said. "I'm married."

Shooting up out of his lap, Cherry grabbed the nearest cushion and threw it at his head. "You piece of shit! You—"

Too late, she realised that he was laughing. Hysterically.

Cherry threw another pillow. "You're not married at all, are you?"

"Of course not," he choked out. He was still laughing. Smug fucking dick.

"It's not funny!"

"Yes it is," he wheezed. "'*You can tell me,*' she says. Christ, does anyone fall for that?"

"Yes, actually." She crossed her arms and lifted her chin. "Plenty of people."

"*Plenty*, hm?" He caught his breath, still smiling. Then he held out a hand and said, "Come here."

She ignored the way her pulse leapt at his command. "No. Tell me what's going on."

"I will. If you come here."

"Tell me, or the next thing I throw at your head won't be a pillow."

He arched a brow, but let his hand drop. "Fine. You should sit down, though."

Oh dear. That sounded ominous.

Before she could really start panicking, a knock came at the door. An inappropriately loud knock, the kind made by men with large fists and underdeveloped common sense. She let out a huff. "Would that be your mysterious bodyguards?"

"Yes," Ruben said, without a hint of apology. Had she really been ready to sleep with this man? He was bloody irritating.

Cherry stomped out into the hall and yanked open her front door. A huge man stood in the doorway, dressed entirely in black. The man who'd been in Chris's office with Ruben just that morning. The man who'd stormed into the alleyway after that photographer.

She eyed him warily. "Do you speak English? Because I don't speak Swedish."

His thin lips twitched into something that might have been a smile. "Danish," he said.

"Oh, sorry. I'm not big on languages."

"It is no problem. I am Hans. May I come in?"

Cherry, who had given up on all pretence of charm—surprise photographs and denied orgasms would do that to a girl—stepped aside with an ill-mannered sigh and said, "If you must."

The huge man dwarfed her tiny flat's narrow hallway. He headed towards the living room as if he'd been here a thousand times before, not bothering to take off his shoes.

Bloody men.

Cherry slammed the door shut.

When she returned to the living room, she found Hans standing by the window, peering out into the night, and Ruben on the sofa with... her cat, Whiskey. The fat little tabby was stretched out on Ruben's lap, purring. Getting fur all over his £3,000 suit. He didn't appear to mind. He rubbed her belly, and didn't even flinch when she dug all of her claws into his hand.

Cherry tried not to be impressed.

"So," she said, clapping her hands together. "This is cozy."

Hans turned away from the window to look at her dispassionately. Ruben continued playing with Whiskey, who hadn't even acknowledged Cherry's presence. Bloody traitor.

Scrabbling for the remnants of her poise, Cherry picked up the pillows she'd thrown. "I'd offer you both a cuppa," she said, "only I don't really want to."

Hans inclined his head. "That's quite alright, Madam."

How irritating.

But Ruben turned wide, hurt eyes on her. "Really, Cherry? Denying us tea? Is that necessary?"

It took her a second to realise that he was taking the piss. She shot him a glare. He responded with a lazy smile that had her treacherous heart leaping even as her temper rose.

"Will someone tell me what the hell is going on?" she snapped.

Hans blinked. Then he frowned at Ruben. "You didn't tell her?"

"I was easing into it."

"No you bloody weren't," Cherry spluttered. "You haven't told me shit!"

With a sigh, Ruben plucked Whiskey off of his lap and set the cat down on the floor. She, mortally offended, stuck both nose and whiskers in the air before sauntering off.

"Okay," Ruben said. "I'll get on with it, if you like."

"Yes, please."

"I'm a prince."

CHAPTER EIGHT

C herry blinked. "No you're not."

"Yes I am."

"No," she insisted. "You're not. There are, like, five princes. Charles, Philip, Will, Harry—"

"I'm not an *English* prince." He rolled his eyes. "Obviously."

"Oh, right. I forgot we're not the only ridiculous country in the world."

He arched a brow. "I take it you're not a monarchist?"

"Are you offended?"

"No." A corner of his mouth kicked up into that lazy, half-smile. "I'm not a monarchist either. I'm not much of a prince."

From his place by the window, Hans let out an irritated huff. "Yes, you are. You are His Royal Highness Prince Magnus Ruben Ambjørn Octavian Gyldenstierne of Helgmøre and you are very much a prince."

Cherry's brows shot up. "*Magnus*? Your name is Magnus?" For some reason, the idea that she'd been calling him the wrong name all this time bothered her more than the fact that he was, appar-

56

ently, royalty. And where the fuck was Helgmøre? She'd been hoping he was from Monaco.

But he shook his head vehemently. "My name is not Magnus."

"Hans just—"

"My name is *not Magnus*. My name is Ruben." He lost his cool all at once, like the breaking of a dam. His eyes burned bright and his fists were clenched by his sides.

Well. It was about time someone else lost their shit, since she'd been losing hers for the past twenty minutes.

"Fine," she said. "Ruben. Whatever." She shook her head, trying to capture all of her scattered thoughts. "Look, what really matters here is... Christ, you *are* famous. Like, *really* famous. Right?" She looked at Hans for confirmation. The huge man nodded. "So where's Helgmøre? Will those pictures show up in the British press? Because—"

Ruben held up a hand. "You don't need to worry about the pictures."

"I don't? Why not?"

He and Hans shared a look. "They've been dealt with."

Cherry frowned. "Jesus Christ, what did you do?!"

"Nothing! Nothing bad." Then he appeared to reevaluate that sentence. "Well, actually..."

She didn't like the sound of that. Or the way he was looking at her, with wary concern, as if she was a dangerous animal that could turn on him at any moment. Her eyes flew to Hans, and he seemed to share Ruben's worry.

"What?" she snapped. "Just tell me!"

"Well... We may need to get you a security detail or... Something. Not sure. Now I think about it—" He frowned suddenly, as if pained, pinching the bridge of his nose. "Hm. This could get complicated."

"*What?*"

He ignored her, turning to Hans. "What do you think we should do?"

"*What?*" Cherry repeated.

Hans scowled. "Don't ask me. Clearly you've lost your fucking mind today, so I doubt you'd listen to my advice."

"Oh, don't be a bore, Hans. This really isn't a good time."

"You're telling *me* this isn't a good time? I told *you*—" Mid-sentence, Hans switched languages.

Cherry pursed her lips, listening to their rising voices for a moment. Then she searched the living room for something to throw. She marched over to the bookcase, hefting an ency-clopaedia with both hands. Was she strong enough to throw it at someone's head? She wasn't sure. It was rather heavy.

"Cherry."

She moved on to an ornamental bulldog her dad had given her as a kind of weird flat-warming gift. It had a decent weight to it. Hefty, but light enough for her to throw it with some force. Now to choose the first victim.

"*Cherry.*"

She looked up, the bulldog in one hand. "What?"

Ruben looked at the ornament warily. "Could you put that down?"

"Why?"

"Please?"

She watched his jaw clench. And said, "No."

"Fine," he sighed. "Okay, here's the thing. I told the photographer that you were my fiancée—Jesus fucking Christ, woman!" He leapt aside as she launched the bulldog at his head.

It landed on her coffee table with an ominous thud. Hans walked over to the table and picked up the ornament to reveal a slight dent and a mess of chipped varnish.

Cherry glared at Ruben. "You owe me a new coffee table."

"What?"

"Shut up. Why would you say that?"

"Because—"

"I said *shut up*! Jesus," she spat, throwing up her hands. Without permission, her feet began to pace. She didn't really mind. It seemed appropriate. "So what happens now? A load of foreign paps come over here and stalk me? Camp outside my flat? Brilliant, *bloody* brilliant. Jesus Christ, I didn't even get a shag out of it."

"Well, we could still—"

"I swear to fucking God, shut the fuck up or I will gag you with your own *fucking dick*." Had she screamed that last part? She rather thought she might have.

Oh, dear. She was losing her temper.

But Ruben didn't seem to comprehend the danger. He crossed his arms and stared her down and said, "I did it to protect you. Okay? You don't know how—" He broke off, and for a minute he looked almost... lost. So lost that she forgot to be furious for a second. When he spoke again, his voice was stiff and formal. "No, you're right. I—I have put you in an untenable position, without your knowledge or consent, and for that I apologise."

"Oh," she said sweetly. "You *apologise*. Well that's just grand. Can you also guarantee that my life isn't going to change because of your big fucking mouth?"

He swallowed. "No. I really can't. But I—"

She held up a hand. "I think that's enough talking for one day. You can see yourself out."

"Wait, Cherry—"

"Get out." Her voice was hard. "Now."

She didn't expect him to listen. Not really. But after a moment, he nodded tightly and turned on his heel, barking, "*Kom,*" at Hans.

The large man hesitated by the window for a moment, his eyes on Cherry. Then he said, his voice soft, "We will return tomorrow."

"I won't be here."

"Yes," he said firmly. "You will."

Before she could work past the outrage blocking her throat, he left.

Fuck. Fuck, fuck, fuck.

Cherry threw herself onto the sofa, sinking into cushions made soft with age. Her parents had given her this sofa when she'd moved out. Almost all of her furniture was second-hand.

Jesus fucking Christ, he was a *prince.*

Cherry sucked in her cheeks and bit down, hard. Nothing about her current situation became any clearer.

He'd said the pictures were dealt with, but he couldn't know that for sure. This was the modern age. Cloud technology and all that shit meant nothing was ever really gone. And even if it *was* gone, did that matter? He'd told some journalist or whatever that they were engaged. A journalist who'd found them between two blocks of flats. All the guy had to do was hang around until morning, and he'd find out quickly enough who Ruben's so-called fiancée was.

Of course, that might not matter. She'd never heard of Ruben, or Helgmøre—geography wasn't her strong suit—so however famous he was over there, no-one in England would care, right?

But *she* was English. So maybe people *would* care. Crap.

Cherry heaved herself up off the sofa and snatched her phone out of her bag, opening up her messages. The first thing that popped up was her family group chat.

Mum: Netflix date tonight, Maggie.

Magz: I haven't forgotten!

Dad: Cherry where r u. We start at 10 o'clock.

Dad: Here.

Dad: Maggie we start at 5 o'clock for u.

Cherry checked her watch. It was just past five, GMT. Lunch for her sister. Their parents, as usual, were worrying over nothing.

Imagine how they'd worry if they found out about tonight.

Cherry: Don't worry, I'll be there

Having committed to their virtual Netflix date, she left the chat and pulled up Maggie's name.

Cherry: Problem.

She bit her lip, then continued.

Cherry: Secret.

Magz: Shit, you never pull secret. Finally done something wrong?

Cherry: Shut up. Not exactly.

Magz: So spill.

With a sigh, Cherry typed out an abbreviated version of the afternoon's events. She didn't mention Ruben's *fiancée* comment. Maggie's outrage would be a fearsome and tiring thing.

One minute passed. Then another. And then the phone rang.

"Oh my God. A *prince?*"

"You shouldn't be calling. It's too expensive."

"Relax. It's an internet call and I'm on wifi." Cherry could almost hear her little sister's eye roll, and it set her teeth on edge. She loved Maggie—but sometimes she envied her sister's ability to 'relax'. It was hard to chill out with financial ruin breathing down your neck.

But then, Maggie wouldn't know anything about that. No-one wanted her to.

"Yes, he's a prince," Cherry sighed, pushing her envy away. "And knowing my luck, there'll be pictures of us splashed across the papers tomorrow morning."

"Hardly," Maggie snorted. "I've never heard of him, so I doubt anyone else has. It's not like he's a *prince* prince. You know people only care about Brits."

Cherry had had the same thought herself, but hearing it from Maggie's lips steadied her rocketing pulse. She took a deep breath and let those words sink in. "You're right. No-one will know. No-one will care. It'll just blow over."

"Exactly. Don't worry about it. But, while we're on the subject, how long have you and him been—"

"I should go," Cherry blurted out. Anything to avoid telling her little sister that she'd been planning an impromptu one night stand. "Still in my work clothes. And I can practically feel my makeup clogging my pores."

Maggie, who never wore makeup and would happily roam the streets in stained pyjamas, tutted. "Take that shit off. Eat some ice cream. But don't think you're off the hook with this, and don't miss the family date, okay?"

"No-one would know if I did. I could just Google the episode synopsis."

"Mum would know. She'd sense it with her weird magical mum instincts. And then you'd be in deep shit."

Cherry rolled her eyes. "Okay, true. But before I go, how are you?"

She almost *felt* Maggie stiffen through the phone. "Checking up on me?"

"I'm your big sister. Of course I'm checking up on you."

"Well, you don't need to. I eat my vegetables, I take my medicine, I keep my doctor's appointments—I am a model citizen." She said this with a vaguely wounded air, as if it were unreasonable for Cherry to worry about her chronically ill baby sister.

"Any pain, recently?"

"What would you do if I said yes?" Maggie demanded. "Fly out just to force-feed me some painkillers? I'm fine. Now go and get ready. Or unready. Whatever."

"Okay, okay! I'll talk to you later."

"Bye, Cherry Pie."

"Goodbye, Magnolia." She hung up on her sister's indignant sputtering.

CHAPTER NINE

R uben slid into the back of the waiting Hummer, his heart in his throat. Trouble wasn't an unusual state for him to be in, but over these past months he'd started to outdo himself.

This time, as always, it concerned a woman. No matter what he liked to think, he was clearly doing something wrong in that department.

Hans settled in beside him, spearing him with a glare that would freeze hell. "I warned you."

"Don't start. I'm thinking."

"For a change."

"Will you *stop?* I had to say something. I couldn't let him splash pictures of the two of us all over the fucking news. You *know*—"

Hans placed a calming hand on Ruben's shoulder. "Yes. Yes, I know. I'm sorry. But Christ, Ruben, you do realise that you can't take this back, right? Your brother probably knows already. *Everyone* probably knows already. In fact..." He reached for his phone, but Ruben shook his head sharply.

"Don't. Don't bother. We both know it's everywhere by now." He knew from experience how fast these things spread. Although, last time he'd been burned by the press, it'd been for something far more salacious. Perhaps that sort of news spread more quickly...

Ah, who was he kidding? The black sheep of the royal family, engaged? Hans was right. His brother would know. Everyone would know.

He let his head fall back against the headrest, releasing a sigh. "I've fucked this up, haven't I?"

"Which part?" Hans said mildly.

"Don't be smart."

"One of us has to be."

Perhaps it was a blessing that his phone rang at that juncture. Or at least, that's what Ruben thought, until he realised who must be calling.

Hans stared at Ruben's jacket, where the chirping ringtone emanated from, like there was a bomb hidden in the silk lining. Ruben, unsurprisingly, shared the feeling.

"You'd better answer," Hans said, "or it'll ring out."

And then the king will lose his shit with all the grace of a machine-gun-toting toddler. And everything will be a million times worse.

"Right," Ruben said grimly and fished out his phone. He took a second to collect himself before he answered the call. He'd probably still fuck up, though. His brother had that effect.

Resigned, he brought the phone to his ear and said, "Ambjørn."

"You do that purely to irritate me. It's pathetic." The voice was a deep baritone, the kind that should've been soothing. It went through Ruben like nails on a chalkboard.

"Believe it or not, brother, not everything about me is designed solely to disappoint you."

"If that's true, why do you insist on calling me *brother*?" The King of Helgmøre sneered the word. "Provincial to the end. If bonds matter so very much, then please, use the correct term."

Ruben bit down on the inside of his cheek. "Half-brother? Bit of a mouthful."

"Then I suggest you stick to *Your Majesty*." King Harald's words were whip-sharp. So sharp, Ruben thought he felt the ghost of his brother's switch against his calves. Even servants were pressed, charmingly, to call the king *Harald*—though of course, they never would. But Ruben wasn't a servant.

In his brother's eyes, he wasn't a person at all.

"Your Majesty," he gritted out. "Oh, great one, how may I serve you?"

"You may serve me," Harald said, "by explaining your latest disgrace. According to the media, you are engaged."

And Ruben, memories suffocating him and hatred burning like acid in his veins, said with utter nonchalance, "Yep."

Beside him, Hans stiffened.

His brother expelled a noisy breath, like a dragon preparing to lay waste to some village. "And this is the first I'm hearing of it, *because*?"

"I understand your concern, Harald. You and I are so close, after all."

"I am the head of this family, and you are lucky to be acknowledged at all." His brother's voice was a venomous hiss.

He could picture the exact expression that went along with this particular tone: lips peeled back from teeth as though they were fangs, blue eyes narrowed dangerously in a way that still set

Ruben on edge. Still made him anxious. Still reminded him of days when he'd been so much smaller, and his brother had seemed like a mountain.

But he was the mountain now.

"With all due respect, Your Majesty, what the fuck do you want?"

"Careful boy. Whoever this woman is—it *is* a woman, isn't it?"

"Yes," Ruben said stiffly. "She's a woman."

"Thank Christ. You're not a complete idiot, then. Whoever she is, I have not agreed to the match."

"I wasn't aware that I required permission to marry, Your Majesty." *Lie.*

"You require my permission to breathe. Count yourself lucky that you still have it."

Ruben clenched his teeth so tight, his jaw clicked with a burst of pain. He didn't stop. He couldn't stop. Because the one thing he absolutely would not do was give his brother the satisfaction of a response. Harald hated silence. When he spoke, what he wanted, more than anything, was a reaction. So, once the quiet stretched out and Ruben held his tongue, it was the mighty king who broke first.

"Well," Harald said finally. "At least this one's cleverer than the last."

Ruben swallowed, his own rage souring his throat. "What do you mean?"

"Unlike Kathryn, this one actually managed to trap you. Lydia is most concerned."

Ruben ignored the reference to Lydia, his sweet sister-in-law, doubtless designed to keep him off-balance. Harald didn't value his wife highly enough to mention her without an ulterior motive. "Cherry didn't *trap me*," Ruben said, his voice purposely flat.

And then he kicked himself. Fuck.

"*Cherry*?" Harald barked out a laugh. "The fruit? *Kirsebær*? What, do you fuck strippers now?"

"Watch your fucking mouth."

"Put down your sword, Prince Charming. It is just a plank of wood and you are just a peasant boy." Harald snorted with delight at his own joke. "Whatever. It is too late now; we must project unity. You will pretend that I met this Cherry long ago. And you will bring her to me."

"No."

"That wasn't a request, boy. Don't forget: you *do* need my permission. Unless you'd like to renounce your claim on the throne of Helgmøre?"

Ruben gritted his teeth, the pulse thudding through his head so strong that it was painful. This was the game he played, the line he danced across. He was fifth in line for the throne of Helgmøre, which gave Harald a certain legal amount of control over him. Escaping his brother's power would mean renouncing his claim.

And he would never renounce his fucking claim. He would not be struck out of history books and swept aside, no matter how many people thought his existence was a mistake.

"No," he said. "I will not renounce my claim." Now, he would tell his brother the truth. He would never hear the end of it, of course —would be summoned home immediately, have his activities with the Trust curtailed, and yet again, the press would spend months breathing down his neck. Tearing him apart and glorying in his bloody entrails. At the thought, his skin became too hot and tight for his body. His heart rate thundered and his breath came fast, shallow and sharp. Again. It would happen all over again.

He couldn't tell his brother. He couldn't tell anyone. He couldn't go through another fucking scandal. They'd eat him alive.

"I will bring her," he choked into the phone. "Okay? I'll bring her. Soon. At some point. I'm going now."

"I beg your pardon? Ruben—"

"I have to go!" He put the phone down and threw it into the car's footwell. Then he stared down at it, that innocuous little rectangle of glass and plastic with which he'd just dug himself into an even deeper hole.

Fuck.

He looked over at Hans, searching for some kind of reassurance. Instead, he was faced with the sight of his bodyguard and lifelong companion wide-eyed and open-mouthed, looking at Ruben like he'd just grown another head. Out of his arse.

"What the fuck did I just do?" Ruben rasped.

"I don't know. Shit. I don't know. What the hell were you thinking?"

"I... I realised that if I take this back, it could start all over again. Just like before. And I can't deal with that. I can't." Memories rampaged through his mind, blurring together like a countryside viewed from a speeding train. The headlines, the articles, the fucking documentary, all the shit that had popped up over the last eight months. People dredging up the drama of his past, his origins, the story of his parents—his mother. All because he'd dragged the family name through the mud and turned out to be exactly what people always thought he'd be.

Unworthy of the Royal House of Helgmøre.

"Hey." Hans's voice was as hard as the grip he had on Ruben's shoulder. He squeezed, his fingers grinding into muscle and bone, until the pain brought Ruben back into the present. "Stop panicking. You don't need to panic. This is fine."

Ruben huffed out a laugh. "No it fucking isn't."

"It is. So you told the world that Cherry is your fiancée. You know what that makes you?"

"What?"

"Boring. Normal. Something other than the royal family's black sheep. And it protects her from too much media interest, too—as long as they think she's yours. So... why don't you make it real?"

Ruben stared at his bodyguard. "What the fuck are you talking about?"

"Make her your fiancée. Then everything is simple, yes? No lies. She's just your fiancée."

"Hans," Ruben said patiently. "I realise that you don't know much about women—"

"Incorrect."

"—But Cherry does *not* want to marry me. At all. Not even close."

"Actually, I did notice that." Hans said this a little too smugly for Ruben's liking. "But I am not talking about a *real* engagement."

Ruben eyed his friend warily. "Continue."

"I mean, you ask her to play the role of fiancée. For a period of time, I don't know; a long engagement. Long enough for the press to become bored of her, and for your brother to forget you exist."

"I wish," Ruben muttered.

"Then she leaves you, yes? And you are a tragic figure. Everyone feels sorry for you. It blows over. Understand?"

Ruben tapped his fingers against his thighs as he mulled that plan over. "I don't know. It's kind of ridiculous."

"You have a better idea?"

"It's *extremely* ridiculous."

"Okay. Give me an alternative. Another way to extricate yourself from this situation without a repeat of the last eight months."

Ruben clamped his teeth together. "I don't know. She'd never agree to that."

"She might. If you offer the appropriate motivation." Then, at Ruben's baffled look, he added, "Money. People need money, *Your Highness*." He was still angry, then, despite all his advice.

"Oh. Right. Of course. Do you think she'd do that? For money? Put herself in that position?"

"You've already put her in that position. She might as well get something out of it. And I think you'll find that most people, these days, are in desperate need of money. Offer her enough, and see what happens."

The silence stretched out between them as seconds crept into minutes.

Then, finally, Ruben spoke. "You might be onto something."

CHAPTER TEN

C herry spent the next day on edge. She was waiting for someone with a camera to leap out from the bushes and call her a slut in Danish. Or for Chris to sack her for inappropriate fraternisation with the Academy's personal prince. Or something.

None of that happened. In fact, nothing unusual happened at all. Until she left work that afternoon.

She chugged down the long, gentle hill towards the outskirts of town, turning the corner before her flat—only to brake sharply when she came car-to-face with a horde of shouting people.

She blinked, confused. What the fuck were they doing, crawling across the street like a nest of ants? That was a sharp bend; she could've hit someone. Did they have no sense of self-preservation?

Then the first camera flash popped into view, sending stars across her vision.

No way. No fucking way.

"It's her! That's the car!"

Oh, fuck.

A fist banged against her window, and then one guy sprawled his whole damn body across the hood of her poor little Corsa, camera flashing right in her face.

Looked like Maggie's confidence had been misplaced. Apparently, some people *did* care about foreign royals.

Cherry smiled. It was her prettiest smile, not seductive or charming but delightful and demure. She turned her head slightly to display the left side of her face. If she was about to play a starring role in some gossip rag, they should at least get her good side.

She gave them a solid three seconds of beauty. Then she slammed the accelerator.

They scrambled. She had to hand it to them; they were quick. Although, the guy who'd been lying across her hood rolled off the car and right onto the road. Oh, dear. That *had* to hurt. Maybe his fancy fucking camera had broken the fall.

She sped the rest of the way home, skidding into her flat's car park and swinging recklessly into a parking space. Well—three spaces. Horizontally. Whatever. She hit the brakes, then flipped down the visor mirror, checking her reflection. Still perfect. Good. Because there, loitering near the entrance of the car park, was a black, stretch Lincoln MKT. *Gag.*

Well. Hans had told her they'd be back.

With a sigh, Cherry got out of the car, striding over to the limo just as its door opened and Hans's huge body emerged.

"Madam," he said.

"Have you come to kidnap me? I have to warn you, my scream has been known to burst eardrums."

His lips quirked, but his gaze remained blank; he was all smooth professionalism and intimidating silence.

"Fine," she sighed. "Be that way." She slipped past him and climbed into the car.

He shut the door behind her.

"I'm glad to see you," Ruben said.

Cherry closed her eyes, just for a second, as she reined in the feelings that sentence had set off. There were many of them, bright and varied as a Bonfire Night sky, but the most pressing emotion was rage.

She was still angry, then. In case she'd been in any doubt.

When she opened her eyes again, he was frowning at her. He lounged against the limo's leather seats, his right ankle crossed over his left knee, the fabric of his suit trousers pulling tight over powerful thighs. He wore no jacket, and his shirtsleeves were rolled up to expose his forearms. For a moment, she considered allowing herself to enjoy the sight of those forearms—objectively, you know. Separating the art from the artist.

Then she pulled herself together and clutched her anger close, a burning barrier against the twisted attraction she still felt. Clearly, his looks did terrible things to her head. And she needed her mind clear for this conversation.

Cherry tore her gaze from his face and forced herself to speak. "I thought you said the press would leave me alone?"

"In Helgmøre," he said, "there is an understanding between my brother—the king—and the media. The royal family are protected from certain invasions of privacy. That agreement does not, unfortunately, extend to the activities of the British press."

"Great," she said woodenly. "Perfect. Just what I need."

"I know," he said softly. "I'm sorry."

She pursed her lips. Frankly, that wasn't much of an apology. It had all the key parts: 'I'm' and 'sorry'. But she wanted something a bit more impactful. Something involving sky-writing and a grand band, perhaps. Just a few ideas. Maybe she should write him a list.

"Cherry," he said, after her silence went on a little bit too long. "Are you going to talk to me?"

Before she could stop herself, she tutted. And then was utterly mortified. God, she sounded like her mother.

The corner of his mouth tugged up into a smile. "I take it that's a no." At her blank stare, his smile faded. He sighed, sitting up straighter, planting both feet flat on the floor. "You're right, obviously. Why should you talk to me?" His tongue snaked out to wet his full, lower lip. "But I have a lot to say. Do you mind if we drive?"

She shrugged. He reached over and pressed one of the buttons lined up by the nearest blacked-out window. "*Køre.*"

The car slid into movement, so smooth she almost didn't notice.

"Alright," Ruben said, clasping his hands together. "I know you like to keep things to the point—"

"And yet," she murmured, "you continue to babble."

He grinned. Apparently, he didn't care what she said, as long as she spoke. "I do, don't I? It's natural, I'm afraid."

She arched a brow. "Now you're doing it on purpose."

"What can I say?" His voice deepened, became darker, rich as molasses. "I seem to behave badly around you."

Cherry swallowed, hard. She clamped her knees together and tried to forget the feeling of his hands tugging at her suspenders. Didn't work. So she talked over the images crowding her brain. "Whatever you're trying to say here, get on with it. Please. Before you bore me to death."

His eyes captured hers and didn't let go. They were steady, impenetrable, unavoidable, even as he gave her that devastating little half-smile. "Certainly. I'm here to make you an offer."

Oh, dear. "An offer, as in…?"

"You have a problem," he said, which was an understatement if she'd ever heard one. "I do too. My… indiscretion affects both of us, believe it or not."

She snorted. "Not."

But he watched her steadily, unsmiling. "I have no wish to draw attention to myself, Cherry. I had a bad experience, not so long ago, that left me with little desire to cause another…" His mouth twisted as he searched for the word. "Another *scandal*. So, yes, this affects me. I have a certain reputation, one that I cannot seem to escape and desperately want to. You can help me change the narrative. And, in return, I may be able to help you. Understand?"

Cherry rolled her lips inwards, her toes curling inside her shoes. In less than a day, she'd managed to forget how it felt to bear the full force of that intensity. But she forced herself to concentrate on what mattered; on the meaning behind his words, not the thread of steel in his voice or the aura of authority that twisted something in her chest.

"So what did you do?" she asked.

He frowned. "What do you mean?"

"What did you do? To get this terrible reputation of yours?"

He pinched the bridge of his nose. "Nothing… immoral."

"Well, you know, people rarely consider themselves to be immoral. Hitler thought of himself as a great guy. So, I'd kind of like to know."

She could practically hear him grinding his teeth. "It was… related to my sexual proclivities." Then, when he saw the look on her face, he hurried to add, "Nothing like that. I didn't hurt

76

anyone. I don't..." He sighed. "Jesus, Cherry. I had sex. That's what I did."

"Oh, please," she scoffed. "You're a man. You could fuck the Queen and they'd pat you on the back."

"Well," he said wryly, "*my* queen is also my sister-in-law. So perhaps not."

"You know what I mean. The only time men get shit for sex is if they're on some truly twisted shit, *or* they're anything other than laser straight." She looked up to find him watching her with quiet amusement, and something in his eyes made her realise... "Oh. You—"

"*I*, what?" He demanded, one brow raised. "I fuck who I want, how I want? Correct. That's what I did. Are we done?"

Cherry bit down on the inside of her cheek, suddenly feeling kind of... shit. "Yeah. Okay."

He inclined his head, and his voice was soft when he murmured, "Good." But his eyes skated away from hers again, and he seemed to reel himself in. The air between them no longer swelled with the force of his personality. Everything was still and quiet and precisely as it should be. He reached for a case of black leather beside him, revealing that it was actually a huge folder. He slid open the silver clasp and pulled out a thick sheath of papers, half of which he gave to her.

"This is my offer," he said. "You can study it at your leisure, but the long and short of it is—well. I'd like you to become my fiancée. For a year."

In the ensuing silence, Cherry became acutely aware of the low hum of the car's engine, its smooth glide forward. She wondered, suddenly and pointlessly, where they were. Was the driver circling the block? Probably not. That would cause unnecessary attention. Maybe they were heading towards the city, where a car like this wouldn't garner as much notice. Maybe—

"Cherry," Ruben said gently. "Are you alright?"

Was she alright? Now she thought about it, she was tapping her foot rather rapidly. And clenching her fists kind of tightly. Her nails must be carving some serious crescent moons into her palms right now. It would probably hurt, if her mind wasn't too busy freaking the fuck out to notice minor things like pain.

"Cherry." His hand came to settle on her shoulder again, squeezing this time. Hard enough to capture her attention, to drag her out of her own head.

She blinked at him. "Could you repeat yourself? Please?"

He swallowed. "I asked you to be my fiancée for a year."

"I thought you did," she nodded. "I really thought you did. But then I thought, why the fuck would you ask me to do that?"

"Well… there are, ah, several reasons…" He sat back in his seat, clearing his throat.

"Is this a joke?" she asked sharply. "Because it's not very funny. I just had photographers crawling over my car like ants, and I am waiting, just *waiting* for a hysterical call from my mother—"

"It's not a joke," he interrupted. "I told you; I need your help."

"Well, no, you didn't say that at all. You said a load of mysterious, complicated shit that made no sense whatsoever—"

"Maybe you just weren't listening."

"And maybe you're shit at explaining things."

He smiled, sudden and unexpected. "You're right. I am terrible at explaining things. I have no finesse."

"Really? I would've said your problem was getting to the point."

"Fine." He held out his hands as if in supplication. "The point is this: I need a fiancée—specifically, you—because of yesterday's shit-show. And, yes, I realise it was mostly my fault."

"Completely your fault."

He winked at her. *Actually* winked at her. "Well, maybe. But I never take full responsibility if I can help it."

"Wow. You really are a prince."

"Yep. Now, I realise there's not much in this deal for you—"

"There's *nothing* in this deal for me."

"—So I added a financial incentive."

Cherry paused. She looked down at the paper in her hands. Then she flicked through, faster and faster, until she came to the part that mattered.

The number on the page made her brows shoot up. Then Ruben leant over and shook his head. "No, that's not it. That's how much I'm going to give you if you refuse."

Her head snapped up. "I beg your pardon?"

"If you don't sign. That's the amount I'm giving you anyway, you know, to make up for the probable media fall-out." He shook his head, flicking forward another few pages. "But you forfeit that if you sign, and instead you get this."

She blinked. "Isn't that the same amount?"

"Monthly."

Cherry stared.

Her mind ran through calculations in a split second. Maggie's healthcare fees in the States—her blood transfusions, her antibiotics, her hydroxycarbamide—and the tuition fees that her scholarships didn't cover...

Cherry could pay them. Easily.

No more debt. No more panic. Her whole family—her parents, her uncle and her aunts—could stop pouring all their money into

Maggie's education and healthcare, could stop hiding the way it gutted them all. And her sister could continue to live the life she deserved, without worrying about her illness.

But it couldn't be that easy. Could it?

She licked her lips, which felt suddenly dry. "I don't know if an engagement with me would... would help you avoid a scandal. Or whatever it is you want."

He crossed his arms, watching her with all the patience in the world. "And why not? Please, explain."

"Well..." She floundered, awkward. What did he want her to do? Lay out all the things about herself that most of society found distasteful? Remind them all that she wasn't considered princess material? Fuck that.

But then he pushed. "Tell me. What is it about you that's so terrible?"

"Nothing," she said immediately. "I'm fine. I'm great. Doesn't mean everyone *else* sees me that way. You're a prince, and I'm, you know, normal." She winced. "No offence. Plus, I'm not really considered ladylike. Because..." She waved vaguely down at her body.

He followed the motion of her hand, his eyes cool and assessing as they travelled over her. Then he said, his voice bland, "I see no issue."

She glared. "Jesus fucking Christ, you're annoying."

"So I'm told. Really, stop worrying. I know how these things work."

"Believe me," she said grimly, "so do I."

He sighed. "Cherry... People, generally speaking, are amoral, arse-licking hypocrites. If you're some woman I kissed in an alley, they'll despise you; once you're a princess-to-be, they'll discover boundless liberal sentiment. I'll be a pioneer of the modern age.

You see what they're saying about your country's royal family, don't you?"

She set her jaw, refusing to allow that point. "But I'm *not* a princess-to-be. I haven't agreed to this."

"But you will," he said softly. "If you weren't going to, you'd have told me so already. Wouldn't you?"

Cherry looked at the contract. She looked at her hands. She remembered her mother's face two years ago, the day Maggie had received her acceptance letter from Harvard. She remembered the last time she'd stayed with her parents, over Christmas, when they'd refused to turn the central heating on. Acting like they didn't need to.

When really they couldn't.

She said, "How do I know this contract is real?"

"You know it's real," he said calmly. "But it's just a draft of the version we would sign, should you agree to this. I'm sure you understand it."

She pressed her lips together. She worked in HR; so yes, she could read a damned contract. But she relied on people assuming that she couldn't. It was always easier to control a situation when no-one thought you were capable of doing so.

"Take a look," he said, nodding towards the papers in her lap. "See if the whole arrangement is to your satisfaction."

She flicked through, scanning each page with an ease born of practice. It wasn't the kind of document she came across often, but that didn't really matter. These things were all based on the same principles, and she knew those principles like the back of her hand.

It wasn't tricky. There was no double-talk, nothing to suggest he was trying to confuse or manipulate her. Just basic terms, caveats, detailed specifics. They would remain engaged for a year, at which point *she* would leave *him*—interesting. During that year, she would be bound by the same obligations as he was, so far as royal duties went. *Royal duties*—wasn't that a fucking trip? She'd spend most of her time in Helgmøre, but not all of it. She could visit with family whenever she wanted for up to two weeks at a time. She couldn't tell anyone of their agreement, blah blah blah...

Cherry looked up. "You know you've forced me into this. You understand that, right?"

He looked stricken. "I—"

"You let me think you were just some guy. You kissed me knowing that something like this *could* happen. Then you opened your big mouth and made it happen. You have all the power in the fucking world compared to me, and I..." She huffed out a laugh. "I need money. Have you ever needed money?"

His face was solemn as he said, "No. I have never needed money."

"Lucky fucking you." She stared down at the contract. "I don't want to do this."

"Cherry—"

"But I'm going to. I'm going to lie to everyone I know, lie to the *world*." Just the thought of it turned her stomach. "And *you're* going to pay me. And in a year, I will walk away and do my best to pretend this never happened, even though everything about me will have changed. So just know that I will sign this contract, and I will fulfil my obligations, but... you and me? That's not happening. Not even a little bit. Not anymore."

He swallowed, hard. Nodded. And said, "Yes. I understand. I do."

"Good." She slapped the contract into his lap. "So we're going to Helgmøre, then?"

"As soon as possible, yes."

"Crap." Various problems sprang to mind, though they seemed

mundane in light of what she'd just agreed to. "I'll have to take Whiskey, obviously. God, I'll have to quit my job. Rose will be scandalised. But I'll never have to work with Chris again." She smiled. "Hm. Silver linings, and all that…"

Ruben leaned forward, his brow furrowed as he asked, "Whiskey?"

Oh, right. "My cat," Cherry explained.

Ruben sighed. "I see."

CHAPTER ELEVEN

The private jet descended bit by bit, and Ruben kept his eyes on Cherry. She, despite her obvious disgust for him, did not look away. No; she stared him down like they were rival gunslingers in the wild west, and she was shooting to kill.

It might turn him on if it weren't for the fact that she genuinely disliked him. And she had a damned good reason to.

As the plane circled his family's little landing strip, Ruben fought the sense of dread that had been growing since the moment she'd agreed to this charade. It made no sense—she'd done exactly what he'd hoped she'd do. Exactly what he'd wanted her to do. But he couldn't stop thinking about the way she'd smiled at him when they'd first met—just three days ago. He already knew that she'd never smile at him like that again.

This was probably the fastest he'd ever fucked something up. Dragging Cherry into his life felt like dragging a princess off to his lair. He was almost certainly the dragon in this fairytale.

When the plane finally landed, she collected herself with brisk efficiency. It had only been a two hour flight, but Ruben felt like... well, he felt like he'd stepped into a giant metal cage, crossed the world at an unnatural height and speed, and been dumped on the ground again. Cherry, however, looked like a slightly more casual version of her usual glamorous self. Her hair was a riot of curls and coils, her face was as perfect as ever, and her glare was colder than the January air that hit them when an air hostess opened the plane door.

"Welcome to Helgmøre, Madam," the hostess said with a sunny smile.

And Cherry, damn her, dropped the ice in an instant and answered with a devastating smile of her own. "Thank you, Ida." She paused, looking out of the open door at the bare tarmac, crawling with security, and the frosted field beyond. "It's so… refreshing. What a beautiful country."

Ida's smile widened and her pale cheeks flushed with pleasure. She stared at Cherry as though hypnotised. "Thank you! You are very kind."

Ruben moved forwards to help Cherry down the plane steps, and for one fraught moment he thought she might resist his touch— might protest, or jerk away, or do something to alert the plane staff of the chasm between them. But thankfully, she allowed it, though her hand was rigid and unyielding in his.

He, feeling utterly pathetic, bathed her in warmth, in smiles, in consideration, as he led her down the steps. Hans's disapproving stare was a knife at his back, sharp and impossible to miss. Ruben barely cared. It was galling to realise how desperate he was for even a single ray of the sunshine Cherry gave out so liberally. If she shared a drop of that charm with him, he might die of gratitude.

How did she do this? How did she do this to him?

"You like my country?" he asked, trying to inject some humour into his voice. He wanted to make her laugh, for reasons he couldn't quite explain. He'd done it before, so surely he could do it again.

She smiled and murmured, "Oh, yes." It was a practiced smile, and they were practiced words. Indistinguishable from the facade she'd offered the air hostess moments ago.

So this was how it would be. Ruben cleared his throat awkwardly, shame creeping down his spine like a centipede, making his skin crawl. What had he been thinking? That she'd soften, that things would go back to the way they were? The way they might have been? Her life was forever changed because he'd chosen her, and been too arrogant to consider the consequences. He'd taken away her power, her control—the things he already knew that she valued the most. And now he was using her to boot.

They descended the steps in silence. Thank God that, when they reached the bottom, Demetria was there waiting.

"Hello!" she cried, flashing her blindingly white teeth. "I'm Demetria Karzai, Ruben's assistant!" Ruben had never heard her sound so chirpy in his life. And he'd known her for many, many years. "You can call me Demi. It's so nice to meet you!" She stepped forward to shake Cherry's hand, and her hijab sparkled in the sunlight. Why the hell was she wearing a *sparkling* hijab? And where were her glasses? Was she really wearing contacts just to meet him at the damn airport?

As the two women exchanged greetings, Ruben turned a questioning look on Hans. The big man shrugged helplessly.

Then Demi finally released Cherry's hand and gave Ruben a hard, sideways look as she trilled, "I've heard so much about you!"

Ah.

"Demi," he said. "Get in the car."

Cherry frowned. "Don't be rude to her."

Oh, so now they were best friends. Bloody women.

"*Both* of you get in the car. Come on." He stalked forward, Hans bringing up the rear, Cherry muttering acidly about autocratic arseholes. Ruben bit back a smile.

Once they were safely ensconced in the back of the limo, he said, "We're not really engaged."

"Oh, for fuck's sake," Cherry muttered.

But he barely heard that over Demetria's shrieked, "I *knew* it!" Then she turned to Cherry with an apologetic look. "No offence."

Cherry said, very sweetly, "None taken." She was almost certainly lying.

"What Demi means is that if we were really engaged, she'd already know who you were. She's my friend."

"I'm your P.A. And your babysitter."

"What, you're not my friend?"

"No comment."

Cherry's icy demeanour thawed slightly, and she offered Demi something approaching a smile. "I see."

Demi nodded. "I woke up the other day to a thousand headlines about Ruben's mysterious fiancée, and he wouldn't even answer his phone!"

"I had a lot on my plate," Ruben murmured wryly.

"Yeah, whatever. So I texted Hans and he said, 'Ruben is engaged'."

All eyes swung to Hans, who was sitting silently in the corner. He raised his brows. "What? You *are* engaged."

"Anyway," Demi said, her tone long-suffering. "I thought either something was up, or... I don't know, that Ruben met his soul-mate and fell in love at first sight."

Hans snorted. "Is that why your hijab is all… glittery?"

"Awww, you noticed!"

"You look like a disco ball."

"Don't hate me cuz you ain't me."

Cherry, Ruben realised, was watching the pair trade barbs with the strangest little smile on her face. Then she met his gaze, and instead of looking away, she arched a brow. Almost conspiratorially.

Now, if he could just figure out what the conspiracy was…

When he could only stare blankly in response, she rolled her eyes heavenward and looked away.

Shit.

"So anyway," Demi said, turning pointedly away from Hans. "What's going on?"

"Yes, Ruben," Cherry said sweetly. "Tell her. Explain the situation. Please."

Ruben stifled a sigh. This was not going to be easy.

THE SUN WAS SETTING by the time they reached Ruben's estate. Because that, Cherry decided, was the only appropriate word for it: estate.

They may be in Scandinavia, but the imposing grey-bricked mansion looming in the distance seemed as English as steak and kidney pie. Or classism. Or fish and chips.

A huge wall surrounded the property, passing further than Cherry could see, but the car stopped in front of a pair of gothic, iron gates. The gates swung open unassisted, like something out of a horror film, and they drove in.

Why did it feel like Cherry was marching headfirst into her own doom?

A tense discussion raged in the car. Demi, unsurprisingly, had been horrified at Ruben's explanation and was now berating him quite passionately for putting Cherry in 'such an awful position'.

Cherry rather liked Demi.

But the argument was cyclical, like siblings bickering during a road trip, and Cherry's nerves were strung tight enough as it was. Earlier that day, before leaving for the airport, she'd had a quick and unpleasant phone call with her parents.

It hadn't gone well. Not that they were *angry* with her. No. But when she'd awkwardly lied about a whirlwind courtship and sudden engagement—things she'd *never* do—they'd decided that she was having some kind of early mid-life crisis, and that Ruben was taking advantage of that crisis for his nefarious, princely purposes.

She'd been hoping that his royal status might get her parents onboard. Apparently, the opposite was true.

So she took deep breaths and tuned out the argument filling the car, squinting out of the darkened windows as they drove up the gravel path. She could hear it crunching beneath the car wheels. Who the fuck had a gravel path, for Christ's sake? And the thing was miles long, too, with a turning circle. A bloody turning circle!

She bit the inside of her cheek as they approached the house. And then...

They drove right past it.

Cherry frowned. "Where are we going?"

Ruben took a break from bickering with his P.A. to say, "Home."

"Isn't that your house?"

He rolled his eyes. "The mansion? No. I hate that place."

"So where do you live?" Cherry demanded. As soon as the words left her mouth, another house came into view. Tucked away at the back of the mansion's vast garden, this house was more of a cottage. Not exactly small—about the size of a family home, really —but cozy. Warm and welcoming and not at all disturbingly gothic.

"I live there," Ruben said.

Cherry nodded stiffly. She tore her gaze away from the house with its cheerful red bricks and wide bay windows and ivy crawling merrily up the walls, and tried her best not to feel pleased.

MAGZ: **Mum thinks you've lost it.**

Cherry lay back on the mammoth, four-poster bed that apparently belonged to her now. It was a nest of thick, deep purple blankets and over-fluffed pillows that she desperately wanted to hate, but found disturbingly comfortable.

Whatever. She still didn't want to be here.

Cherry: I know. Do you?

Magz: You haven't really told me what's happening yet, so I'm reserving judgement.

Cherry huffed out a laugh and settled back into the blankets, the silk of her headscarf sliding against the satiny pillows. There was no lock on the door, so she was lying in the dark at 10 p.m. If anyone came knocking, she could pretend to be asleep. That way, she wouldn't have to display her bare face, wrapped up hair and fluffy bed socks to whoever decided to stop by.

Living with people was strange—people who weren't family, anyway. She'd have to be *on* constantly. For what felt like the thousandth time, Cherry began to wonder if she could really do this for a year.

Cherry: Do you trust my judgement?

Magz: Yes.

Magz: 100%

Cherry smiled. There was something to be said for little sisters.

Cherry: I can't tell you everything, but I want to know what you think... I had a decision to make, and I looked at all the available evidence, and I believe I chose well, long-term. But short-term it's going to be uncomfortable. I keep worrying I've got something wrong and it's too good to be true or it won't be worth it. What do you think?

She lay there, her arms aching from holding her phone up over her face, waiting for Maggie's response to that cryptic mess.

Magz: That was an essay, lol.

Cherry rolled her eyes.

Magz: You're super smart. You're the sensible one. You probably chose right.

The idea that her little sister, who was studying Biomedical bloody Engineering at *Harvard*, thought Cherry was smart, made her grin. But still, she couldn't stop herself from asking...

Cherry: Probably? What if that's not good enough?

Magz: Probably has to be good enough. Life is probability, sis.

Cherry: Wow. You're really learning shit over there.

Magz: Whatever. So are you gold-digging your prince or what?

Cherry snorted. If only she fucking knew.

Magz: Cuz if you are, hook me up with a cousin first.

Cherry: Hook you up?! You better face your damned books!

Maggie replied with several eye rolling emojis. Cherry snorted.

Cherry: I should go. Beauty sleep.

Magz: But you don't need it cuz you're already sooooOOooooo-OOoooo beautiful.

Cherry: Girl shut up. I'm not staying up to text you about Teen Wolf.

Magz: Wow, you don't love me at all, do you?

Cherry stared at that message for way longer than she should have. It was a joke. The kind of throwaway comment they made all the time, totally sarcastic. But it struck her all at once just how much she *did* love Maggie. How happy it made her to think of her little sister living her best geeky life across the pond, going to school every day with all the other geeks, learning to be the greatest geek she could be. Or something. And while the whole family had moved heaven and earth to make that happen, the possibility that one day they might run out of heaven and earth had always existed.

But it didn't exist anymore.

Cherry: You take your meds?

Magz: I'm the one who suffers if I don't, so what do you think?!

Cherry: LOL. Down, girl. Night x

Magz: Night sis, love you x

Cherry: I really love you too.

CHAPTER TWELVE

T he next morning, Hans dragged Ruben to the dining room bright and early for 'a meeting'.

He found a council of war seated at the mahogany table, sunlight streaming through the tall, glass windows like a hazy spotlight. Demi sat at the head of the table, the set of her shoulders and her dark, winged brows giving her a militant air. She was wearing her glasses again, and her usual plain hijab, so she looked both familiar and austere all at once.

To her right was a round, faded old woman wearing a floral apron and a warm smile: Agathe. And to Demi's left was Hans, who was staring at the side of Demi's head with a brooding expression. Probably because he hated meetings, Ruben thought. Those two really were polar opposites.

At the end of the table, two more seats faced each other. One was empty. The other was occupied by Cherry, and the sight of her was like a punch to the gut.

Her lipstick was peachy today, instead of red, and glossy instead of… whatever the opposite of glossy was. Her velvety skin shone in the sunlight and her tight curls quivered with every movement of her head, like countless little springs coiled up with energy. He remembered how soft those curls had felt in his hand and wanted to kick himself. How had he fucked things up so royally with this woman? *This* woman, of all women?

Her eyes settled on him, gleaming copper in the light, and he tore his gaze away. He may be infatuated, but there was no need for her to know that. It would only make her uncomfortable.

Ruben bent over the old woman's shoulder on his way to his own seat, pressing a kiss against her soft, wrinkled cheek. "Agathe."

"Good morning, lazy boy."

He clapped a hand to his chest, feigning pain. "*Lazy*? Me? How could you say such a thing?"

"You are late," Agathe sniffed.

"Yes," Demi said. "So sit *down*, Ruben, *please*." She reminded Ruben of the staff at the Trust corralling younger kids with a rictus-grin. "I thought we could have this little meeting to, ah, collect ourselves! Get our house in order. You know, since—"

"Since Ruben dived into a shit show and dragged the rest of us along with him," Hans said darkly.

There was a slight pause. Agathe looked aghast. Cherry appeared to be fighting a smirk. He wanted to kiss that smirk off her face. Then he remembered that he was supposed to be glaring at Hans.

"No," Demi said, dealing with Hans on her own. "I was *going* to say, since we want to be at the top of our game for the ball next month."

Ruben sat up straight. "Ball?"

"Yes," Demi sighed. "You didn't check your emails?"

"I've been busy."

"Really?" she asked sweetly. "During that two hour flight yesterday?"

He pinched the bridge of his nose. "Demetria."

With a sigh, she let it go. She knew how much he hated fucking balls. And soirées. And garden parties. And—

"Harald is holding a ball to introduce your fiancée to society. He expects you at the palace within a week of the event, to get Cherry settled in." She said these words matter-of-factly, as if they were actually true. As if Harald cared about things like *settling people in*. More like he wanted ample time to tear Ruben apart. "So we have about three weeks to prepare. If this is going to work..." She looked at Cherry, who looked back with an arched brow and lifted chin. It was vaguely terrifying and unfairly attractive.

Demetria seemed to agree, because she snatched her gaze away and began shuffling awkwardly through the papers in front of her. "If this is going to work," she repeated, "you two need to pass as a couple. Harald is very observant—which you already know, Ruben, but it bears, ah... *at understrege*?"

"Emphasising," he offered.

"Yes! Emphasising." She threw Cherry an apologetic look. "I read better than I speak."

"You speak beautifully," Cherry murmured. And then, God damn her, she smiled. Dimples and everything.

Demi blinked, slightly dazed. Was Ruben mistaken, or was his stalwart assistant actually blushing? He looked at Hans. Hans, his bad mood momentarily forgotten, looked back at him with raised brows.

He wondered if Cherry was capable of toning down her charm, or if she just exuded it like a rose exuded scent. Then he remembered how frosty she'd been on the flight over and decided she could definitely turn it off when necessary.

But if he asked her to be less devastatingly lovely around his assistant, she'd probably kick him in the shins.

"Right," Demi muttered, shuffling through her papers. He had no idea why paperwork would be necessary for this kind of thing, but Demi loved paperwork.

"Well," Agathe rasped into the silence, her voice roughened by the youthful smoking habit that had never quite let go. "This is very exciting, but I think not so related to me. It is breakfast time. Ruben, you want to eat?"

If he said no, she'd force feed him anyway; she had that determined gleam in her wintry eyes, the kind she got whenever he'd been travelling or 'working too hard' and she was convinced only steak and plenty of vegetables could possibly reinvigorate him. Luckily, he was actually rather hungry. So he said, "Yes, please."

"Good. Demetria, Hans, have you had breakfast?"

"Oh, sorry, Agathe," said Demi. "I have. And I've got a lunch meeting anyway…"

"I am fine," Hans rumbled.

Unusually, Agathe appeared quite pleased by that fact. "So just Ruben and you, Cherry?" she asked. "What do you like to eat, *min kære*? We have eggs and bacon or we have, ah, the cereals, or something else? Pastry?"

Cherry pursed her lips in thought and tapped a pink tipped finger against her chin. She looked like a fantasy, even though the pose should have seemed ridiculous. Or at least vaguely pretentious. Finally she said, "I bet you're an excellent cook. And I'm not picky. I'm happy to have whatever you'd like."

Agathe's wrinkled face split into a wide grin as she stood, smoothing her hands over her apron. "*Vidunderlig*! I'll start breakfast. Ruben, be good, *ja*?"

He rolled his eyes. "I'll do my best."

"Hm," she sniffed, clearly dubious. But she hurried from the room anyway.

"So," Demetria said brightly. "Moving on. I'm sure that the two of you will get to know each other very well, rattling around this house, but—"

"Wait," Cherry interrupted. Not in her usual charming manner, either, so smooth you wouldn't realise she'd cut in. No; the word was blunt, almost blurted out. "We're not going to be the only ones here," she said. Her voice didn't rise in question; rather, she seemed to be saying the words as if she could make them true via sheer force of will.

For what had to be the fiftieth time, Ruben was struck by just how much he wanted this woman.

"You kind of are," Demi said. "Hans and I are here most of the time, and so is Agathe, but we all live in the main house, so—"

"Why?" Cherry demanded, her brow furrowed. She looked adorable. When did she *not* look adorable? Of course, she also clearly did not want to be alone with him. But for now he'd think less about the stinging implications of that and more about the little line between her brows.

"Well..." Demi began. She looked at Ruben. And so Ruben, with great effort, dragged his brain into gear.

"We can arrange for a lock on your door," he said to Cherry, his voice brisk. "If that's what you want. And I can give you a guard. Or whatever you'd prefer."

"What? Wait, no—that's not what I meant. I don't—I mean, I wasn't saying—" She broke off, and for a moment he thought he'd somehow managed to render the formidable Cherry Neita tongue-tied. But no. She shook herself and said, much more calmly, "A guard is unnecessary, and we don't need any more people involved in this deception. I just... so, no-one was here last night? Except us?"

"No," he said. "No-one. But the estate's security is excellent. You're completely safe here."

Cherry huffed. "I know that. Never mind." But then she added, "Why does everyone stay in that house except you?"

Ruben shrugged, trying to hide the fact that her simple question had his skin crawling. Familiar anxiety ground against him like sandpaper, but he sounded as collected as ever when he said, "I'm one person. I have a lot of staff. This house is small. That house is big."

She arched a brow, expecting more, but that was all she'd get from him. After a moment, she clearly realised that, because she gave a little shrug. It was the tiniest lift of her shoulders, her gaze flat, as if she'd barely cared at all. So cool he almost forgot the hint of panic in her voice just minutes ago.

She didn't want to be alone with him. Why?

"Well," Demi said. Hacking away at the awkwardness again and again, bless her. "As I said, I'm sure you'll get to know each other. *But* I thought we could cover the basics and make sure everyone is on board with the plan!"

Hans groaned, dramatically, rubbing a hand over his jaw. "Plans, always *plans* with you, woman."

She narrowed her eyes at him, all chirpiness gone. "*You* don't have to be here, you know."

"Good." Slapping his hands on the table, Hans heaved himself out of the wooden dining chair. It creaked slightly, freed of his vast weight. "Ruben, you know where to find me." Then he turned a winning smile on Cherry. Or rather, a close-lipped grimace, which was his best effort. "Ms. Neita."

She gave Hans the dimples. Ruben was now convinced that she was flaunting them at everyone but him, purely to piss him off. It was working.

"Hans," she murmured, her voice all whiskey and honey, rich and raw and sweet. "Call me Cherry."

Ruben tried not to think unreasonable thoughts. Still, images of punching his best friend in the gut assailed him. When had he become the jealous type? And over a fake fiancée who could barely stand him?

Hans strode from the room, leaving Ruben, Demetria and Cherry behind. Poor Demi. Her smile was melting away like plastic left on the hob.

But still, she tried. "So you'll need to get the basics down—background, interests, and so on. A backstory that we can all agree on, you know, when and where you met. And—"

"Demi," Ruben interrupted. He was talking without thinking again, but he was too tired to care. He needed a shave and a platter of bacon before he could have this sort of conversation. "You should go and do... whatever it is you're doing today."

She blinked. "But—"

"It's fine. You have plans. Cherry and I can muddle along." He looked at the sheets of paper trapped in her capable hands. "You made lists, I assume?"

"Oh, yes," she admitted, looking down as if she'd forgotten they were there. "But—"

"We'll follow the list," he said, "and report back later. Promise."

She released a long-suffering sigh. It was a familiar sound. "You're sure?"

"Yes, Mother."

She rolled her eyes. "Fine. If you insist." She slid the papers over the table at him before giving Cherry a nod. "You have a phone in your room. You can call me at the house if you need anything—anything at all. Just press '02'."

"Thank you," Cherry said, and she really did look grateful. Because she was in a strange house, in a foreign country, with a man she barely knew and didn't trust, and he should have thought this through, shouldn't he? Why didn't he think anything through?

The thought shimmered, twisted, transformed in his mind, reborn with his brother's voice and his sister's quiet spite. *Do you have half a brain in that head, Ruben? Does the peasant part even function, little brother?*

"See you later!"

He blinked back to reality just in time to see Demi leave. Which meant that he and Cherry were alone. Utterly alone. Well; except for Agathe's singing, floating down the hall from the kitchen. He held on to that hoarse, wavering voice like a talisman. *Pull yourself together.*

"So," he said, scanning the papers. And now he sounded like Demi. "We have the, ah... the list. Basics, background, things like that." He looked up. Cherry was sitting directly opposite him, her arms folded under her breasts, looking at him from beneath her long, long lashes. If it weren't for the hard line of her mouth, she might look seductive.

Ruben gave his head a firm shake. If he couldn't stop thinking about her like this, they'd never get anywhere.

"So," he began. "How long have we been together?"

She shrugged. "Up to you."

"You're sure? You don't have a preference? Something you'd like to tell your parents?"

"Oh, yes," she murmured. "It matters so much that I tell my parents the most *tasteful* lie possible. I *really* give a shit."

He bit back a smile. "Point taken."

"Look," she sighed. "I'm not trying to be awkward. It's just... You know what you need out of this, right? I don't. So when it comes to backstory and all that shit, it's up to you. As for the rest, the personal information—if you give me the list, or whatever Demi made, I'll write it down for you."

"But if we don't talk," he said, "we won't become comfortable together. That's important too."

She arched a brow. "You think I can't turn it on? You think I can't flirt with you?"

I know you can. I wish you would. I wish you could mean it.

"No," he admitted. "I know you'll be fine with all that. But I—"

"*You* are a bigger flirt than I am," she said. "And we both know it."

Ruben considered feigning outrage. Then he saw the dangerous gleam in her eye and decided not to bother. "Okay, fair enough. But if we were engaged, I wouldn't just pull all my usual shit on you, would I? I'd be different."

"How romantic," she drawled.

At that moment, Agathe swept back into the room with a plate in both hands. "Here we go," she trilled, setting them down with a flourish. "Now, I will be right back—"

Ruben stood, intending to help with the rest of the plates—Agathe had a rather poor grasp on appropriate portion sizes. Then he realised that Cherry was also standing, and his eyes narrowed. "You sit," he insisted. "You're a guest."

"Exactly," she countered. "Guests help. It's polite."

"No, *hosts* do everything."

"That's ridiculous. You—"

"See, this is the kind of thing Demi means. We can't just write down the shit on her list and get to know each other," Ruben insisted. "We have to spend time together."

Agathe appeared again. In the time it had taken them to have their ridiculous argument, she'd fetched a small mountain of muesli. And a platter of fruit salad. Jesus, she was really going for it.

"Fine," Cherry said, sitting down slowly. She murmured her thanks to Agathe and grabbed a piece of toasted rye bread, looking at it as if it was some kind of alien substance. Finally, she shook her head and met Ruben's eyes. "We'll do this, then. We'll eat together. We've both got to eat, after all."

Ruben's heart leapt. He was relieved, he told himself. He wanted this to go smoothly. That was all. "I'm usually out for lunch. And breakfast. Dinner?"

She arched a brow. "What do you do at lunch?"

"I'm at work."

"*Work*?" She spluttered, reaching for a glass of orange juice. "You have a *job*?"

He shrugged. "I have an occupation. Every man needs one."

"Right... Okay. So, um... What should I do?"

Ruben tried not to be disappointed by the fact that she hadn't asked about his job. "That's up to you. You can go anywhere you want as long as you run it by Hans first, so he can deal with the security. And Demi will give you access to my bank account—"

"Why would I need access to your bank account? Aren't you paying me?"

"Of course. But if you decide you want to spend the next few weeks, I don't know, re-decorating my library—"

"You have a library?" she demanded, her voice sharp. "Where?"

"Ah, it's nothing major. It's just a room with a ton of books."

"Whose books?"

102

He shrugged. "No-one's. Agathe's. I mean, she chose them, her and Demi."

"Okay," Cherry nodded. "Cool." She downed her orange juice and stood. "I'm gonna go."

"Um..."

"Bye!"

Ruben sat and watched as she hurried from the room.

This was not going well.

CHAPTER THIRTEEN

A nd so it went on. And on, and on, and on, for almost a week. Cherry avoided him with impressive conviction and iced her way through their dinners; Demetria scolded him about checklists and convincing performances like a schoolteacher; and Ruben became desperate. Really fucking desperate.

He didn't want it to be like this. Fuck, none of it was ideal, and it was completely his fault, but...

He kept thinking back to the woman he'd first met at the Academy. Her spark, her knowing humour, the confidence that danced through everything she did. Now that woman was trapped in *his* gilded cage, doing everything she could to keep him at arm's length, and it was taking its toll. She seemed a little more tired, a little more subdued, every day. So one night, about a week after they signed that damned contract, he made a decision.

Was it a sensible one? Probably not. But then, he wasn't known for his sense.

Ruben lay in bed, staring up at the ceiling, wondering what it said about his life that he was tucked beneath the sheets before 10.30 p.m. Nothing good, probably.

And then the idea bit him. Bit him, and wouldn't let go.

You should see Cherry. Talk to her without Demi's list and Agathe breathing down your neck.

But Agathe's the only thing that makes it bearable. If she's not around, Cherry probably won't talk to you at all.

Or she'll lose her temper and scream at you for half an hour.

Now *that* sounded good. That sounded *great*. Ruben didn't want her blank stares or her polite answers or her pointed avoidance. He wanted her to bite his fucking head off.

Maybe she'd feel better afterwards.

He leapt out of bed and yanked open his door, striding out into the hall. Then he remembered that he was naked, and turned right the fuck back around. If he showed up at her door without any clothes on, there was a 98% chance he'd leave with his balls stuffed up his backside.

Throwing on some pyjama bottoms and a dressing gown, he started the short journey again. He was marching down the hall with a discipline he hadn't felt since his rather uneventful time in the air force.

But when he reached her room, the fire in his gut was snuffed out as reality flooded in.

This wasn't going to work. What was he going to do, force her to speak? Prod at her until he got the response he wanted? Because that would make her feel *so* much better.

With a sigh, Ruben rested his head against the cool surface of her firmly closed door. She was so fucking close, and it didn't even matter. He'd dragged her into his bullshit and fucked up her life, just because he wanted her. No matter how different he liked to think he was, in reality he was just like his siblings: an overgrown, spoilt brat who treated people like toys.

Why would Cherry want anything to do with him?

He turned, ready to leave. But then a thought captured him: if he wasn't enjoying this, she wasn't either. But if they got to know each other, perhaps they could rub along for a year without her feeling trapped, always being on her guard.

Maybe someone just needed to make the first move.

He hesitated, hovering at the door like a ghost. His common sense was telling him to turn the fuck around and go back to bed, but his instincts disagreed.

Always follow your instincts.

Funny; that mantra kept failing him recently. But it had served him so well for so long, he couldn't give it up after a few failures, could he? Maybe something good was waiting at the end of all these apparent mistakes.

Taking a deep breath, Ruben knocked gently on the door.

For a moment, nothing happened. But then a voice called, "Demi?"

Ah, fuck. He definitely should've left. "It's me."

Another pause, and then she said, "Oh." That was it. *Oh.* He couldn't tell if she was pissed or just surprised. He couldn't tell if that single syllable meant *I see,* or *Screw you.*

So he said, his voice embarrassingly tentative, "Um... Can I come in?"

"Why?"

"Cherry," he sighed. "Let me come in."

For a long, long moment, he thought she'd tell him to fuck off. He wouldn't be surprised. But when she did finally speak, all she said was, "Fine. Come in."

He froze. Did she really mean that? Had he misheard? Or—

"For fuck's sake," she snapped, "hurry up. Before I change my mind."

For once, Ruben did as he was told.

The room was veiled with inky darkness. As he shut the door behind him, his vision blanked out completely. But he waited, knowing his eyes would find the faintest scrap of light somewhere, if he gave them a chance. He'd spent a lot of time locked in dark rooms as a kid.

Sure enough, the outlines of furniture came into view, so faint and shadowed he wasn't sure if he really saw them, or somehow sensed them. But those were the kinds of fanciful thoughts he'd taken comfort in as a child—*maybe I'm special, maybe I have powers, and one day I'll use them to make everyone pay.*

Now he was an adult, and he knew that his supposed night vision was thanks to cracks in the curtains and underneath the doors, and pupils wide enough to drink in those drops of light and put them to use.

He moved gingerly through the room, still managing to catch a side table with his hip, but not falling over anything or otherwise disgracing himself. When he reached the foot of Cherry's bed, he felt a little presumptuous sitting down—but the darkness was too disorientating for him to stand on ceremony.

"Oh, by all means," she said acidly as he sank onto the mattress. "Make yourself at home."

"There's at least four feet of space between us, so don't have a fit."

"Why the hell did I tell you to come in?"

Ruben sighed. "I don't know. I'm insufferable. I apologise."

He received nothing but silence in reply. He couldn't quite grasp the quality of that silence. Was she agreeing, or simply surprised by his words, or too tired to bother with conversation? He supposed it didn't matter.

"Believe it or not," he said, "I didn't come here to irritate you." The words reminded him of conversations with his siblings. He was beginning to think he had issues. He felt the sting of rejection too keenly, and yet, he chased it down.

"So why did you come?" she demanded. Even though she'd been lying in the dark, she didn't sound tired. But then, as far as he could tell, she spent all day in the library reading books and playing with her cat.

So he just said, "Our meetings aren't going well."

"Meetings," she murmured. "Is that what we're calling them?"

"I don't see what else we could call them," he said reasonably. "Preparation for the Grand Deception?"

She snorted. Which was close to a laugh, right? He'd made her laugh once. Before she'd learned to be wary of him.

Spurred on by that snort—edged in derision though it was—he tried again. "Improving Cherry's Ruben-Threshold?"

"Something like that," she admitted. She shifted slightly on the bed, and he felt the motion through the mattress as if they were lying side by side. He'd said there was distance between them, but he had the oddest feeling that if he reached out, his hand would find her ankle, or her calf. He laced his fingers together and put them firmly in his lap.

"I know this is hard," he said. "And I know you don't like me, and you don't trust me. But this will go easier on both of us if we know *something* about each other once we leave this place. And fuck, I wish we didn't have to, but we do. *I* do."

"And I do too," she murmured. "I decided to do this. I agreed to it. And I suppose I have been... shirking my obligations. Which isn't the way I usually behave."

He chose his words carefully. "I think you could be forgiven for feeling unlike yourself, at the moment."

"I'm sure you're right," she said dryly. "But the world keeps turning, and all that. I think I've wallowed long enough. It doesn't really suit me."

"If you've been wallowing, it was the most graceful and glamorous wallowing I've ever seen."

She did laugh at that; an adorable little giggle that bubbled out like water from a fountain. She tried to hide it; he could tell. He couldn't see her, but he'd bet money on the fact that she'd put a hand over her mouth. Didn't matter. In the quiet of the night, and with the way she captured his attention so very thoroughly, he couldn't miss it. And the sound made him bold.

"I want to know you," he said, honestly enough. But he clambered up the bed as he said it, finding the headboard with outstretched hands before settling down beside her.

She tutted. "You think you're so smooth."

"I don't know what you mean."

She tugged at the covers. "You're hogging the blankets."

"I'm not even *under* the blankets."

"I should bloody well hope not. But you're lying on them and it's pulling them off me." He felt her foot knock into his calf through the covers, a glancing blow. He wasn't sure if she'd kicked him on purpose or if she'd come across him by accident and snatched herself away in the next breath. He wanted her to do it again.

But that wasn't why he'd come, he reminded himself sternly.

"I think we should play twenty questions," he said.

Her reply was doused in sarcasm. "Oh, *really*? Are you going to ask me if I've ever kissed a boy?"

"No. I save that sort of thing for truth or dare."

"You're ridiculous."

"I certainly am. Shall I go first?"

"You can ask. No guarantee I'll answer."

"Fair enough." He paused, pretending to think of a question. In reality, he didn't have to think. His mind was nothing but a jumble of questions when it came to her; there were a thousand things he wanted to know, and as soon as his questions were answered he'd think of a thousand more. For some reason, he'd developed a mild fixation on this woman. Probably because she didn't want him.

But, once upon a time, she did want you. And you were no better back then.

Firmly ignoring the voice in his head, Ruben said, "First question. Who's your favourite person in the world?"

"My sister," she said immediately. "Who's yours?"

"Agathe," he said, just as fast.

"The housekeeper?" She sounded incredulous. "I mean, she is really lovely, but—"

"She's not the housekeeper," he laughed. "She's my grandmother."

"Um... What?" Her voice came out as a squeak. "Wow. We really *do* need to get to know each other. What the hell? Why does she do all your cooking?"

"Because she's my grandmother."

She scoffed. "I'll ignore that. Why don't you call her grandma? Or whatever you guys say?'"

"*Mormor*," he supplied. "And I never got into the habit. I only met her..." He calculated quickly. "Seven years ago."

"What?"

"Well, no, that's not accurate. I knew her for the first five years of my life. Then I didn't. Then, seven years ago, I did."

She shifted beside him, the mattress rolling. He imagined she was looking at him now. So she hadn't been before. "Forget twenty questions," she said. "Explain that."

"Well... She's my mother's mother."

"Okay. And?"

"Did you... Google me at all?"

He could almost *hear* her eye roll. "You think that's what I do with my free time? Research you?"

"Truthfully, I had imagined you would. I mean, why wouldn't you?"

She paused. Then, with a huff, she admitted, "I kind of did. I started to, but the first thing that came up was—"

"Kathryn," he finished grimly. It may have been eight months, but that particular scandal would never fade. He wondered how much she'd seen. How much she'd read. If she'd watched...

"I didn't look," she said quickly. "I wouldn't do that. I just saw the headlines. And then I stopped."

"I see." He lay back, staring up into the darkness. Waiting for questions. But none came.

Apparently, she wasn't going to push that particular issue. Still, he felt the need to move on before she changed her mind. "So, my brother, Harald. The king. And my sister, Sophronia. They're my half-siblings. We have different mothers."

"Okay," she said, softly. As if she was treading carefully. As if she could already tell this was a difficult topic. Had his voice given him away? He'd thought it was admirably steady.

Actually, it was probably the fact that he'd been separated from his own grandmother for most of his life that clued her in. Yes. That made sense.

"My mother was a maid. Then she met my father, and I suppose they fell in love. He divorced his wife, the Queen Consort—my brother's mother. This is when my brother was, I suppose, fifteen, and Sophronia must have been thirteen. My father abdicated the throne, and my parents married. I arrived soon after."

"Your father abdicated," she murmured. "Doesn't that mean—"

"Harald's mother was Queen Regent for five years," Ruben said. His tongue felt dull, numb, too thick for his mouth. "Then Harald became king."

"Only five years? That's a lot of responsibility for a twenty-year-old."

"Yes. But there wasn't much choice. After five years, Johanna—the Queen Regent..." He hesitated. "Well, she took her own life."

Cherry exhaled softly. It was barely a breath, but it contained a wealth of meaning. Before she could say anything, he forged on.

"She did so the day after my father's death. My father and my mother."

He heard her swallow. The tiny sound was loud as thunder in the stillness of the room. And then, out of the black emptiness, her fingers came to brush against his cheek. Tentative, searching. After that first contact, she touched him fully, her soft hand cradling his face as if he were a child. He realised too late that she would feel the dampness there. So much for keeping his voice steady.

"What happened?" she asked softly.

Ah, what a question. Still, he'd come this far in the spirit of honesty. And something told him Cherry valued that.

Ruben recited the story that had changed his life with as little inflection as possible. "They liked sailing. Had a house on the coast. And my mother liked to sneak out—that is, she hated being watched all the time, followed all the time." He hated it too, even if he understood the need for security. He should learn from his parents' mistakes and stop trying to disappear.

But then, if he wasn't his reckless mother's reckless son, he probably wouldn't be here with Cherry right now. "They went sailing in the middle of the night, a storm struck, and they drowned. Tragic accident. Mundane, really."

"I see," she whispered. "I... I'm sorry."

"They only married because of me. I was born six months after the wedding. Eight months after the divorce. And they only died because they were together—"

"Stop," she said softly. "That's enough."

He sucked in a breath, familiar dark thoughts like a jagged knife scoring his gut. Slicing open the same scar tissue. "Is it? I should tell you all the sordid details, really—"

"Ruben."

"At least then you'll understand why I can't—why I have to avoid disgracing myself any further. The family name, you know. My existence alone already makes things... messy. If I could, I'd renounce my title completely. But I can't. Because then I'd be just like—"

"*Ruben.*"

"I'm too much like my parents—like my mother, that's what Harald always says. Reckless. But I know that, and I handle it. I had everything under control. It was all going well, until I chose wrong."

Her breath caught, and her hand pulled away, and it took him a minute to realise what she thought he meant.

"No, not you!" He caught her hand, tugged it back to his cheek.

113

As if he needed it. As if he needed her. "I'm not talking about you. I meant something else. Before." He didn't want to say Kathryn's name. He was tired of hearing it, even from his own lips.

"Okay," she said finally. The tension in her wrist eased, and she touched him again. He fought the instinct to rub against her like an animal. He'd embarrassed himself enough for one night.

They were silent for a while. So long, in fact, that he might have thought she'd fallen asleep, if it weren't for the slow glide of her thumb over his cheek. Then, suddenly, she said, "I've been trying not to like you. But I've decided to stop."

He hesitated. "What do you mean?"

"You know what I mean." There was a smile in her voice. "I wanted to hate you for making everything so complicated, but honestly, I'm bored of it. Being angry all the time is exhausting. And you're right; we need to get to know each other."

"We do," he said slowly, fighting to calm the rapid beating of his heart. "But it's easier like this, isn't it?"

"Of course it is," she said simply. "Everything's easier in the dark."

Ruben rolled towards her, wrapping an arm around her waist. And for once—even when he felt the soft curves of her body beneath the blanket—his mind stayed out of the gutter. He pulled her close and whispered against her forehead, "I'll come back. If you want. Tomorrow."

He didn't think he imagined the way she leaned into him. "Okay."

"Okay." He pressed a kiss to her brow. Then he let her go, and got up, and left.

It didn't feel right, but he did it anyway.

CHAPTER FOURTEEN

T he next morning, Cherry spent an extra fifteen minutes on her makeup. Not for Ruben, she told herself hurriedly; men never appreciated winged liner. She was just in that sort of mood. She studied herself in the bathroom mirror, the spotlights in the ceiling casting rather unflattering shadows across her face. But at least the light was good: white-ish, rather than yellow or orange. And her liner was razor-sharp. She was most definitely ready.

She swept out of her en suite, pointedly ignoring her bed. The bed where, just last night, she'd actually talked to Ruben. Touched him. Comforted him.

Also, where she'd thought about fucking his brains out. But that, she reassured herself, was a natural urge when faced with a painfully attractive, domineering arsehole. Well, for her, anyway.

A weakness isn't a weakness so long as you accept it.

For the first time since she'd arrived, Cherry left her room without a feeling of overwhelming dread. She wasn't afraid of bumping into Ruben in the halls, or sharing a meal with him. She wasn't dreading the moment she'd have to push down all the feelings he caused in her gut and replace them with a show of disdain.

Yes, she'd needed to be miserable for a while, if only for her own peace of mind. And yes, she had resented him. Because despite the fact that she had agreed to all this, it still felt like a trap. But this was her reality, and would be for the foreseeable future, so she might as well get something out of it. Like… flirting with a man who was gorgeous enough to make her heart stutter. Yeah, that felt like a solid benefit.

And the money, of course. But currently, her parents were being awfully stubborn about taking it.

She entered the kitchen in search of breakfast, her anticipation spiking when she heard someone rooting around in the pantry. But then the pantry door opened, revealing Agathe, not Ruben, inside. The older woman's face split into a smile when she saw Cherry. It was almost sweet enough to make Cherry forget her disappointment.

"Good morning!" Agathe's voice was rough, her sing-song accent soothing. "How are you? Did you sleep well?"

"I did," Cherry smiled. She studied Agathe's face for echoes of Ruben's and found a few; the hawkish nose, the thick brows— though Agathe's were blonde.

"Sit down, sit down. I'll make you breakfast."

"Oh, no, that's okay." Cherry was sure that she'd put on five pounds in the week since she'd come here. Which would be fine, if her clothes weren't so… tailored. Then again, she was rich now. She could buy more clothes. "Actually, that would be great. But I can make it."

"No, no, don't be silly!" Agathe cried.

"Really, I like to cook."

That gave the woman pause. "You do?"

"Yeah. I mean, mostly baking, but—"

"Oh, you bake?"

"Yeah, I—"

"*Demetria*!" Agathe bellowed, her raspy voice suddenly strong as a herd of elephants. Jesus Christ. Cherry resisted the urge to cover her ears as the woman shouted again, "*Demetria*! Come here!"

There was a pause. Then the soft sound of feet padding down the hall. "What?" Demi cried, rushing into the kitchen. "What's happening?"

"Nothing, nothing. Calm down. Cherry just tells me that she likes to bake."

Demi exhaled. "Agathe, we've talked about this. When you shout like that, people think something is wrong."

"Oh, hush. Your nerves are so delicate. Young people." Agathe clucked her tongue and rolled her eyes heavenward. "Anyway, I know you want to learn how to bake, yes? But my baking is a steaming pile of horse shit."

Cherry blinked. Okay; so Ruben's elderly grandmother, with her floral apron and love of cooking, had a potty mouth. Sure. Why not?

"You girls," Agathe said, "neither of you have any fun. You should have fun together. Bake, *ja*?"

"Um…" Demi winced down at her watch. "I'm kind of—"

"Oh, stop. All my grandson does is pander to children all day. You cannot have so much work."

Children? Cherry realised that she'd never actually asked about Ruben's so-called occupation. When he first mentioned it, she'd been desperate to get away from him—to end their conversation before he did something utterly adorable or unbearably sexy and ruined her decision to hate him.

Maybe I can ask him about it tonight.

But her mind didn't envision their standing dinner date when it thought about 'tonight'. It envisioned darkness, and the heat of his body and the low, smoky hum of his voice.

"Fine," Demi sighed. "I do want to learn how to bake."

Cherry shook her head slightly, pushing her highly inappropriate thoughts aside. The man's grandmother was standing right there, for Christ's sake. "Bake, as in?"

"Cake," Demi said. "I love cake. So I thought I should learn how to make it, but... Well, I'm not good at following instructions."

Cherry found that rather surprising, considering how great Demi was at *giving* instructions. But the prospect of having something to do other than play with Whiskey or text Maggie or avoid calls from Rose—who was much harder to lie to than Jas and Beth— made Cherry's day seem brighter. "Okay," she said. "I'd like that. When do you want to start?"

Demi studied her watch. It was black and sleek and expensive and it had no numbers whatsoever on the smooth, shining face. "An hour?" she said.

"Sure. An hour," Cherry smiled.

As she left, Agathe slapped a plate of bacon and rye bread on the table with a grin. "There. Is all good, *ja*?"

"Yeah," Cherry murmured, something happy and hopeful blooming in her chest. "It's all good."

RUBEN CAME HOME in a foul mood.

It was funny; he'd been so worried about Cherry for the past week, he hadn't even noticed the fact that Hans was still pissed with him. But now that Cherry didn't want to kill him anymore—

he hoped—his eyes were being opened to all sorts of things. Like the fact that his best friend was still on the edge of fury.

"Will that be all, Your Highness?"

"Stop *Highnessing* me," Ruben growled, yanking off his hat and scarf and tossing them by the door.

Hans sent the scarf a speaking look. "If you leave those there, Agathe will tidy them up."

"I keep telling her to stop fucking cleaning." Ruben glared down at the pile of wool. "I live here because I don't want people tidying up my mess."

"Then you shouldn't have given her a key."

"Oh, for fuck's sake." He snatched the hat and scarf from the floor and hung them up by the door. "Happy?"

Hans simply sniffed before letting himself out.

Something had to be done. Bickering was one thing, but Hans was clearly still furious. Which was fair enough. If Ruben had listened to him from the start, none of this would be happening.

He wandered down the hall, forcing his mind to focus on simpler topics—like the meeting he'd just had with a local headteacher. He didn't want to speak too soon, but he rather thought he'd found another partner for his scholarship scheme here in Helgmøre.

His trust had six international branches—so far—and he'd started offering scholarships nationally just last year. It was going well and growing fast. So he'd turned his sights to the U.K., his second home…

And found Cherry. Cherry whose laughter floated down the hall like music. Ruben's focus danced away, and his mind became a whirlpool of fantasy and memory, the two intertwined like lovers. Cherry in the dark, touching him out of kindness, became Cherry in the daylight, touching him because she simply couldn't stop.

Her laughter sounded like the ocean used to, when Ruben was a kid and his parents would take him to the coast. He'd roll down the window and listen eagerly for that distant, soft rush to grow louder and more powerful, excitement humming through him.

His feet followed the sound and his mind didn't bother to argue.

She was in the kitchen, her back to him, an apron tied around her waist. The bow at her back draped over the swell of her arse and her curls bounced as she laughed. Ruben crossed his arms and leant against the doorframe, taking the opportunity to watch her undetected.

At least, he thought he was undetected. He hadn't even noticed that Demi was in the room too, not until she said, "Hi, Ruben." Her tone was slightly mocking, slightly smug, and when he finally placed her, standing over by the fridge, her smile was sly. Who needed little sisters when they had uppity personal assistants?

"Hi, Demi," he sighed, just as Cherry turned around.

God, she was so fucking beautiful. She flashed him her perfect smile, the beauty pageant one, with just enough teeth and the hint of a dimple. If he'd wondered how she'd react after last night, he now had his answer: she was nervous.

Good. He was nervous too.

"Hi," she said, sounding slightly breathless. Which, he told himself, could have nothing to do with his arrival. There was a huge mixing bowl clutched to her chest, and she was stirring its contents with alarming vigour. So maybe she'd been standing there, stirring and laughing and talking to Demi and now she was out of breath.

Or maybe she was remembering the way it felt to touch him in the dark.

"What are you doing?" he asked, trying to sound casual. He thought he managed it. So why did she look down at her bowl instead of meeting his eyes? Was that good or bad?

"Baking," she said.

"Baking…?"

"Nothing exciting. Fairy cakes, you know."

"Cupcakes," Demi supplied.

"They're not cupcakes!" Cherry smiled at Demetria, *really* smiled. Her cheeks plumped up and her dimples flashed and everything about her relaxed. "Fairy cakes are smaller. And less sweet. And just… better."

"How can *less sweet* and *better* come up in the same sentence?" Demi sounded outraged.

"Subtlety is everything," Cherry said pertly. "I wouldn't expect you to understand."

"I *will* put icing in your hair, you know. I'll do it."

"You wouldn't dare!"

Ruben watched them banter with an unfamiliar feeling in his gut. It took him a good few seconds to identify that feeling as jealousy.

He was losing his fucking grip. He gritted his teeth and told himself firmly not to be ridiculous. But now the little voice in his head was whispering, *She's not really yours, and Demi knows that. You have no claim on her whatsoever…*

"Demi," he said sharply. "The meeting went well."

She put down a jug and the bottle of milk she'd been pouring into it, her grin fading as she looked up at him. "That's… good."

"I want them involved."

She stared at him for a moment, her face blank. But then her lips curved into a slight smile and she said, "Want me to start on the paperwork?"

The paperwork she'd done twelve times before and could prepare in her sleep? "Yes, please."

"Aye aye, Captain." She pulled off her apron, dusting her hands on the back of her jeans. "I'll see you later, Cherry. Duty calls."

"Oh, okay. Later, then."

Cherry sounded far too disappointed for Ruben's liking. But Demi looked oddly pleased, her dark gaze scanning him with an intensity she usually reserved for official correspondence and football matches. She bumped into him slightly as she passed him in the doorway, and when he looked over his shoulder, she was sticking her tongue out at him as she walked away.

He was a fool. As if Demetria of all people would try it on with Cherry.

Clearly, jealousy was an unpredictable emotion.

Still, there was an upside. Now, he had Cherry alone. She had turned away from him again, and she was stirring the contents of that fucking bowl as if her life depended on it. But he could tell by the set of her shoulders, by her uncharacteristic silence, by the way the air shimmered between them as if the room were heated, that she was waiting.

And he'd never make a lady wait.

He crossed the room before he could second-guess himself. His hands came to rest on the swell of her hips and it felt like everything he'd ever needed, but that didn't make any sense. Nothing made any sense. Until she put the damned bowl down and turned around in the circle of his arms and looked up at him with eyes that were wide and dark and endless. Then, all at once, everything was perfect.

"I still don't like you," she whispered, her lips pursed.

"Yes you do. If you don't, my heart will break."

"Boo hoo. Buy a new one." She pressed her hands to his chest and he thought, for one world-ending moment, that she might push him away. But she just fiddled with the buttons of his shirt, slipping her fingers under his tie. Then she said, "Where did you go?"

"To a school in the city."

"Why?"

"Same reason I was at the Academy. I put together scholarship programmes for the kids who attend my A.P.s."

She raised her brows, and he thought that she might be impressed. "You run alternative provisions?"

"Yeah. For kids from disadvantaged backgrounds who are disengaged or have unique learning needs and so on. But some of them are really fucking smart, and I started to think about what they'd get out of attending schools like the Academy. I mean, not schools like the Academy—they'd probably suffocate."

"True," she murmured. Her eyes were pinned to his chest, and now she was fiddling with his tie. He looked down at the sweep of her lashes. She had some kind of dark makeup around her eyes that made her look like a cat. Well—even more like a cat than usual. "So why were you looking at a school in England?" she asked.

"The Trust operates across a few European countries."

She looked up, finally, her eyes warm. "The Trust?"

"The Ambjørn Trust."

"Ambjørn is your family name, right?"

"My mother's."

"Ah." She was looking at him with an expression he didn't recognise. Her eyes were bright, her lips slightly parted and tipped into a half-smile, as if she was seeing him for the first time.

But then a tinny *ding* popped the bubble around them, and she threw up her hands, pushing him away.

"Where's that bloody tea towel," she muttered, marching around the kitchen. "Ah!" She snatched it off of the island and bustled over to the oven. Ruben leant against the counter and watched her bend over. Yes, he was a pig, but it was definitely worth it.

She produced a tray of little cakes, and then another, popping them onto the counter with a flourish. "There! Three and four!"

"Three and four?"

She turned around and nodded towards a cupboard. "One and two are in there."

He pulled it open to find two plastic containers full of little cakes, decorated in lavender and pink and cream, with glitter—*is glitter edible?*—and pearls and tiny stars scattered across the icing.

"You've made a lot of cakes," he said finally.

"There's a ton of stuff in here. Do you bake?"

"Ah, no. I can cook, but I don't really bake. Agathe tries, but she's kind of terrible at it."

"Hm." She had returned to her bowl, but now she was spooning its mixture out into trays full of little paper cases. "You know, you never got around to explaining how the two of you... grew apart?"

"We were separated," he said. Then he realised that his voice had been too sharp, too hard. "I mean... I just mean, she wouldn't have left me."

"No," Cherry said mildly. "I'm sure she wouldn't. Separated by whom?"

He sighed, wandering over to stand beside her. She scooped out the mixture with sure, practiced movements, not spilling a drop as she transferred it to the cake cases. Clearly, she did this a lot. "My brother," he finally said. "My brother cut off all contact with my maternal family, after my parents died."

It wasn't something he liked to tell people. It revealed a little too much about the direction his life had taken, once he'd become his brother's property. Or *responsibility*, as Harald would say. But Cherry made no expression, didn't say a word, didn't even look up. She just nodded and kept spooning out the cake batter.

"So... so when I was older I asked Hans to find her. Of course, she was where she's always been. This town." He wet his lips. His throat felt dry, all of a sudden. "The main house was my father's. A country getaway sort of thing. It's where he and my mother met."

"I see. And this house?"

"Oh, I built this myself. I didn't want to live in there."

"Why is that?"

"I don't like—" he broke off, suddenly realising that he'd said way too much. But the movement of her hands and the softness of her voice were almost hypnotic, and she still wasn't looking at him, and the words were suddenly desperate to escape. "I don't like big houses. Feels like a palace."

Finally, her dark gaze turned on him, and she might as well have pinned him to the wall. "Did you grow up in a palace?"

He swallowed. "Yes."

She nodded thoughtfully. Then she said, her tone suddenly bright, "Do you want to help me decorate these cakes when they cool down?"

He hesitated. Not because the answer was no, but because he was suddenly afraid. Afraid of the words she pulled from him without even trying, afraid of the way she looked at him as if she read the meaning behind his every breath. The last thing he needed was someone *understanding* him.

Anyone who understood him would leave.

But she raised her brows and said, "I told Demi we'd decided to spend time together. So now we have to do it, or she'll be *very* disappointed."

"Fair enough," he said, and in spite of his worries, he felt himself smile. "Tell me what to do."

AFTER A COUPLE of hours in the kitchen with Cherry, Ruben could see why she loved to bake.

It was almost therapeutic, following her murmured instructions, stirring ingredients and setting timers. After he proved less than effective at the cosmetic side of things—his icing arrangements looked more like accidents—Cherry put him to work on a sponge.

Her directions were clear and she smiled when he mucked things up. She made him wash his hands before and after cracking eggs, and swatted his arse with a wooden spoon when he didn't get out of her way fast enough. And she laughed when he streaked icing sugar down her nose—though, to his disappointment, she didn't retaliate and start a food fight. He'd been hoping to rub icing into her cleavage in the name of war.

Somehow, she coached him through the recipe for chocolate puddings while she sat at the breakfast bar and messed about with marbled icing. He had no idea what that meant, but it looked damned good.

"You should be a teacher, Cherry."

"Oh, no," she scoffed. "Bugger that. I don't do well with kids, hence why I stay in the tower as much as possible."

Ruben laughed. "Okay. Fair enough. A lecturer, then."

She arched a brow. "Really, Ruben? Doesn't that require three or four or however many degrees?"

"You could do that."

"In a thousand years, maybe. I'm hardly the brains of the administrative outfit."

He sighed, the exhalation punctuated by the trill of the timer. His puddings were ready.

"You're smarter than most people I know," he said lightly. "You can do whatever you like."

She didn't answer. He looked over to see her faffing about with a handful of blueberries, holding back a smile. Satisfied that she was at least listening, Ruben whipped his puddings out of the oven with a flourish and presented them like an offering.

"Oh, well done," she said, sounding surprised. The little sponges had all risen, unburnt, and even looked somewhat light and airy. He was rather surprised, too.

"Thanks," he grinned, setting them onto the counter. "It's all thanks to your expert guidance, of course."

She snorted. Then she leant over the chocolate puddings and closed her eyes, inhaling the scent of almonds and cocoa with a look of pure pleasure on her face. For the past hour, Ruben had been too busy following instructions to remember how badly he wanted the woman in front of him. Now it was back to the forefront of his mind.

The warmth of the kitchen left Cherry's rich skin glowing, and tiny little coils of hair sprang out around her face with particular enthusiasm. When she opened her eyes again, Ruben was staring at her with what he knew was plain lust.

She bit her lip.

He moved closer, his voice low. "What *do* you want to do? Professionally, I mean." He asked because he'd been curious for a while. She hadn't seemed upset about quitting her job, and she wasn't enthusiastic about education, clearly.

Cherry blinked. That probably wasn't what she'd expected him to say. But even when he wanted her, when desire rode him relentlessly, Ruben still wanted to know her. He wanted that more than anything else.

She shrugged, turning away slightly. "I don't know."

"Oh, come on. You must."

She flicked a dark look his way. "*Must* I? I suppose I should. I'm a grown woman after all."

"...You really don't know?"

"Well," she sighed. "I have a few ideas. When I was a kid I wanted to make wedding cakes, actually. But then I turned eighteen, and I needed a job, and... Well, I'm good at telling people what to do and charming them into doing it. So, to Rosewood I went."

He nodded slowly. "HR, right? You didn't like it?"

"I liked it fine, and I really am good at it. But I've been thinking... I'm rich now. You know, thanks to you." She flashed a wry smile. "I can do whatever I want. Like... start a small business? I don't know. I'm just playing with ideas. I have a year to plan."

Ruben ignored the reminder of the time-limit on their... *association*, because it made him somehow uncomfortable. But everything else she'd said intrigued him. "I can see you as a businesswoman. Thinking about your wedding cake dream, are you?"

She rolled her eyes. "It's not a *dream*. It's just an idea."

"Right." He grinned. "But even if it was a fully-fledged business plan with start-up capital, would you tell me?"

She gave him a pert look. "I wouldn't tell anyone. Not until I made my first million at least."

Ruben laughed, sliding a hand into her hair. He couldn't help himself. "You really are something, Cherry."

"Yes. So I'm told."

CHAPTER FIFTEEN

H e didn't touch her in the kitchen. He didn't touch her when they passed each other in the halls, or when they sat down to dinner with Demi and Hans and Agathe. But that night, when he came into her room, he lay down beside her and prayed to every god he could think of that she might touch him.

She didn't, of course. But the smile in her voice when she spoke felt almost as good as her hands might have. "I called my parents today."

"Yeah?" He laced his fingers beneath his head to stop himself from reaching out. "How are they?"

"Good. Still vaguely confused about this whole thing, but my mother is enjoying bragging to the neighbours. My dad's still kind of stuck on the fact that you've never met."

"Mmm. I bet he is." The easy comfort of Cherry's company wasn't enough to dampen the alarm that fired in Ruben's gut. She was a daddy's girl. And her dad almost certainly hated him.

"Everyone's been debating you in the family group chat."

"You have a family group chat?"

"Yep. Maggie started it."

He tried to sound casual as he said, "So what does your dad think of me?"

"Um… He's reserving judgement."

"Is he?"

"No. He thinks you're an evil playboy who's going to break my heart, but he's glad I'm getting to travel."

Ruben couldn't help himself. He laughed. "I take it you get the practicality from his side of the family."

"Something like that. Although he's being very uncooperative about…"

Her voice trailed off into silence, and Ruben frowned, turning towards her. So much for keeping his hands to himself; he reached out and settled his palm against her waist, soft and perfect. "About what?"

"Um… My sister's tuition and… things. I mean, I told you Maggie's in America, didn't I?"

"Yes. Your genius little sister."

"Right. Well, we all contribute to her tuition and her… Well, she has sickle cell. Do you know what that is?"

"Ah…" He searched his mind. Came up blank. "I've heard of it, but not really."

"It's a genetic thing, a life-long illness, and she needs medicine and regular doctor's appointments and so on. But, you know, in America, you have to pay. A lot. And with the kind of studying she does, and her illness, we don't want her to work. She couldn't earn enough money to cover the bills anyway."

"Right. So…" He closed his eyes as the truth sank into his gut like a fist. "So that's why you needed the money. For your sister."

131

"No," she said seriously. "I'm spending it on my shoe collection."

He snorted. "Sure. So what's up with your dad?" If he kept talking, his mounting guilt might take a little longer to suffocate him.

You dragged her into your issues to save your delicate fucking feelings, and she's doing it for her sick sister. You are a fucking Disney villain.

"Well," Cherry said, "I was going to use the money you're giving me, but—"

"But he doesn't want you to." Ruben's voice sounded as grim as he felt. Every time he allowed himself to forget what an arse he'd been, something happened to remind him. This time, it was the realisation that he'd trapped her with the offer of money more than he had with his words to that damn reporter.

"I'll pay the fees directly," he said. "You shouldn't be spending your money on that anyway."

"What are you talking about?"

"The money is for you. It's what I owe you. I'll pay your sister's tuition and whatever else."

She scoffed. "That doesn't make any sense. The money's for me, and I want to spend *my* money on—"

"I'll talk to Demetria about it. And she'll talk to you. Okay?"

There was a pause. He could almost hear her mind ticking over, considering the offer from all angles. Because she probably didn't trust him, or his motivations.

He slid his hand from her waist.

But then she said, "Okay. You're right. You do owe me."

He exhaled, relieved. "Good. I'll sort it out tomorrow." Then a thought hit him. "Your dad's going to hate me even more, isn't he?"

"Oh, yes."

"Great." He huffed out a laugh. "I suppose fathers never like their son-in-laws." He froze as he realised what he'd said. "I mean— not that we're—obviously we're not really—"

"I know," she interrupted. "We're not really getting married. Don't worry. I'm not likely to forget that." Her voice was strained, slightly distant, and even though they were close enough that he could feel the heat radiating from her, the gap between them widened. Because, of course, she had no idea what a mess his mind was in. How easy it would be for *him* to forget. How much he wanted her, even though he shouldn't.

"Cherry," he said, and then his breath caught in his chest as his mind fumbled. The moment stretched until he had to speak, but he knew his words would be inadequate. "If I say things like that," he explained, "it's not because of you. It's not for your bene- fit. It's for me. Okay? It's just for me."

She sighed. "What does that mean?"

"Just that... I like you. If I hadn't fucked things up so badly, I'd have tried to... I don't know. See you again, definitely. The day we met, I felt like I'd been hit over the head." He was relieved to hear her laugh at that. "I shouldn't have done any of the things I did that day. I made a shit ton of mistakes. But taking you out wasn't one of them." Because it was important that she know that. Very, very important.

She reached out and fumbled around for his hand. He let her struggle for a second, her fingers brushing against his bare chest, along his arm, before he captured her hand with his. But, to his surprise, she didn't hold it like a mother offering comfort. No; she put it back on her waist, as if it belonged there. As if she wanted it there.

The last vestiges of awkwardness disappeared as Ruben's desire flared to life. He pulled the blankets away; if she was going to give him this, whatever it was, he'd take advantage while it lasted. The covers dealt with, he explored the deep curve of her

133

waist, the swell of her hip. With her breath loud in the silence and her warmth searing right through him, he tugged up the soft, worn cotton of her T-shirt until his palm met bare skin, her hips edged by the lace of her underwear.

But he wouldn't spend too long thinking about her underwear. If he did, the ache of his cock would sharpen into something really unbearable.

So he focused on her waist. On the little hills and rolls of her flesh, and the silken texture of her skin. "You're so fucking soft," he whispered. "I want to touch you everywhere. I can't even tell you."

She stretched out like a cat, a little sigh floating into the darkness between them. She said, "You owe me, Ruben." There was something in her voice, a desperate edge, a touch of amusement, that captured his attention and tightened his balls. When she spoke like this, he thought she might be everything he'd ever wanted.

"What do I owe you, sweetheart?"

"Anything I want." She pressed her hand against his chest, her fingers playing lightly with the hairs there. "But I don't know if you can handle what I want."

He wrapped a hand around her wrist, his grip hard, and she gasped. It was the sweetest little sound, barely a breath, and still it went straight to his cock.

"I know what you want," he said. "And you know I can give it to you. Don't you?"

He expected her to argue. To fight back. To give him that fucking attitude, the one he loved so much even when she used it to push him away.

But she didn't. She just said, "Yes. I know."

And his control snapped. With a growl, he rolled on top of her and captured her mouth with his.

CHAPTER SIXTEEN

Cherry buried her hands in the silky strands of Ruben's hair and wrapped her legs around his waist and tried not to lose her head. It wasn't easy.

His lips were insistent, devouring her with every inch of the passion she'd seen simmering beneath his surface. The single-minded intensity he displayed with every look, every touch, every word, was channeled through his kiss. She'd hoped for this all day and all night, lay here thinking about it while she waited for him to come, and now it was really happening.

His hands roamed her body like he owned it. He grabbed at her thighs, her hips, fingers digging into flesh for a heartbeat before skating away, sliding up her waist, along her ribcage, perilously close to her breasts—and then, once more, they disappeared. He was a fucking tease. But he was panting against her lips, pressing his hard cock into the ache between her legs, and his tongue caressed hers as if the opportunity was a gift. He wanted her. He wanted her in a way that made her shiver, made her belly tighten and her clit swell and her nipples tingle. And he was taking her.

He pressed her into the mattress with the sheer size of his body, and his bare torso felt like heaven against her skin. For the first time she wished that they weren't in the dark. She wanted to see him. But no; it was better like this. Because if they'd tried it in the light she'd never be able to say…

"You like control."

He laughed darkly. "I'm glad you noticed. Have you been watching me the way that I've been watching you?"

She bit her lip. "You've been watching me?"

"All I can fucking do is watch you. You're magnetic. But you know that, don't you, sweetheart?" He captured her chin with his fingers, turning her head to the side. First his teeth closed around her earlobe, then his tongue traced the contours of her ear. "Tell me."

She wet her lips, tried to ignore the thundering of her heart and the throbbing between her legs and the desperate need to blurt out her every secret. "Stop trying to make me say things. I can't say things."

"You say whatever you want," he whispered. "We already know that. Are you asking me to stop?"

She took a breath. "No."

"Good. Roll over."

She didn't disobey, because the iron voice with which he issued his commands got her wet.

She rolled over beneath him, and he didn't make it easy. Every inch of her hips, of her arse, of her thighs came into contact with the thick ridge of his cock. He ground into her, and when she finally ended up face down on the pillow, he placed a hand on the back of her neck to hold her still and said, "Good girl." She bit down a whimper at the sound of that deep voice, the feel of his hand. Controlling, demanding, protecting.

He settled his cock in the cleft of her arse and thrust back and forth, rolling his hips, showing her in no uncertain terms that he knew what he was doing. His weight pushed her hips into the mattress, created a sweet pressure against her swelling, aching clit.

He leant over her and whispered, "I can hear you moaning. Did you know that?"

She gritted her teeth. "I'm not."

"You are." His hand slid under her scarf, dislodging it slightly, to grasp at her hair. He jerked her head up off the pillow and said, his voice firm, "I'm in charge now. Don't bullshit me. Stop fucking around and take what you need."

She swallowed. "What do I need?" As if someone else had to say it for it to be real.

But his words weren't exactly what she'd expected. *To obey. To submit. To yield to me.* He said, "You need to know I've got you. And I do. You know that, don't you?"

"Yes," she admitted. Her voice was a whisper. It felt like a shout. Right here, right now, in this bed, she knew without a doubt that he absolutely had her.

"I could pull out my cock," he said, "and push your underwear aside, and fill you up right now. And you'd let me. You'd take it beautifully, I already know. Your pretty cunt would swallow up my cock, and you wouldn't even flinch." The pressure of his hardness moved from her arse to her pussy. He ground into her, as if to prove the point, and that little movement almost drowned her in desire. His arms were still braced around her and the hard length of his body pressed into her, suffocating her until all that was left was sensation. Sensation, and the feeling of being protected.

Protected and owned.

He slid a hand beneath her, lifting her hips and reaching between her legs until the heel of his palm pressed into her clit. She moaned, ragged and desperate, and he laughed low in her ear. "There we go, sweetheart. That's what you want. Be a good girl and ride my hand."

She obeyed, forgetting to feign hesitancy. Any embarrassment or nerves or awkwardness she might have felt were no longer an issue, because he was the one in control. Cherry rolled her hips against the pressure of his hand with nothing in her head but the pursuit of pleasure. He kissed her neck as she rubbed her aching clit against him, the movement bringing the head of his cock against her cotton-covered pussy again and again, until she felt almost delirious with sensation.

"You feel so fucking good," he growled. "So good. I can feel how wet you are. Soaking through your fucking underwear." He twisted his hips, his hardness parting her folds even through the cotton, and she moaned helplessly.

Beneath her, his hand began to move, as if he couldn't help himself. He rubbed her clit roughly through her underwear, fast and hard, and she gasped, arching against him, urging him on without words because she could barely catch her breath and every nerve-ending lit up like a white-hot fucking flame until she—

Her orgasm was fast and hard and disorientating. The only constant as she was hit by wave after wave of ruthless pleasure was Ruben, covering her body with his, soothing her fevered skin with his kisses, whispering adoration into her ear.

"Cherry," he murmured. "We're going to do this again, you know. In the daylight."

"Ummm..." She tried to protest, but her mind had turned to mush. Tiredness dragged at the edge of her senses.

He pressed a soft kiss to her cheek. "We are. Now go to sleep."

She'd never been good at following instructions, but clearly she did fine with commands. She obeyed immediately and without effort, surrounded by him and satisfied.

CHAPTER SEVENTEEN

C herry perched on a stool at the kitchen island and ate her cereal. She kept her eyes glued to the little TV on the counter, and her spine straight—well, slightly arched—and her ankles crossed. She was wearing jeans, turned up a few times over her calves, and silk camisole beneath a buttoned-up little cardigan. Her hair was piled on top of her head in the kind of style that looked casual and effortless but actually took an industrial-strength hair tie, fifty hair grips and half a tub of product.

"We're going to do this again. In the daylight".

Oh, it had seemed so simple. In the dark.

But now she felt caged, waiting to bump into him in his ridiculously normal house. She would, sooner rather than later. Why couldn't he have a damned mansion, for Christ's sake?

She caught herself. It didn't matter. It didn't matter that, now she wasn't avoiding him or sticking to her room, they'd almost certainly be on top of each other. It didn't matter that he could come in here at any minute, or that she wasn't entirely sure what she'd say to him if he did. It would be fine. It would be—

"Morning, Cherry Pie."

She clamped her teeth together, but that didn't stop a strangled yelp emerging from her mouth. It also didn't stop her dropping her spoon into her cereal, sending the milk flying.

In an instant, Ruben was beside her, a hand on her shoulder. "Are you okay?" He frowned down at her, taking in the milk splatters on the table and—oh, dear. On her cardigan. So much for the perfect sartorial armour.

"Fine," she managed. God, she could do better than that. She forced her smile into place, forced her voice to become light and airy. "I'm fine. You surprised me. Whoops!" A soft little laugh floated from her lips, and she let her fingers drift up to her cheek. Then she waited for him to look enchanted.

He did not look enchanted.

He continued to frown, looking at her as if he could see right through her. No, not through her; into her. Behind the carefully put-together version of herself she'd chosen to wield, right to the real, actual person. She waited for him to call her out. He didn't.

Instead he said, "I'm sorry. Agathe always says I need bells." And then he smiled. It was lovely and charming and devastating. A gift.

"You do. Someone so big shouldn't be so quiet." She gave him a smile of her own, a real one, and he reached out and slid his hand over the back of her neck. Cherry tried not to arch into him, but she rather thought she failed.

For a moment they stayed that way, connected by the warmth of his skin against hers, by secrets whispered into the darkness and looks shared in the daylight. But then he pulled away, shaking himself slightly, and strode across the kitchen.

"Here," he said, grabbing a cloth from beside the sink. But he didn't give it to her; he wiped up the mess she'd made of the table. Then he lifted the cloth towards her, hesitated, lowered his hand again. All at once, Cherry registered the cold wetness spreading through her clothes. *Oops.* Annoyed at herself—really, she was staring like a widgeon while milk soaked into cashmere— she hurriedly unbuttoned the cardigan and tugged it off.

The milk wasn't bad at all, she decided, examining the splatters. She could rinse it out. Setting the damp fabric aside, she turned back to Ruben, a *thank you* on her lips.

The look on his face wiped her mind clean. And then made it filthy.

He was staring down at her chest like he'd never seen tits before. Sure, her bra was kind of visible through the white silk, but it was hardly erotic. And yet... he looked down at her, his jaw set, his grey eyes thunderous. His nostrils flared slightly as he took deep, hungry breaths, his fists clenched tight. If she didn't know him, she might think that he was angry.

He wasn't angry. He was focused. So, so focused.

"What?" she said softly, arching a brow.

His movements were fast and sharp, predatory. He bent over her, resting a hand against the island, his other hand grabbing a fistful of her piled-up hair.

"You know *what*," he rasped, his eyes boring into hers. Then they dropped. "No lipstick?"

"It's 9 a.m.," she breathed. "Why would I—?"

"You always wear lipstick."

"I'm relaxing," she drawled, as if he wasn't filling her space and exposing her throat. "At home."

He smiled, the brightness of the expression cutting through his intensity, softening the harsh lines of his face. "Home, hm? Interesting."

"Oh, don't be smug." She rolled her eyes.

"So sorry," he murmured mockingly. His hand shifted, dragging her head back. She swallowed, painfully aware of the vulnerability of her position, of the control he had over her movements. Aware and… aroused. Fuck. Was it really that easy? Surely it shouldn't be that easy.

But it was. He bent over her, his lips hovering an inch from hers, his gaze inescapable, filling her vision like a stormy sky. "I didn't mean to do this," he whispered. "I'm trying to go slow."

"Go slow?"

He smiled. Her eyes were closed now, but she felt it—felt his lips skate against hers as the corners tipped up. "Yeah. Slow. We get to know each other, and you trust me, and then I kiss you under some mistletoe—"

"Mistletoe?"

"I thought the trust might take a while. I was aiming for Christmas at the latest."

She could tell he was trying to make her laugh. Instead, her stomach sank like a stone. Because Christmas was almost a year away. By the time it came, there'd be 30 days left of their sham relationship.

"Don't," he whispered. "Stop thinking about things."

"You know I can't."

"You can. I could make you. Should I make you, Cherry?"

"Try," she whispered back, the words disappearing like smoke against his lips.

He kissed her. That's what it was called, one person's lips against another: a kiss. He had one hand in her hair, and the other floated across her cheek, and his mouth slanted over hers, and that was a kiss.

142

But it felt like something more than that. It felt like he was pouring himself into her, and she didn't want him to stop.

The hand on her cheek disappeared, returned at her waist. He hauled her off the stool and pulled her against him, holding her tight. His body was hard against hers, his erection harder. He reached down and grabbed her arse, his big hand clutching as much firm flesh as it could manage, squeezing and kneading through the stretchy denim of her jeans, staking his claim.

He dragged his lips away from hers, his hot mouth tracing her jawline, leaving brightness in its wake like the tail of a shooting star. "I like the hair," he growled.

"I don't care."

"Liar. I like the way your lips taste, too. Never wear lipstick again."

She sighed as his tongue flicked out to slide along the line of her throat. "Are you sure about that?"

He paused for a moment, as if thinking. She tried not to whimper and demand more of his mouth. "No," he said finally. "I leave all lipstick decisions to you. Clearly, you know what you're doing." And then, blessedly, he sank his teeth into the softest part of her shoulder.

She let out a cry, and he froze. Then he released her hair, grabbed her waist, turned her around and lifted her onto the island. His hands went to her knees, forced them apart. He stepped into the space between them before she'd even fully registered the fact that they'd moved.

He grabbed her jaw, the tips of his fingers digging into her cheeks, forcing her to meet his eyes. His voice was raw and strained as he said, "I want to take your jeans off and get on my knees and lick your cunt. Tell me you want it."

"What if I don't?"

"Then tell me what you *do* want, and I'll give it to you." He reached down and grabbed his cock through the thick cotton of his joggers, the muscles of his biceps rippling as he squeezed himself. Hard. His hips jerked forwards between her legs and he rasped out, "Tell me. Or at least tell me to fuck off before I come in my pants like a teenager."

"Maybe I want you to do that."

He pressed a thumb against her lips, forcing it between her teeth. "Tell me what you want, and I'll give it to you. Anything. Right now. *Tell me.*"

She gazed into his eyes, her breath coming in ragged pants, her pussy clenching as if desperate to be filled. The way her legs were spread made her jeans tighter, creating the barest hint of pressure over her clit. The kind that made her want more. He was staring at her with eyes heavy-lidded and lustful, his full lips parted, his hips still jerking as he stroked himself roughly through his clothes. He'd do anything to make her come—she knew that as surely as she knew her own name. He'd make her come, and he'd fucking enjoy it.

She made her decision.

"I want—"

The front door slammed shut, the noise reverberating through the house. "Yoo-hoo! Where is my *guldklump*?"

"Shit." Cherry shoved at Ruben's chest, laughter bubbling up inside her where there should only be panic. "Agathe has a key?"

"Of course she has a key." He pulled back, straightening her camisole. "She's my grandmother."

"Which is why you need to disappear," Cherry whispered, casting a meaningful glance down at his crotch. Then her brows shot up as she finally caught sight of the erection she'd only felt before now.

Jesus Christ.

He shoved a hand through his hair and took a deep breath. As if they had all the time in the fucking world. Agathe's heavy steps echoed through the house. "Ruben? Hans?"

Jesus, Hans. How had she forgotten that he could be around here somewhere?

"Go," she hissed, smacking Ruben's shoulder. "Now!"

"Okay, okay!" He stepped back. But then, with a mischievous smile on his face that was way cuter than it should be, he leant in again and pressed a kiss to her cheek. "Want to come to work with me today?"

She blinked, stunned. "Um…"

"Say yes, or I'll stay here."

"You wouldn't."

"Try me."

"Fine," she whispered, holding back her laughter. "Yes. Now fuck off."

He kissed her other cheek. And then he left.

When Agathe came into the kitchen, Cherry was still sitting on the island like a damned fool. And she didn't even mind.

CHERRY DIDN'T KNOW what she'd expected, but it wasn't this.

She stood in the bright, January sun, wrapped up in a thousand and one layers—Ruben had insisted—and leaning against a huge maple tree. If she raised a gloved hand to protect her eyes and squinted just a little, she could watch a gaggle of children running around on the white-frosted grass, laughing and screaming and chasing a football.

A gaggle of children, and Ruben.

In the car over, he'd told her that these kids were aged 9 to 12. Some of them looked tiny; a few seemed huge for their age. She'd worked in a school long enough to notice that some of them probably had learning difficulties, and one of the girls might be autistic. But they were surrounded by staff members in matching purple jackets who made sure that everyone was involved, and that every child was comfortable.

It was as different from the Academy's approach as anything she'd ever seen. She remembered her first date with Ruben—their only date, she supposed, since lying in bed with your fake fiancée, whispering your feelings into the dark, didn't count. Ruben had seemed uncomfortable with the idea of sponsoring the Academy, had pushed for her opinion on the matter. She, of course, hadn't wanted to badmouth her place of employment.

But when she thought about education, this was her personal ideal.

Not that she knew shit. She was just HR.

The kids clearly loved it, though. And when they'd seen Ruben approaching, they'd all run to him like he was their long-lost-father.

It was disturbingly sweet.

"You are impressed?"

Cherry jumped slightly, even though she recognised that impossibly deep voice. Hans. He was standing beside her, his arms folded, his eyes on Ruben and the kids. And his thin lips were tilted slightly into that half-smile he occasionally displayed.

"Yes," she said, truthfully. "I didn't expect him to…"

"To give a shit. I know. People are always surprised." He leant back against the broad trunk of the maple, like her, as if they were friends. At first, she'd thought he didn't like her at all, but recently she'd realised that he was just a prickly guy. She liked prickly people. She liked people who couldn't be charmed.

"You and Ruben are close," she said.

There was a slight pause, as if he were surprised. Then he said, slowly, "Yes…" And she *knew* he was surprised. "We haven't been acting like it," he added. "Since you came."

"I know," she said. "That's why I noticed. Absence takes up a lot of space."

He grunted.

"So what's up? You're still angry with him about… This?"

Hans sighed. "I am angry with him because he never looks out for himself. He thinks he can handle anything. He thinks if he *can't* handle something, it's a weakness and the end of the world, instead of a normal human limitation."

"Always slaying dragons?" she suggested.

"And coming home half-dead, thinking no-one will care."

She digested that for a moment. Then she said, "Tell me about his brother."

And Hans said, "No."

Cherry nodded slowly. "So it's bad?"

His voice became almost small, hesitant. "You understand, Ms. Neita, my loyalty is to the crown. If it weren't, I would not be fit for this position. If it weren't, I could not stay with him."

Strange, the many ways that people could be trapped.

She turned away. Watched Ruben laughing in that cold, cold sunlight, letting the children foul him left and right, separating them when they got too rough or over-excited. He was beautiful. He was wonderful. He was perfect.

Oh, dear.

"I THINK this has gone on long enough."

Ruben looked up from the stack of cones he was putting away. Hans was looming over him like a giant, his face serious as ever.

Ruben raised his brows. *"What's* gone on long enough?"

"Don't be petulant." Hans shifted slightly, the only sign of his discomfort. The sort of sign only Ruben would notice.

Still, he turned away, stacking the cones neatly. "Use your words, Hans. I believe in you."

His bodyguard released a sigh so loud, Cherry probably heard it from the classroom down the hall. The classroom where she was currently getting to know the children while Ruben helped put away this morning's sports equipment. Every so often, he heard her laughter. Far more often, he heard the children's.

"I think we should get over this... disagreement," Hans finally said.

Ruben stood, dusting off his hands. "You want to kiss and make up? Already? Usually, you last longer than this."

Hans shrugged. "You need me."

"Oh, I do?"

"Yes. You want to talk to me. About her."

Ruben grinned. "I *do?*"

Hans rolled his eyes. "Fine." He turned to leave, but Ruben grabbed his old friend's arm in a move they'd executed countless times over the years. They were both too stubborn for this friendship to work, and yet, somehow, it did.

Sometimes, people were meant to be in each other's lives, and nothing else really mattered.

"Stay. You're right. I want to talk to you."

Hans sighed again. He was a master of sighs. Then he shut the door of the little equipment room and leant back against a shelf. The shelf, sturdy as it was, creaked dangerously under his weight. Hans stood. "So talk."

Funny. All of a sudden, Ruben had no idea what to say. But in the absence of certainty, his mind spit out a thought that seemed both ridiculous and true. "I don't want her to leave."

"She's not going to leave. You've got a year."

"I *never* want her to leave."

Hans looked slightly alarmed. "You've known her for—"

"Less than a fortnight. I'm aware."

"Hm." The rough-hewn lines of Hans's face appeared blank as stone, which meant that he was thinking. "You know, your father once said he fell in love with your mother at first sight."

Ruben arched a brow. "Have you been reading interviews?"

"Please. You know my mother is obsessed with yours. The beautiful and tragic Lady Freja."

"Still?"

"Of course. The people loved her."

"Thank God somebody did." Ruben felt traitorous as soon as the words left his mouth. Plenty of people had loved his mother. *He* had loved his mother, more than anything else in the world. So had his father. "I don't think emulating my father is a good thing, when it comes to love. Things turned out badly for him."

"I don't know about that," Hans said slowly. "He got everything he ever wanted. He died, but everyone must die. And not all die happy."

Ruben turned those words over in his mind, but couldn't quite get a handle on them. They felt ephemeral, like something beautiful but impossible to hold. Something that didn't apply to people like him. He put the problem away for later and focused on a more pressing issue.

"I don't want her to meet my brother."

Hans shrugged. "That is natural. I wouldn't want Demetria to meet a python."

"...Demetria?" Ruben frowned. "What does Demi have to—"

"You know, people you care about," Hans said. "Would you want her to meet a python?"

"I—what?"

"Would you lock Demi in a room with a python?"

"What the fuck are you talking about?"

"No! You wouldn't! No-one would. That's all I'm saying."

Ruben stared at his friend. Hans was almost... emoting. And right now, he looked panicked. "Are you okay?"

"I'm fine. Look, don't worry about Cherry. You have a whole year to convince her that you're the love of her life."

"Well, I don't know about *love*—"

"Shut up. A whole year, Ruben. If it's meant to be..."

"I don't know about *meant to be*—"

"Shut up." Hans opened the door and strode out into the hall . "Come on. Let's go."

Ruben felt slightly dazed. He wasn't entirely sure what that conversation had been about, or if they'd agreed on anything, or why Hans kept using words like *love*.

But he and his best friend were okay again. So he shrugged it off.

CHAPTER EIGHTEEN

C herry was sitting cross-legged on her bed, her laptop resting on her knees. There was a white ear bud in her left ear and a pink one in her right, and a smile on her face.

"Ooh, shit. I felt that." Maggie's voice came through the pink ear bud. A sickening *crunch* came through the white one, as Jessica Jones crushed some gang member's fist with her bare hand. Then Maggie said, "Would you fuck Jessica Jones?"

Cherry thought. "Hypothetically." Her mild interest in women had never developed into anything more concrete, but Jessica was cute enough.

"What if she, like, accidentally killed you?"

"Ummm..." That was actually a good point. "Okay, maybe not. Imagine the obituary. Mum would die of shame."

"Exactly. I'd fuck the actress, though."

Cherry hesitated. Talking about sleeping with a fictional character was one thing. Talking about sleeping with an actual person, even if they'd never meet, felt the tiniest bit more... real.

And for some reason, kind of like a betrayal. Which was weird. Very weird.

"What?" Maggie demanded. "You wouldn't fuck her?"

"Ah... No, I would." In theory. But when she tried to imagine it, her mind threw up different images. Memories rather than fantasies. Dark hair that wouldn't stay in place and rough hands and hard words.

"Oh, God," Maggie said. "Are you too *in love* to think about fucking other people?"

"What? No. I mean..." She should probably say yes, right? That's what she wanted her family to think. But lying to Maggie felt like that moment when a dentist put cotton or whatever in your mouth to stop it from closing, and you couldn't control your own spit and everything tasted disgusting and you kind of wanted to choke or hit something or down a litre of water all at once.

"You *are*," Maggie insisted. She sounded delighted. Cherry's sister was 23 but she had never been in love and insisted that she never would be. She was probably planning years of sibling torture based around this very moment.

"Oh, shut up. We're missing the show."

"I can multitask, sis. And I am finding this conversation far more interesting than Netflix right now."

"You're the most annoying person on earth, do you realise that?"

"You literally ran off to a foreign country to marry a *prince* without warning. You won't tell me shit about him, and I had to use Biblical quotes about judgement to stop Mum from Googling him, and *I'm* the most annoying person on earth?"

Cherry winced. "Okay, fair."

"Right." Maggie paused. "So he's had it kind of rough, huh?"

"Wait—did *you* Google him?"

"Of course I did. And you should thank your lucky stars I got there before our parents, cuz Jesus Christ—"

"What? What did you find?"

There was a slight pause. Then Maggie said, clearly shocked, "You don't know?"

Cherry stiffened. Her sister meant well, but the incredulity in her tone was threaded with something else—something dangerously close to concern, worry, pity, as if Cherry was in the dark. As if she was a fool. She wanted to say, *I know what I'm doing.* She wanted to say, *You don't even realise how in control of this situation I really am.* But she couldn't, and not just because she'd signed a non-disclosure agreement.

She couldn't say either of those things because she wasn't sure that they were true.

So instead, she said, "Oh, I know about all of that stuff. Just, I heard it from him. I didn't want to invade his privacy." She sounded casual, unconcerned, totally confident.

It worked. She felt her sister relax through the phone, through the miles between them. "Fair enough. Honestly, I feel really sorry for him. I mean, that Kathryn bitch…"

Cherry paused Netflix. She remembered the headlines she'd seen, the one and only time she'd Googled Ruben.

Prince's Perversions Exposed: View Kathryn Frandsen's Social Media Live Stream!

Pushing the memory away, Cherry shut her laptop with a *click*.

"I should go. I'm getting a migraine."

"Oh, God, really? Are you okay?"

"Yeah, I'm fine. I think I've spent too much time looking at screens today. I'll probably go to bed early."

"Okay." It was a flimsy excuse, but Maggie seemed to believe it. Probably because Cherry didn't lie. Usually. "Hope you feel better in the morning, sis."

"I'm sure I will," Cherry said. "Love you."

"Love you. Bye."

Cherry put the phone down and stared at her laptop for a few minutes. It felt like an hour.

But she wouldn't do it. She couldn't. Of course, she probably *should*; Maggie's reaction proved that. Researching Ruben would be the sensible choice, and she could do it while avoiding headlines like the one she'd seen.

But when she thought about his smile and his sweetness and the warmth of his hands against her skin…

She sighed and turned away. It was time for bed.

HE CREPT into her room like it was a habit. Two nights, and they'd fallen into some kind of illicit routine. Cherry lay on her back, staring into the darkness and wondering if she was weak for wanting a man she hardly knew. Maybe. She wasn't concerned about the fact that she wanted his face between her thighs, because that was simply to be expected. He was… Ruben.

But she also wanted him to lie here and tell her everything. Anything. All of it. Like they had that kind of relationship—like they ever could, in this sort of situation.

Yeah. She was probably weak.

She'd never had a chance to be weak before. Maybe she should enjoy the freedom of it while it lasted.

His weight made the mattress dip, and she allowed herself to roll towards him—just a little bit. As if she couldn't help it. But he

155

didn't touch her. He lay down, close enough for the sensation of almost-feeling to prickle across her skin, like that sense of wary excitement before a summer storm, when the air became hot and electric.

If he was surprised to find the blankets turned down—as if waiting for him to appear and slip inside—he didn't say anything. He just lay there. He was going to let her speak first. He was going to let her dictate the tone of this midnight meeting.

So, since she was being weak and all, she said, "Tell me about Kathryn."

He paused. Then she felt movement beside her as he… shrugged? Maybe. That would fit the vague tone of his voice as he said, "We slept together. Repeatedly. It was fun, until it wasn't."

"You got bored of her?"

"Yes," he said dryly. "Like a child with a toy. I got *bored* of an entire woman. That sounds just like me."

She smiled into the dark. "Sorry. You are a prince."

"Hardly."

"Definitely," she said firmly. "Don't let anyone convince you that your birthright is in question."

When he replied, he sounded surprised but pleased. Like an early sunrise, unexpected warmth slowly dawning. "Cherry Pie," he said. "Have you come over all monarchist?"

"Well, no. But as long as you weirdos aren't running the country—"

"Charming, I'm sure."

"—I see no reason for anyone to deny the reality of who you are. Your existence is just as valid as your brother's and your sister's."

For a moment, he was quiet. She started to worry that, in the midst of her unexpected passion on this topic, she'd said the wrong thing. But then his hand came groping towards hers in the dark, bumping against her hip, her shoulder, her forearm. She helped him out and slid her palm into his. He squeezed. He didn't let go.

"Kathryn and I had a disagreement with regard to the, ah, future of our arrangement. She wanted something more serious. I didn't. We argued. It wasn't over—not in my mind, anyway. But clearly it was in hers. She invited me over, initiated our usual… activities. Encouraged me to be particularly vocal throughout, not that I noticed at the time. It was only after, when I came home, that I found out she'd recorded the whole thing. Live. It's all the rage on social media. There wasn't much to see in the video, but there was plenty to hear, and she'd added a few helpful comments. Enough to convince the world of my… perversions."

If that last word sparked an inappropriate flare of curiosity in Cherry's gut, it was overpowered by the wave of outrage she felt as she processed that information. "What the fuck? That's horrible. Really fucking horrible. When was this?"

"About eight months ago. Most of the attention died down recently, but…" Ruben laughed. The sound was bitter. "It'll certainly stay with me for a while."

"I see. Is that why, when we were caught together…"

He sighed. "I don't know. I thought I'd gotten over it. Weathered the storm and whatever. But when I saw that camera I felt like I was choking."

"Jesus. I'm sorry." Cherry bit her lip, her stomach twisting. "Kathryn sounds like a fucking delight."

Ruben squeezed her hand. "I can feel you fuming over there."

"I don't know what you mean," she said brightly.

"I have a theory," he said, his voice mild, "that under the right circumstances, you would be capable of murder. I should add that this aspect of your personality is one I appreciate."

She huffed out a laugh. "Good to know. I can count on your support at my trial then?"

"Cherry." She could hear the smile in his voice, saw him in her mind's eye shaking his head. "Listen. As easy as it would be to let you think that I'm the victim... I'm not. I deserve everything Kathryn did to me."

She frowned. His words made no sense, but his voice was steady. She sensed his unease in the way his hand curled around hers, the way the mattress shifted as he fidgeted. He was serious. He really believed that he deserved it. As if anyone could ever deserve it.

"Ruben," she said, her voice soft. This was a tone reserved for delicate things, the injured and afraid, but she used it with a man as big as a mountain because he needed it.

People are many things at once; that's the beauty of humanity.

"I'm assuming," she said carefully, "That by *perversions* you mean—"

"Kinks," he interrupted, his voice clipped. "And bisexuality. And... no, I think that's it."

Cherry swallowed, her chest tightening as she imagined what that would be like. To have your private self exposed to a nation already slavering to tear you apart. She was starting to think that back in England, when he'd dragged her into his mess, when he'd trapped her and tied her to him... he'd somehow been trying to protect her. Wasn't that a novel fucking idea?

She licked her lips and tried to make him see. "You can't possibly think that anyone deserves that kind of treatment."

"I used her." He said it plainly, without hesitation. "I used her, and I let her think... God, I don't know. Kathryn is a difficult woman. I won't pretend she's pleasant, but no-one forced me to sleep with her. I did it, knowing I felt nothing for her, because I convinced myself that she and I were the same. And really, I was right; we are the same." He barked out a laugh. "We're both pieces of shit.

"When I told her that I didn't want a relationship, she assumed it was because of her position. She's new money, her family is messy, and she doesn't care. That's one of the reasons I wanted her; I respected her attitude. But she thought I didn't want more because I looked down on her. What was I supposed to say? *No, I just don't like you?* What the hell was I doing, sleeping with a woman I didn't like?" He sighed. "I shouldn't be telling you any of this."

"Why not?"

"Because you're not here to listen to my twisted ramblings."

"I'm here to get to know you," she said softly. "And I don't know if you have much experience with the whole *friendship* thing, but it usually involves listening to twisted ramblings."

He rolled onto his side, the mattress dipping as he faced her. She could feel the ghost of his breath against her cheek as he whispered, "Is that what we're doing? The friendship thing?"

Her throat felt dry, scratchy, but she forced the words out anyway. "Isn't that what you want?"

There was a pause. A long, long pause. But finally, he said, "I would be grateful for your friendship."

She didn't miss the way that he'd manoeuvred around the question. And she definitely didn't miss the hope that swelled within her at that realisation.

Fucking ridiculous. He'd just given her a thousand more reasons not to trust him.

Then he lay back and said, "I hope it made her feel better, at least. That would be something."

Cherry sat up, suddenly infuriated by his attitude. She'd heard the waver in his voice when he'd described the situation, but still he acted as if this Kathryn woman was some delicate fucking flower, innocent of all responsibility.

"Are you telling me that you'd do this to someone?" she snapped. "That you'd expose someone's intimate moments like that? Spill secrets and... and do your best to humiliate someone who'd trusted you?"

He shot up too, the mattress squeaking under his weight. "Of course not! I would never!" She'd never heard him sound so vehement.

"Right!" she said, exasperated. "Because it would be fucking reprehensible, and you know that. Some people like to say that all's fair in love and war. Those people cannot be trusted with power. It sounds like you were an absolute arse, and you can feel guilty about that—you should. But what she did to you is a separate issue. You didn't deserve it. No-one deserves that. Do you understand?"

He reached for her. She felt it, the same way she felt his gaze or his smile. Even before his fingers brushed against her cheek, she knew what he was doing.

"You sound so fierce," he murmured. "Cherry Pie."

"You have to stop calling me that." She'd meant to be firm, but her voice was worryingly soft.

"Why?"

"My dad calls me that."

"I could say something inappropriate, but I'll restrain myself."

She burst out laughing. "You're ridiculous."

"Fine. No Cherry Pie. How about... Cherry Blossom?"

She faked a gag as his hand slid from her cheek to the nape of her neck. "No. Another dad name."

"I don't think it's fair of him to monopolise all the cherry-related nicknames. I'm going to file a complaint."

"He did mention wanting to speak with you..."

Ruben froze. "Fuck. How long do you think I can put that off?"

She laughed again. Her chest felt light all of a sudden, but the weight of his hand against her skin felt heavy. Deliciously heavy.

"I don't know. I'll figure something out. He's really not that scary."

"So you say. What about Cherry Pop?"

"Taken."

"Of course it is," he sighed. His fingers found the knot of her scarf at the base of her neck. "What's this?"

"Scarf."

"To sleep in?"

"Yeah. It's silk, so my hair doesn't dry out."

She could hear the smirk in his voice as he said, "So delicate, hm? A born princess."

She rolled her eyes. Tried not to think about the fact that she was a *fake* princess. A fake princess-to-be. Whatever.

"Cherry," he whispered. "I like touching you." His finger trailed down the back of her neck, along her spine. It dipped under her T-shirt, dragging down the fabric. She arched her back and shivered.

"I know you do."

"Oh you *know*, do you?"

"I noticed, yeah."

He wrapped a hand around her throat and pushed, gentle but insistent, until she lay back against the bed. Cherry tried to ignore the way her nipples tightened and her clit throbbed, brought instantly to life by... What? By the casual way he controlled her? By the restrained strength in his grip? Or by the way he lay down beside her, his chest against her side, his muscled forearm lying between her breasts?

His lips pressed against the hollow just beneath her ear, finding the sweet spot with unnerving precision in the pitch-black. "Do you like it when I touch you, Cherry?"

She swallowed, her throat dry. And even though her mind was scrambling and bright white stars were bursting behind her eyes, she forced herself to speak. "It's obvious that I do."

"Is it?" His voice was low and soothing, but with a thread of command that had her pulse quickening. "I don't think it's obvious. Not until you tell me. So tell me." His grip on her throat tightened, his fingers pressing against her pulse.

White fire shot through her veins as she gasped out, "Yes, I like it."

"Tell me what you like. Tell me *exactly* what you like." Always, he wanted more. More of her.

She loved that.

"I don't know," she smiled, her voice hoarse. "Show me what you can do, and I'll tell you what I like."

His tongue slid out to trace circles against her skin, the place where it grew thin and sensitive at the base of her throat. "Is that a challenge, sweetheart?"

"Yes," she breathed. "It is."

CHAPTER NINETEEN

R uben squeezed his eyes shut at her words, willing his stampeding pulse to slow and his lust to fade. Just a little bit, until it became something he could handle, something he was used to. Because right now, his need for Cherry was almost scaring him.

She lay there, the curve of her hip a breath away from his aching cock, her throat shifting as she swallowed beneath his hand. For all her fucking mouth, she liked this. She liked the power exchange.

"I think I know what you want," he said softly. "But thinking isn't good enough. We need to be sure. And you're not sure yet. Are you?"

"I... I don't know. Not exactly. No." Her voice shook. Not much; the slight waver was almost imperceptible, but he noticed. And, because he was a twisted fuck, he liked it.

"You trust me?"

She hesitated.

He ignored the way that hesitation tore into his heart and clarified. "You know I won't hurt you? I won't do anything you don't want?"

"Yes," she said, and the certainty in her voice almost soothed the pain in his chest. Almost.

"Good. Then let me tell you what *I* want." He dragged his hand away from her throat, down her chest, until he reached the soft mounds of her tits through her thin T-shirt. Her nipples were hard and thick beneath the fabric. He rolled one between his thumb and forefinger, and she arched her back and let out a moan. Ruben's cock swelled, almost painful now, and he fought not to release a moan of his own.

Couldn't let her know what she did to him. Not yet.

His voice was calm and steady as he continued. "I want control. I want you to give yourself to me, because you know I'll look after you. Understand?"

She swallowed. "I'm... I can look after myself."

"Of course you can," he soothed. "You always do." He released her nipple, running his hand slowly down her body. "You look after yourself and everyone else. You're the smartest person in every room. You're the most capable person I know. But you don't have to handle everything." He savoured the swell of her belly, the soft rise and fall of her flesh, on the way to his ultimate goal.

His palm slid between her legs, cupping her pussy over her underwear, his thumb and little finger grazing the soft skin of her thighs. "I can handle this. I can make you come. I can make you scream." His fingers explored the cotton gusset of her underwear, the only thing keeping him from what he really wanted.

She was wet. Fucking soaked, the thin fabric damp and sticky. The knowledge made his balls tighten, made his cock ache to sink inside her. "Don't you get tired of thinking all the time, sweetheart? Of figuring out how everything should go and where everything should be?"

"Yes," she sighed. Her hips lifted slightly, pumping against his palm.

He growled, pushing her back against the mattress. "Don't move. You take what I give you. Understand?"

"Yes," she said again, her voice thick with lust.

He rubbed her slowly through the cotton, let her feel how much he adored her. How much he needed her. When had that happened? He didn't have time to think about it. "Let me look after you, sweetheart. You don't have to control everything. Let me do this." He held his breath as he waited for her answer.

Maybe it was counterintuitive, but Ruben had only ever wanted the submission of women who didn't need him. Women who could live just fine without him, but didn't want to. Women for whom handing over the reins was both a relief and a sacrifice. He wanted to own Cherry, because she already owned him. And she didn't even know it.

Finally, she touched him. Her fingers wrapped around his wrist, the one trapped between her thighs. She didn't push him away. She squeezed, as if she wanted more.

He wouldn't give her more. He wanted to tease her. He wanted her to beg. He wanted to spread her legs and fuck her until they both passed out.

Instead, he said, "Have you ever done this before? Power play?"

"No," she admitted, her voice low. "But I know the theory."

That made him smile. "Been researching, love?"

"Of course I have."

"Good. Let's talk about it." He'd meant to go slow, but his control was fraying. She was so fucking sweet, so sharp, and he wanted every piece of her. So he hooked a finger beneath the edge of her underwear, pushed it aside, and dragged his thumb down the hot, slick seam of her pussy.

Jesus, she was wetter than he'd thought. She inhaled sharply at his touch, her fingers tightening around his wrist. He'd be surprised if she didn't cut off his circulation. He should tell her to let go, tell her exactly where to put her hands, but something about her—about the unexpected innocence beneath all her knowing smiles and those swaying hips—got him harder than straightforward dominance. So he let her cling to him as he explored the silken folds of her cunt, spreading her wetness around.

"I like control," he said, his voice slightly raw. "I like rough sex. I don't want to accept your submission. I want to work for it." He hesitated. Forced himself to continue, because truth mattered. "I want to *take* it. Oh, and I have an oral fetish. You understand?"

"Yes," she gasped. But she didn't move. If it weren't for the way her voice unravelled on that single word, he wouldn't even know that she was falling apart.

Suddenly he wanted, more than anything, to see her face.

"Tell me what you want," he said gently.

"I want you to fuck me."

"No." He dragged his thumb up to the swollen nub of her clit. "You have to tell me what you like. And you have to tell me your safe word. Just in case." He hovered over her clit, waiting for her to push up, into him, to force the pressure he knew she wanted. To misbehave.

"I, um… I want you to be in charge."

"I'm always in charge, Cherry. You know that."

Despite her claim, she responded with sharp defiance. "I certainly do not."

"Watch it, sweetheart." His voice was hard, and he felt her shiver. "Now tell me your safe word."

"Milkshake."

"Catchy."

"Shut up."

He lifted his palm and brought it down against her mound, firm rather than hard. Her hips jerked up as she released a low moan, her nails digging into his wrist.

He kept his voice mild as he said, "Hard limits?"

"Um..." She was panting now. "No serious pain. Just a little bit."

He couldn't help himself. He pressed a kiss to her cheek, finding her effortlessly now, even in the dark. "I won't hurt you, love."

"Well," she said. "A little bit."

Smiling, he spanked her pussy again. She yelped, arching into him.

"Cherry," he said softly. "That's the second time you've moved without permission. What do you say?"

"You can't touch me and expect me to—"

Ruben pushed a finger deep inside her. Holy shit, she was tight, and soft and wet and hotter than fucking hell. Her walls clung to him, tightened and released around that single digit as she hissed, "Oh my fucking God, yes."

"You like that?" He thrust back and forth, feeling her open up around him. "Is that what it takes to keep your pretty mouth shut? I just have to fill up your cunt?"

"Fuck you," she panted, a smile in her voice.

He found the line of her throat with his lips, then bit. She gasped, and he bit harder, fucked her faster, turned one finger into two and then three as she spread her legs for him.

"Good girl," he whispered, releasing her neck. His tongue laved the bite mark he'd left, feeling the slight indents in her skin. He didn't think it would bruise, but some dark, possessive part of him hoped it might. He pulled his fingers from her pussy and she whined, rolling her hips. "Shhh," he murmured. "I'll look after you. Remember?"

"Yes," she whispered into the dark. His heart swelled almost as much as his cock. God, he wanted to see her. He wanted to see her so badly.

"Let me turn the light on, Cherry."

"No," she said, her tone slightly panicked. "No. I'll... Not yet. Please—"

"Okay. It's okay." He kissed her cheek, her jaw, the corner of her mouth, until she grew silent and still and the air between them calmed again. "Don't worry. What's your safe word?"

"Milkshake," she said immediately.

"Good. Remember to use it. For anything. I mean that. Anything at all."

"Right," she whispered. "Yeah. I'm sorry."

"Don't be sorry. Never be sorry."

"Okay." Her hand came up to feather across his jaw, and just that touch brought him to the edge of desperation. Touching her was one thing. But having her touch him? The fact that she wanted him? That she wanted him enough to give him everything, including the control she held so tight to her chest? He could come right now.

Then she reached down and grabbed his hand, dragged it up to her lips, and sucked his fingers into her mouth. And Ruben almost *did* come.

Her hot tongue slid across his skin, licking him clean, licking her own fucking juices. Christ, her mouth, her lips, so full and lush and soft, and the pull of each firm suck, almost savage.... He hadn't meant to, not tonight, but Ruben had to pull his cock out of his pyjamas and squeeze, hard, right at the base. She released his fingers with a pop and he said, his voice a ghost, "Good girl. Fuck, good girl."

"Oral fetish, hm?"

Ruben laughed, but the sound was rough and broken. "Oral fetish as in, if I get my mouth on your cunt right now, I'll come."

"You mean—"

"I mean I'll come. Immediately. You're too fucking perfect. Shit, come here." He rolled on top of her, and she widened her legs almost automatically, her body flowering for him. Because she wanted him. This woman wanted him. Her T-shirt had ridden up, so the soft skin of her belly pressed against his naked dick, and Ruben hissed through his teeth. He thrust against her, smearing his pre-cum over her skin, and she fisted a hand in his hair and kissed him.

He would never be the same.

CHAPTER TWENTY

Cherry hadn't meant to kiss him. She hadn't meant to do any of this, but his filthy words were straight out of every fantasy she'd ever had, and the way he touched her—dominant yet caring, desperate and demanding and so fucking hungry—took her close to the edge. So she'd kissed him. And she was glad she had.

His mouth slanted over hers, harsh and commanding, rough as ever. He thrust his tongue between her lips, only to glide it gently along her own as if performing an introduction. If they hadn't been in darkness already, he'd have stolen her sight; he surrounded her, his powerful legs bracketing hers, their foreheads touching lightly. He rested his weight on his elbows, and she felt his forearms either side of her temples. She was caged.

Then one of his hands moved to her throat, his thumb and forefinger bracketing her jaw, forcing her head back. Enough to control, to suggest that he could hurt her and prove he never would. He pressed his advantage, enjoyed the vulnerability of her position, owning her mouth with his tongue. And all the while his hips pumped against her, the searing hardness of his cock pressing into her belly.

His pre-come eased the glide against her skin, smearing her with stickiness, filthy and decadent. She let her hands roam over the ridges and valleys of his muscular back, the skin hot, the flesh beneath it taut. Then she went lower, dipping beneath the waist of his pyjama bottoms, finding the rounded, powerful globes of his arse and squeezing.

He dragged his mouth away from her lips. "Behave," he said, his voice so fucking deep and heavy she felt it right between her legs. Felt her pulse between her legs. Felt everything between her legs.

"Yes, Sir," she teased.

He rewarded her by biting her lower lip, giving her the slightest, sweetest pain to sharpen all this hazy lust. "Good girl." The words sent sparks of heat showering through her pussy, and she felt elated, fucking high, because she'd known. All along, she'd known that this was what she wanted, what she'd eventually find. And she'd known it would be him. She'd known he'd give it to her.

He kissed her again, lighter now, little raindrop touches of his lips against hers, like breadcrumbs showing her the way. The way to desperation.

"Understand this," he said. *Kiss.* "You are mine." *Kiss.* "I know what you need." *Kiss.* "And right now, you need to spread your legs like a good girl and let me do all the work."

"Yes," she whimpered, arching into him, straining against the hardness of his powerful body. "Please."

She felt him smile against her lips. It was the kind of filthy smile she'd seen on his face a thousand times, the kind that had made her desperate for him in the first place.

"Tell me, Cherry. I know you're wet—but how wet?" He trailed his lips across her cheeks, her jaw, whispering as he went. "Is it worse, now? Is it dripping down your thighs? Making a mess for me? Getting ready for me to use you?" He reached between their bodies, and she thought she'd pass out if he touched her. But he didn't; he just tugged her underwear back into place, over her aching pussy. When she whimpered, he laughed darkly. "I'm sorry, baby. But I don't have any condoms, so we need to keep those on. Next time, I'll fuck you. Would you like that?"

"Yes," she blurted out. "Please."

Suddenly, his weight disappeared, and she thought for one terrible moment that he was going to stop. But then his voice broke through the darkness again. "You've been such a fucking brat tonight, I should just leave you like this."

He wouldn't. Would he? She didn't know. Maybe. Her mind was frantic, desperate, but she kept her mouth shut.

Finally he said, "I won't, though. I couldn't leave my baby like this." His fingers traced the swell of her pussy through her underwear, the only point of contact between them, and she shivered. "Fuck it," he grunted, and then his hands, big and brisk, pulled the cotton off of her hips. He dragged the underwear down her thighs, down her calves, pulled it from her feet. She didn't know what he did with it. She didn't care.

Then the mattress shifted as he settled between her thighs, and when he spoke again she felt his warm breath against her bare pussy. *Fuck.*

"The first time I saw you," he said, "making grown men sweat with nothing but a smile, all I could think was... What would I have to do for you to take all of that power and hand it over to me? And ask me nicely to keep it for you? To look after it?" His voice dropped to a whisper. "You're so sweet, Cherry. I bet every man you ever fucked was shit-scared of you."

"Just a little bit," she admitted, her voice hoarse. "That's how I like my men." *Lie.*

"Good thing I'm not one of your men." He ran his tongue over the inside of her thigh, right at the sensitive crease just before it swelled into her mound, and she almost screamed. "You're *my* woman. Understand?"

"Yes," she gasped, arching blindly towards him. She needed more of that fucking tongue, and she didn't care what she had to do to get it. "Please."

"Are you begging me, baby?"

"No."

"Yes." He licked her again, on the other side, his wide tongue straying onto the outer edge of her pussy lips. "Beg. Tell me how much you want it."

She wanted to refuse, to tell him to fuck off. But her clit was aching so badly, and she was so desperate, and it was all because of him.

Did he really know her body that well? Could he really bring her to this point with nothing more than his hands and that filthy fucking mouth? Apparently, yes, he could. So what else could he do?

She thought of what he'd said before. *If I put my mouth on your cunt, I'll come.* Could *she* do that to *him*?

She wanted to. And she knew he'd meant it. She knew he wanted her that much, and nothing had ever made her feel more power-ful, more lustful, in her life. So she begged.

"Please, Ruben. I need..." This was why she couldn't let him turn the lights on. She wanted this, and she knew it, but even in the dark her cheeks burned and her words stuttered.

But he was there, his voice firm, his dominance cutting through her hazy thoughts and leading her straight to the truth. To her truth. "You need to come on my tongue."

"*Yes.* I need you to make me come."

"Good girl. Was that so hard?"

"Oh, fuck off." She didn't know if the words had escaped or if she'd set them free. One second she wanted to push, the next her veins were alight with lust-edged fear, her breath trapped in her lungs as she awaited his reaction. Would he deny her? Would he change his mind?

He sank his teeth into the sensitive flesh of her inner thigh, and she yelped. Then he pushed two fingers into her cunt, spreading them wide, stretching her. "Watch your fucking mouth," he growled, "or I'll put my cock in you. Understand?"

She ignored the flare of arousal, the twisted desire to test him. "Yes, Sir. I'm sorry."

"Good." The rough slide of his fingers inside her disappeared. She almost whimpered at the sudden emptiness.

Then he slid his hands under her arse, squeezing as he pushed her hips up, forcing her pussy closer to his face. She grabbed at the sheets, her fingers twisting the fabric in anticipation. His breath turned cool as he blew against her entrance, and she realised how wet she was. Ridiculously wet. Embarrassingly wet. But all she felt was desperate need.

And then he kissed her.

His lips were soft but firm, parting her folds with the same delicacy he'd use to kiss her mouth. His tongue snaked out to probe her entrance, lapping at her juices, and his fingers tightened around the globes of her arse. He groaned low in his throat, the sound raw and guttural. Then his lips left her and his tongue grew firmer, tracing a path of fire up the seam of her pussy until it reached her clit.

He used the very tip of his tongue, stiff and firm and wet, to circle her swollen nub. She almost screamed. Round and round he went, until she jerked her hips in a desperate attempt to ride his face. It didn't work. He pulled away completely and bit her thigh, a warning. She tried to stay still. Gritted her teeth. Pinched her own nipples in an attempt to feed the lustful hunger inside her.

Apparently satisfied that she'd behave, he returned to her pussy. And finally, blessedly, his tongue pressed against her clit, rolling the needy flesh back and forth, just the way she needed it. Cherry sighed and spread her legs wider to accommodate the breadth of his shoulders.

He laughed, soft puffs of air that felt hot against the wetness of her pussy. "You like that, love?"

"Don't stop."

"Demanding, aren't you?" But he licked her again, and again, and then his finger eased inside her. It was thick and long and deliciously rough, but a single finger after the way he'd stretched her out felt like a tease and he knew it. That fucker. She was ready to scream until he turned his hand, palm up, and curled the pad of his finger against the upper wall of her pussy.

He stroked that soft place inside her, the place that sent electricity sparking through her veins and white-hot fire up her spine, and all the while his tongue rolled at her clit. Then he sealed his lips around the swollen nub and sucked, so, so gently, his finger stroking her with firm confidence.

She came. She came harder than she'd thought was possible, her body fracturing and falling apart and coming back together again, molten and liquid. She came so hard that breathing felt unnecessary, and if she'd had any sight in the darkness she probably would've lost it for a second. She came so hard that everything around her fell away until she was just a body, floating on a breeze of satisfaction.

She didn't realise that Ruben had moved until she felt him kiss her cheek. His lips were soft, but his stubbled jaw was sticky and he smelled deliciously filthy. He smelled like her. Fuck.

"Cherry. You okay?"

"Mmhm." Apparently, she couldn't speak.

He laughed softly. "Good." His fingers trailed over her lips, as if he were learning their shape. He kissed her again, on her forehead this time. "You tired?"

"Mmhm." If he'd stop talking, she'd already be asleep.

"Okay. I should go."

That gave her pause. "Why?" she demanded.

He caught one of her hands in his and dragged it down to his waist. Pressed it against the front of his pyjamas. The soft fabric was marred by a significant wet spot.

"*Oh.*"

"I did tell you," he murmured, his voice tinged with humour.

"Yeah," she chuckled, trying not to sound smug. "You did. Hey, where's my knickers?"

His voice, which had been playful as usual, became iron-hard again. "They're mine now. Okay?"

And even though her whole body felt worn-out, a spark of arousal flickered within her at his tone. "Okay."

He kissed her again, and then she felt the mattress shift as he got up. But she didn't hear her bedroom door open and shut behind him. Instead, she pressed her face into the pillow as the bathroom light came on. Just a flash of brightness before he closed the door on it, plunging her into darkness again. There was the sound of running water, another flash of light, and then he sank back into bed beside her.

She tried to remember why this was a bad idea, and failed.

He gathered her up in his arms and his scent enveloped her, clean linen and spice with the sharp edge of arousal and sweat. She'd done that. She kissed him, and it felt like comfort.

"Go to sleep, Cherry."

"Don't tell me what to do," she mumbled.

He laughed. She slept.

CHAPTER TWENTY-ONE

Ruben always woke up early, but he had the feeling that he'd slept later than usual.

The sun fought its way through the gaps between Cherry's curtains, bathing the room in gentle light. The first thing he felt was the warm weight of her leg, slung over him as if it belonged there. It certainly felt like it did. His hand was resting on her hip, and he realised with a jolt that his fingers were intertwined with hers.

He'd never heard of people holding hands in their sleep. He liked it, though. The panic that usually clogged his throat at the thought of this kind of thing—this kind of casual intimacy—was nowhere to be found. Maybe Hans was right. Maybe he was in love with her.

But he had this idea of falling in love that involved earthquakes and fanfare and, frankly, disaster. This all felt very *normal*. As if he'd been waiting his whole life to feel like this. To want someone like this. Shouldn't love be tragic and fraught and all that shit? He wasn't sure.

Ruben looked at Cherry's head, her hair all wrapped up in a pretty silk scarf. It was slightly wonky. He had a feeling that was his fault. Then he pulled back just a little bit, to see her face. He really fucking wanted to see her face.

She looked the same as always: beautiful. Unusually beautiful. The kind of beauty that people noticed, that they stopped to look at, that they made fools of themselves over. Her face was relaxed in sleep, her full lips pouting slightly and her plump cheeks soft. But her skin was different. Her usually flawless complexion was interrupted by little marks, slightly darker than the rest of her skin. Like freckles, but bigger, softer, less frequent, scattered apart. Scars?

He traced a thumb over a few of the marks, like a constellation across her cheekbone. Her skin felt like silk. He liked it; liked touching her without the makeup she usually wore, the velvety powder or whatever the fuck it was.

He wanted to nudge her awake. He wanted to see her face when she came. But he should let her sleep.

Of course, as soon as he thought that, she woke up.

She let out a few soft sighs, fidgeting slightly, her lashes fluttering. He felt her hand tighten around his, and then her eyes opened all at once and she said, "Fuck."

Which didn't sound good.

"What?" he demanded.

"You're still here."

"Of course I'm still here." He felt the soft, satisfied feeling in his chest drain away. "Did you want me to leave?"

She frowned. "No. But..." Her eyes skittered away from his, and if he didn't know better, he'd have thought she was blushing.

He cupped her cheek, pushing gently until she looked up at him. "What?" he asked softly. He didn't know what to expect. Maybe karma had come knocking on his door, and she was about to give him a speech about how this wasn't serious and she wasn't ready for a relationship. But then, he hadn't asked for a relationship, exactly. Yet. Plus, they were kind of *in* a relationship. They were engaged, for God's sake.

It occurred to him that he hadn't given her a ring. He wanted suddenly, urgently, to give her one. Specifically, the one sitting in his room, in a drawer, beside an old photo album of his parents.

He was in love with her. He was in love with her. *Fuck.*

Cherry bit her lip and whispered, as if they weren't alone: "What if Agathe comes over?"

Ruben blinked. "Well... She comes over every day. To make breakfast."

"Exactly! So she'll notice that we're in the *same room!*

"Why would she notice that?"

"You think she doesn't watch you like a hawk?"

He was trying not to laugh. Cherry looked genuinely worried. He didn't think she'd be pleased if he laughed. "Okay," he said slowly. "But why would she care?"

Cherry blinked. For a second, she looked stumped. Then she said, "*I* care."

"About what?"

"About your sweet little grandma knowing I've been fucking her grandson." She batted at his chest. "Get out. Go back to your room."

Ruben grinned. "But you *haven't* been fucking me. Not really. Why don't we—"

"Ooooh my God, will you stop? Get out!"

"Fine, fine." Ruben threw off the blankets and tried to bite back the huge, shit-eating grin he could feel spreading across his face.

Then he caught Cherry staring at his naked chest with a rather vacant expression and stopped trying to hold back the grin.

He was in love, and the object of his affections didn't hate or regret him, and appeared to enjoy the sight of his chest. Really, what more could a man ask for?

All of her.

He shoved that thought aside.

"Next chance I get," he said, "I'm fucking you."

"Piss off." She sat up, scowled at him, and grabbed her phone from the bedside table.

"Are you saying no?"

She rolled her eyes. "If you don't get out, I'm never speaking to you again."

"You know, Cherry, we *are* engaged. There's really no need to be embarrassed—"

She threw a pillow at his head. He left. He was happier than he'd ever been in his life.

HIS GOOD MOOD didn't last.

Ruben was on his way to breakfast—and already late for his lunch meeting a city over—when Demi appeared out of nowhere to grab his arm.

"Jesus Christ, woman." He slapped a hand over his heart, leaning against the hallway wall. "Where the hell did you come from?!"

"Study," she said shortly. "I need to talk to you." And then she dragged him off into the study he never used, displaying far more strength than was natural for a woman of her size.

He shut the door behind them and frowned down at her. She looked like someone had died.

Then she said, "The king has summoned you."

The last of Ruben's good cheer evaporated. "Tell him I said get fucked."

"Oh, really? *That's* what you want me to do?" Demi threw herself into the chair behind the room's huge desk and gave him a look. "Shall I email his assistant, or call to pass on the message directly? And while I'm at it, would you like me to invite your sister over for tea? Since apparently you're *trying* to make your life hell?"

Ruben pinched the bridge of his nose. He'd been awake less than an hour, and already his head was pounding.

Fucking Harald.

"I thought we had another week," he said finally.

"We did. He's trying to mess with your head." Demi stood, her expression unbearably kind. "Don't let him."

"It's really not that simple." Ruben ran a hand through his hair, looking around the room with unseeing eyes. "He controls almost everything I do—"

"As long as you retain your position in the royal household, sure."

He looked up sharply. "I'm not giving it up."

"Ruben..." She sighed. "You know what Hans and I think. You'll always be your parents' son, title or not. He can't take that away from you."

Ruben swallowed past the lump in his throat. "You have no idea how many things that man has taken from me. I'm not giving up anything else."

She said something, but he barely heard the words. He was already leaving.

WAITING AROUND for a man wasn't really Cherry's thing. So she told herself that she wasn't waiting at all; she was eating breakfast, and if Ruben happened to turn up, so be it.

It's not like she was breathless with anticipation or anything. Aside from the moments when her mind wandered from cinnamon muesli and coffee and the sound of Agathe humming to settle on thoughts of his smile, of the scent of his skin in the morning. *Then* she got kind of breathless.

The sound of rapid footsteps tore Cherry from her mooning and Agathe from her task, which appeared to be bleaching the sink. Cherry was pretty sure the older woman had done that twice yesterday, but to each their own.

Demi appeared in the doorway, her mouth pressed into a thin line, her brow furrowed.

"Demetria?" Agathe frowned. "What is the matter?"

"Ruben isn't in here?"

Cherry's concern spiked at the worried tone of her voice. "No. I think he's upstairs. What's going on?"

Demi shook her head, turning to go, but then Agathe said in a voice of iron, "Demetria. Tell me. What is the problem?"

The two women shared a look before Demi said, "Harald has run out of patience. Either he's brought the ball forward, or he gave us the wrong date on purpose. Whatever the reason, we've been summoned." She hurried off down the hall, leaving those words behind her like a bomb.

Cherry frowned. She already knew that Harald was, frankly, a grade-A cunt. But Agathe's usually ruddy face had turned grey at the news of his so-called 'summons'. The old woman wrung her hands with uncharacteristic worry in her eyes, hunching over at the waist.

"What?" Cherry demanded.

The other woman looked up sharply, injecting brightness into her voice and forcing a smile onto her face with obvious effort. "Nothing. It is just, Ruben hates the palace, and he'll be angry."

"Ruben's never angry."

Agathe gave Cherry a look. A look that said, *Don't think you know him. You don't.*

Something was going on here. Something Cherry didn't fucking like.

"I know Ruben and his brother don't get on," she said. "And I know they kept him away from you."

Agathe flinched as if she'd been hit. When she looked up, her eyes were dark with anger and... something that looked like shame. "They took him away," she said heavily, "but I let them."

Cherry took a moment to adjust to the implications of that statement. "You... you didn't want any contact?"

"That's not it. That's not it at all. It is only..." Agathe trailed off, her face grave. "You know, my family was never wealthy, not before my Freja married Magnus. Ruben's father. But we were always happy. Children were always loved. Always cared for. And I believed—" her voice caught, but she cleared her throat, shook her head. Pressed on. "I believed that everyone would be that way. Especially royalty." She let out a little laugh. "My mistake."

Cherry pushed her breakfast away and leant against the kitchen island, dread pooling in her stomach like liquid concrete.

"I should not have allowed it," Agathe said, almost to herself. "But I was selfish in my grief, too weak to fight for him." She kept on wringing her hands, the movement jerky. "So a year turned into two and then three, and I thought, what claim do I have on him? He will have forgotten me anyway, by now. If they don't want me around him, perhaps they are right."

There was a pause as Agathe swallowed, shook her head. "If I had used my brain, I might have realised. My Ruben, he represented everything that boy had lost. That boy who became king." All of a sudden, the emotions written across her face disappeared, studied blankness left behind. She slapped her hands against her thighs and drew herself up tall. "Well," she said briskly. "Never mind all that. You will go to the palace, and you will see. You will see for yourself."

Cherry opened her mouth to push, to ask, desperate for information she didn't deserve—but Agathe snatched up a cloth and firmly turned her back.

There was a moment of silence before Cherry picked up her half-eaten bowl of cereal, heading to the sink. But Agathe just waved one reddened hand and said, "No, leave that. I will do it. Go and find my grandson."

"But—"

"You are wrong, you know. He is often angry. But only with himself."

Cherry thought about that for a minute. And then she went to find her fiancé.

HE WAS IN HIS BEDROOM. The door was slightly ajar, revealing a slash of cool wood floors and a low bed covered in white linens. A pair of bare feet were visible, resting at its very edge. Cherry hovered at the door, peering through the gap, and caught sight of the ankles attached to those feet. And then the calves. And then the powerful, hair-sprinkled thighs.

185

Ruben said, "I know you're there, Cherry Pie."

She bit back a smile and pushed the door open, stepping inside. "I told you, you have to stop calling me that."

"Fine," he said. He was lying against his bed, arms folded behind his head, his broad chest still bare. His legs were bare too. He wore only tight, blue briefs, so she kept her eyes very firmly away from that area. "I'll call you Cherry Tart," he said. "I bet your dad never called you that."

"Shut up." She came towards the bed, hesitating for just a moment before sitting down on the edge.

He snorted and reached out, wrapping an arm around her waist. "Come here. What, you can't lie with me in the daylight?"

There was something in his voice, something she didn't hear often, if at all. An edge she didn't like, a sharpness that wasn't usually there. He pulled her down beside him, tucking her under his arm like she belonged there. She let her head rest against his chest and tried not to think about the marks her makeup would leave or the fact that her hair was probably tickling his face.

"Did Demi talk to you?" she asked.

He laughed. She felt the sound as much as she heard it, rumbling deep within his chest, but there was no light to it. No humour. "Yeah, she talked to me. You don't need to worry, love. I'm fine."

Carefully, she said, "What's wrong with your brother?"

He sat up slightly, propping himself up on his elbows, looking down at Cherry with confusion in his eyes.

"Why would you say that?" he asked, his voice hoarse. "What's wrong with Harald? Why would anything be wrong with Harald?"

She cocked her head. "He summons you and Demetria panics, your grandmother almost starts spilling family secrets—"

"What did she say?" he demanded, his voice sharp.

Cherry held up her hands. "Nothing. Don't be angry with her."

"I'm not," he sighed, deflating before her eyes. "Of course I'm not. I'm angry with him. I'm angry at the way he can disrupt a perfectly good fucking morning from miles away, and I'm angry at myself for letting him."

"Don't be." She bit her lip, oddly unsure of herself around this new, darker Ruben. But then she pulled herself together and decided to be brave. She reached for his hand, and he met her halfway. Their fingers twined together, his palm dwarfing hers, his skin oddly cold. "Listen," she said. "Emotions are natural. Reacting is a part of living. What I'm asking is... What is it about this guy that causes such chaos? You can't tell me there's no reason. I mean, it's not like he really has any power—"

Ruben cut her off with a snort. "You're smarter than that, Cherry. Don't think that just because this is the modern age, a man with wealth and a title and endless connections and centuries of good fucking breeding is powerless."

"Fair enough," she murmured. "But aren't you the same?"

He let go of her hand. "No. I'm not the same." For a minute he looked so bleak, his features so drawn and harsh, that she thought she'd said something terrible. But then, all at once, his face smoothed out and he gave her something approaching a smile. "Don't worry about all of this, Cherry. I'll need you to pack again. I'm sorry to keep moving you around. But the sooner we introduce you and see what else he wants, the sooner we can come home."

She tried not to think too hard about the fact that, when he said *home*, this place sprang to mind before her old flat did.

No. Not this place. Her bed, in the dark, with him in it.

"Now?" she asked. "We have to go now?"

"No. The monarch has legal power over the rest of the royal family in a lot of areas—including marriage, by the way." He frowned, shook his head. "Not that we're getting married. What I'm saying is, if I don't come when he calls, there'll be consequences. But..." He settled back onto the bed, pulling her down with him. "I don't have to come immediately. I'm not a fucking dog."

Funny. It sounded like he'd said those words before.

"Tomorrow," he said finally. "We'll go tomorrow."

Cherry stared up at his ceiling. He didn't have a grand, four-poster bed like she did. His room looked almost normal. She put her hand against his chest, felt his heart beating, and said, "Okay. Do you think Agathe will look after Whiskey?"

"Of course." Ruben smiled slightly. "Although that creature doesn't need much looking after. I barely see her."

"She is the queen of stealth."

"Right." He chuckled, but then his humour faded. "I'm supposed to be getting ready for work," he said.

"Seriously? You're going out today?"

"I'll have to rearrange a shit-ton of meetings while I waste time pandering to my brother's whims, so yes. I'm going out. I might be late back." He pulled away from her, gently enough, but it hurt just the same. "Demi can help you pack. She mentioned the two of you ordered some clothes?" He got up, leaving her behind on the bed, wandering over to his wardrobe.

"Yeah," Cherry said, sitting up. "For court. Or whatever. Most of it's already here, so..."

"Great." He pulled out a steel-grey suit, looked at it for a moment, then shrugged and threw it on the bed. "I'm sorry about this, Cherry. I really am."

She shrugged. Tried to smile. "It's okay. I don't mind."

"I do," he said darkly. Then he sighed and forced a smile of his own. It was strained, too bright, too wide. He reached for her, and she came, because maybe that would help him shake off the worry he wore like chains.

He pulled her into his chest and buried his face in her hair, his arms iron bands around her body. For a few long minutes, she wondered if he'd ever let go. And if she even wanted him to.

But then, with a sigh, he released her. Kissed her forehead. And said, "Can I come and see you tonight? When I get back?"

If she'd had to describe the way that question made her feel, Cherry would have failed. There were too many emotions, hitting her too fast, merging into one another to create a maelstrom of pure feeling, the kind she'd never experience before.

The only thing she was sure of was her answer.

"Yes."

"Good," he whispered. "Good." He kissed her. His hands cradled her face, his lips gentle and searching. He touched her with every inch of his formidable focus, as if she was the only thing in the world that mattered. Then he pulled away and said, "Leave the lights on. Okay?"

She licked her lips, tasted the ghost of his desire. And she said, "Okay."

CHAPTER TWENTY-TWO

C herry was wearing her pyjamas—or rather, an old Dolly Parton tee and some underwear, which passed as pyjamas for her. As much effort as she put in during the day, she didn't want to look good just to go to sleep.

And yet, she was wearing a full face of makeup.

She sat in the centre of the bed, the main lights off but the bedside lamp on. That counted, right? She was pretty sure that counted. A lamp was a light.

This was ridiculous. As if she'd never had sex with the lights on before.

Never like this. Never with someone like him.

Cherry knew that she was insecure. Frankly, she didn't think it mattered. She liked herself, and she knew exactly who she was, and she knew exactly how she looked. So if she preferred to face the world with a solid inch of foundation as her shield, who gave a fuck? It wasn't that she cared about her scars, exactly. Or even that she cared what other people thought of them. Christ, she'd had acne long enough as a teen to get over that.

But what she did care about was control. Controlling perceptions of herself. And she couldn't control what people thought, how they looked at her, unless she was flawless. Because once she was flawless, what could anyone think except... *Wow. That's Cherry fucking Neita.*

She had no middle name. But *fucking* did well enough.

The only problem was, Cherry didn't go to sleep in makeup. She didn't sit in her room and go about her business in makeup. And if Ruben came home to find her sitting in bed with a smoky eye and red lip, he'd probably think that meant something. Like... that she didn't trust him. Or some shit like that. People had thoughts. Those thoughts didn't always make sense.

But maybe she *didn't* trust him. Cherry really wasn't sure.

So she did the only thing she could do—or rather, the only thing she felt like doing. She picked up the phone and called Rose.

It rang three times. Just long enough for her to think, *What the hell are you doing? You're the worst kind of friend. You practically disappear, and then you call her when you need her—*

"Cherry, darling. Goodness me, it's been a while."

Cherry sighed. "Hi, Rose. I know. I know it has."

"Well, Lord, don't sound like that. You're not up for execution, you know." Rose's voice lowered slightly. "Or *are* you? I have friends in Finland, my dear. If you require an emergency rescue—"

Cherry laughed. Rose laughed too. And everything was easier.

"I really *am* sorry," she said, the words running into each other. "I wanted to call more, but everything's so fucking weird and I'm never quite sure what to tell you."

"Don't worry, love," Rose soothed. "I understand. It's all rather overwhelming, isn't it?"

If only she fucking knew.

"Yes," Cherry said, her eyes running over the room she'd come to think of as her own. The casual luxury of the furniture, the velvet drapes, the four-poster bed on which she was now sitting. And yet, the thing that concerned her most of all was...

"When did you know that your husband was different?"

Rose's voice was careful when she said, "Different?"

"Like, that things would be different with him. That he wasn't like anyone else you'd ever wanted. That he was special."

"Ah." Rose sounded vaguely amused. "I see." For a moment, she was quiet. But then she said, "I think the first sign was that... well, I started asking questions like the one you're asking now. First to myself, then my friends, my mother. He turned my mind towards the issue of forever. Of trust, of togetherness. No-one had made me think about things like that before. Not really."

"Right." Cherry nodded, as if Rose could see. Then, remembering herself, she added, "That makes sense." And it really did.

"Are you sure? Because I thought it sounded like utter rubbish."

Cherry chuckled. "No, I liked it. And I got the point."

"Oh, good. Now, tell me; what's it like being a princess?"

"I'm not a princess, Rose."

"You might as well be. Is it awfully glamorous? Tell me, or I'll torture you with stories of your replacement."

Cherry winced. "Is it bad?"

"It's bloody awful. She doesn't have the sense God gave a goat. Chris *insisted* we hire her; I don't know *what* he was thinking."

For the next half an hour, Rose regaled Cherry with tales of Rosewood Academy's admin floor, and Cherry tried to come up with stories interesting enough to entertain her slightly high-maintenance friend.

And when they eventually hung up, Cherry headed to the bathroom and washed her face.

"IT'S BEEN a hell of a day. Get some rest."

Ruben rolled his eyes. "Aye aye, Captain." Then he tried to stay on his feet as Hans whacked him on the back with one brick-like hand.

"I mean it, *Your Highness*. I'll see you tomorrow."

Which would be even worse, since they'd spend half the day travelling and the other half with Harald. Fan-fucking-tastic. Ruben's already foul mood sank further into the murky depths as he waved Hans away and let himself into the house.

Then he remembered, all at once, who was waiting for him. And just like that, he felt himself smile.

He was headed upstairs when he saw the library door ajar, light spilling out like a golden trail. Ruben's heart thudded against his rib cage as he stepped towards the little room, pushing the door open. All of the dark thoughts that had spent the day chasing him were destroyed, set aflame by that slice of light. There was nothing left in him but hungry anticipation.

Cherry lay curled up on the loveseat in the centre of the little, book-filled room they called the library, a paperback in her lap. Her hair was piled up on top of her head the way he liked it, and in the low lamplight, he could see the T-shirt whose soft, worn cotton he'd once pushed aside in the dark.

"Dolly Parton? Really?"

She looked up with a start, a little smile curving her lips. "You're back."

"And you're not in bed."

She put the book she was reading aside. "Couldn't sleep."

"Right." He moved closer, felt himself prowling the room like a predator but couldn't stop. He could see the outline of her nipples through that T-shirt, thick and dark, dragging his mind into dangerous places. Her legs were bare, and only her soft, blue underwear hid her pussy from his gaze.

It was very thin underwear. The kind he could rip right off her, if he really wanted to. His cock went from interested to painfully hard in the space of a second.

She gazed up at him with eyes turned obsidian in the low light. "You look…"

"What?" His voice was almost a growl, but he didn't care. There was no hiding his feelings now, if he'd ever managed to.

Cherry shook her head. "It's late. We should go upstairs." She started to rise, but Ruben pressed a hand to her chest and pushed until she sank back down onto the loveseat. He took off his suit jacket and dropped it onto the floor, rolling up his shirt sleeves. Then he sat down beside her and picked up the book she'd abandoned.

"*Devil's Embrace*," he read out. "Sounds… Actually, I'm really not sure how that sounds."

Cherry grinned, snatching the book out of his hands and putting it down on the floor. "It's a real bodice-ripper. Very dramatic. Very old-fashioned. I don't know how I feel about it."

"You found that in here?" He put her legs in his lap and she allowed it, relaxing into him. Forgetting to be self-conscious. Her toes were painted the same pink as her nails.

"I did. I think Agathe—"

"I really need you *not* to finish that sentence."

She laughed. "Fair enough." Then she shifted in his lap, and her laughter faded, her eyes widening slightly as her bare foot nudged the unmistakable swell of his erection. He tried not to moan at the contact, but he couldn't stop his eyes from sliding shut or his hips from jerking towards her.

He was more on-edge that he'd thought. He needed her more than he'd thought. No surprise there.

But it was a surprise to feel her come to him. It was a surprise when she rose up onto her knees, when she put her hands on his shoulders and straddled his thighs. Ruben opened his eyes to find Cherry watching him with that dark, endless gaze.

He leaned forward and kissed her, quick and gentle. Just a taste of her sweetness, his tongue feathering along her lower lip until she moaned softly, rolling her hips.

He caught the hem of her T-shirt in his hand and whispered, "Let me see you. Please."

She let her forehead rest against his for a moment. Then she straightened up and pulled the fabric away from his fingers.

She took it off on her own.

He didn't look. For some reason, he just *couldn't*. So he kept his gaze on her face as she shifted against him, fiddling with something he couldn't see. "What are you doing?"

"I'm trying to take off my underwear."

Ruben slid his hands down the smooth plane of her back until it curved into her arse. She had dimples everywhere, it turned out. He grabbed her underwear in both hands and tore.

She gave a little yelp, then looked down. He wanted to look down too, but he thought he might die if he did.

"You know," she said, "I think you have to tear both sides."

He moved his hands to the front of her body. Caught the fabric there. Tore.

"That better?" he rasped out.

She smiled. Then she reached between her legs and produced the remnants of her underwear, waving it around like a flag. "Very efficient."

He slid his palm down over her mound, his middle finger easing between her swollen folds. All he could say was, "You're wet."

Her hand cupped his jaw, and he felt like he belonged. "I was waiting for you."

"Good." Ruben pushed his finger into her, revelled in the clench of her walls around him, stroked until the tightness eased and his skin was soaked in her desire. Then he slid out of her velvet cunt and rubbed his slick finger over her clit, massaging the stiff nub in a slow, easy circle.

She clutched his shoulders and moaned for him. Her hands floated to the buttons of his shirt. He let her undo the first, the second, before he captured her wrist in his free hand and said, "No." He stopped touching her clit.

"Why?" she demanded, frustration in her eyes.

"You're not in charge, sweetheart. Remember that."

With a little growl, she caught his face in her hands and kissed him. He allowed himself to enjoy her lush mouth, her hot, searching tongue for a few seconds before he pushed her away. Then he brought his palm down against her arse. Hard.

She bit her lip on a moan, grinding her pussy against his erection, through his clothes, and he spanked her again. "You're going to mess up my suit, love."

"Fuck you."

Another slap. Before she could react, he grabbed a fistful of her hair and pulled her head back, his grip just tight enough to stop her moving. "Don't push me, Cherry."

She laughed, the sound breathy and hoarse. "But that's what I do. I push."

His hands couldn't stop roaming over the cool silk of her skin, but they might as well still be in the dark, because he still hadn't looked down. Her face was devastating enough, beautifully bare, her lust impossible to miss.

That animalistic voice in his head, the one that had come to life the moment he'd first set eyes on this woman, chanted in time with his ratcheting pulse: *Take her. Now.*

He'd wanted all of her. Now he could have it.

"Stand up," he ordered, sounding as desperate as he felt. So much for fucking control. "Let me see you."

Her tongue slid out to wet her lips, and he imagined the way her mouth would feel on his cock. He wanted that. Then she eased off his lap, and he released her hair, and she stood. And he couldn't look away.

At the sight of her naked body, his mouth went dry and his mind went fucking blank.

Jesus Christ.

Fully clothed, Cherry was already a walking fantasy. Naked, she became something unimaginable. However hard he tried, Ruben could never have dreamt this up. His eyes followed the curves of her body, from those wide hips to that soft, rounded belly, to the gentle sag of her heavy breasts with their thick, dark nipples. She was like a rose in full bloom, delicately decadent.

She trailed a hand down her stomach, towards the apex of her thighs. "You better have condoms."

"I have fucking condoms." He reached down to fist his cock

197

through his clothes, squeezing hard until the pain of his own grip took the edge off of his savage desire. He wasn't about to shove his dick in her like a fucking animal, but that's what his balls were demanding.

All at once, he stood, intending to get the damn condoms from the suit jacket he'd discarded. But it turned out he was physically incapable of walking past her at that moment. When he tried, his feet refused to move, and his hands brought her to him. Ruben clung to his control as if it were a cliff's edge, clung to her as if she were sanity. And he kissed her, and kissed her, and wondered how the hell he could want one woman more than anything in the world.

CHAPTER TWENTY-THREE

Cherry arched into Ruben's powerful body, the press of her nakedness against his clothes strangely erotic. His kiss was hard and unrefined, his hands roaming over her body as if he'd never felt it before, grabbing at her arse, her thighs, her belly, her breasts. As if he were hungry. As if he were desperate.

But slowly, gradually, something changed. Shifted. His kiss softened, his tongue sliding over her lips as if he were tasting her, savouring her. He slid a hand into her hair, angling her head back until the line of her throat was exposed. When he dragged his lips down that sensitive column until his mouth settled over her pulse, she felt his hot tongue as if it were between her legs.

Then he kissed lower, trailing over her chest. He pushed one of her breasts up and sucked the aching nipple into his mouth. She moaned, the sound ragged and uncontrolled, and he looked up at her with that infuriatingly sexy smile, completely at odds with the lust in his eyes. "I like it when you moan for me," he growled. He caught her other nipple between finger and thumb, rolling the tight nub. "You like this, my love?"

"You know I do," she panted.

"But I want to hear you say it. I need to hear you say it." Before she could think about that too hard, he pulled her nipple into his mouth again, suckling her, each pull somehow tugging at her clit as well as her breast. *Fuck.*

His hand slid down her body, tracing the contours of her waist, her hips, as if he couldn't stop touching her. As if he had to remind himself that she was still there, that she was real. The feather-light touch of his fingers felt like the sweetest torture, an electric charge ratcheting up with every second, skating across her nerve-endings.

Then, as suddenly as he'd started his erotic torture, he pulled away. Her eyes slid open to find him staring down at her, his jaw set, something dangerous in his dark gaze. "Come here," he said, and the command in his voice sent a thrill through her. He settled a hand against the back of her neck, led her to face the loveseat they'd just left.

"On your knees," he ordered, his voice sharp as a whip.

She knelt on the plush, velvet cushions, her hands settling automatically on the loveseat's high back.

He stood behind her and reached between her thighs, his big hand cupping her, warm and intimate. Then he bent over her and whispered in her ear, "Spread your legs, love. As wide as you can. I want to see everything."

Cherry shivered as his breath skated over the sensitive skin just below her earlobe, as his hand cupped her firmly, intimately. The touch was so casual and yet so complete, as if the space between her legs was his to use as he wished.

She had given him this. She'd given him control. And he knew how to use it.

"Good girl," he said, his voice so deep, so rough, it was almost a growl. That was the only indication that he was losing it, just like she was. She liked the idea of them both unravelling together. If he felt the way she did right now…

He sank to his knees behind her, his shirt brushing her back as she moved. Then the hand between her legs disappeared, leaving her oddly cold. A second later, she felt it again, pushing her forwards this time, so that her breasts pressed against the back of the loveseat. And now, on her knees, her legs spread wide, her body arched like a bow, she was completely exposed.

She could feel her folds parting, her hot, wet entrance sensitive to the cool air. Her breath stuttered and her heart pounded as anticipation rose. Raw desire suffocated her like sultry heat on the hottest summer day.

His voice was hoarse when he said, "You're so fucking beautiful."

She swallowed. Tried not to strain towards the source of that sound—towards his mouth, the mouth that she already knew was capable of wonderful things.

Fuck, what she wouldn't give for his tongue right now.

"So pretty," he whispered. She could feel his breath against her pussy, and she was so desperate for him that the warm, barely-there air felt like a touch. Then he said, "I want to see your cunt stretched out around my cock."

She moaned.

"And you do too," he said. She could hear the smirk in his voice. His fingers, long and thick, traced her folds, so light she barely felt it. "You're so wet, you're dripping. Did you know that, love?" He pressed a kiss to the small of her back, then another, lower, and another. Creating a burning trail down her spine. He spread her arse with both hands and kept going, his lips brushing along the sensitive cleft.

And then, all of a sudden, he disappeared.

Cherry couldn't stop herself from growling out her protest, the sound mindless and raw. He laughed. "Don't worry love. I'm coming back."

She fucking hated him. Almost as much as she wanted him. If he didn't fuck her soon, she'd hate him more. But every moment of torture drove her higher, tightening the knot of desire at her core, increasing the need that coursed through her body.

When he came back, he'd changed his position, turned around. He must be sitting on the floor, because he slid his face between her thighs and she felt the soft brush of his hair against her clit, like a whisper, his breath against her entrance.

She almost screamed when his tongue slid over her folds, so hot and so fucking good. Her clit ached, but he didn't touch it. Instead, he lapped at her entrance, growling low in the back of his throat. "I love the way you taste," he murmured. "You're always so wet for me, sweetheart. You're perfect. You're so fucking perfect." He licked her again, then eased his fingers into her pussy, parting her swollen, sensitive folds. And finally, finally, his tongue flicked at her clit.

Again and again he licked the tight little bud, his fingers fucking her harder as she opened up to him. Cherry threw her head back and rolled her hips against his tongue, riding his face, fucking herself back on his hand, unable to care about anything but the delicious sensations he created between her thighs.

He worked her swollen, fevered flesh until it became almost unbearable, her clit breathlessly sensitive. When her hips bucked away from the rapid, unyielding rhythm of his tongue, he wrapped an arm around her, pinned her to him, fucked her harder, licked her faster, until she shattered. Completely, utterly, helplessly.

Her cries rang out in the little room, almost loud enough to bring her to her senses—but not quite. Because he kept licking, kept stroking, and the pleasure swelled like waves crashing against the shore. By the time he let her go and eased back, Cherry was exhausted.

She sighed and let her head fall forward, onto the loveseat, as he slid out from between her thighs. Exhaustion and satiation created a heady cocktail.

But then she felt the cushions shift slightly as he covered her body with his own. She looked down to see him sink his foot into the loveseat beside her knee, his powerful thigh, thick and dusted with dark hair, bracketing her body. His arm snaked over her torso like an iron band, holding her steady, his hand grabbing hold of her breast. His other hand came to rest beside hers on the back of the loveseat. His lips pressed against her neck, his chest warmed her back, and his hard cock pressed against her entrance.

Fuck.

His voice rumbled low in her ear. "Put me inside you."

She closed her eyes, biting back the whimper those four words teased out of her.

Ruben kissed the sensitive spot beneath her earlobe, his tongue flicking out to tease her skin. Then he said, "Cherry. I want you to put my cock inside your pretty cunt, to feel the way I stretch you. So don't make me tell you twice."

She released a shuddering breath. "I think I hate you."

"Hate me all you want, as long as you come for me."

With a moan, she reached between her legs and found the thick, pulsing length of his shaft, the condom tight and slick over his skin. And then she guided him into her aching pussy, unable to hold back her little, whimpering sighs.

He pressed into her with searing heat, slow and steady and fucking perfect. His cock filled her, inch by delicious inch, the slick friction almost unbearably good. Ruben sank into her with the same focus he used to lick her to orgasm, the same focus he used to kiss her senseless. By the time she felt the velvet nudge of his balls against her clit, he was so deep she could barely draw breath. Even the slightest movement sent sparks of pleasure straight to her core.

Then he kissed the back of her neck, and the strong arm holding her up tightened almost imperceptibly, and he whispered her name as if it was a prayer, his voice broken. "God," he breathed raggedly. "I—I need you so fucking much."

"You have me."

"Do I?" He pulled back, moaning at the slow glide. "Fuck. You're unbelievable. I knew as soon as I saw you. I knew you were mine."

He thrust into her and Cherry's mind scrambled, all her focus stolen by the rising crest of pleasure within her. "Ruben. More."

He took her hand and pushed it between her legs. "Play with yourself. Come on my cock." She rubbed her clit in rough, desperate circles and he hissed, thrusting into her again, harder this time. "Good girl. Good fucking girl. Jesus Christ, I can feel you tightening on my dick—" He broke off with a groan, and his grip on her breast became savage. His other hand clutched the back of the loveseat so hard his knuckles whitened.

And then he really fucked her. Harder than anyone ever had, harder than she even thought she could take.

He grunted over her with each powerful thrust, his cock spearing into her, forcing her to open up for him. She spread her legs wider, arched beneath him, welcomed each ferocious pump of his hips with a mindless cry. Her fingers circled her clit frantically, and her second orgasm hit harder than even she'd expected.

She moaned helplessly beneath him as he fucked her through every shudder, the loveseat, heavy though it was, edging across the floor with the force of his movements.

"God, you feel so fucking good," he panted, his voice almost unrecognisable, he was so close to the edge. "Look at me. *Look at me.*"

Cherry's eyes had slid shut under the sensual force of his touch, but she opened them now and turned her head to meet his gaze. His eyes were inky in the shadows, his features harsh with lust. He kissed her, hard and rough, his unrestrained thrusts setting her aflame even as his tongue plundered her mouth.

Cherry gasped against him as another orgasm shook her, and he growled deep in his chest, tearing his lips from hers. "Fuck," he rasped out, his thrusts stuttering, his breath ragged. "*Fuck, I—*" His words turned into a harsh cry as he came, holding her tight against his chest. He sank his teeth into her shoulder as his cock jerked inside her, his hips bucking.

Then he stilled, the tension draining from his muscles. His hold on her gentled, became almost protective as he released a long, shuddering breath. He kissed her shoulder, brushing his lips over the skin he'd bitten.

"Holy fuck," he sighed.

Cherry slumped against the back of the loveseat, still on her knees, their bodies still joined, his skin hot against hers.

He pressed a kiss to the side of her face. "You okay, love?"

She forced her eyes open, even though exhaustion had settled over her like a blanket some time in the last few seconds. "Yes," she whispered. "I'm good. I'm great."

He grinned. In an instant, he went from the man who'd just fucked her senseless to the man she…

Well. She wasn't sure how to finish that sentence. She just knew that the sight of his smile did things to her heart, set butterflies free in her stomach, and made her want to kiss him. On the nose. And call him *baby* or *sweetheart* or something equally embarrassing.

Oh, dear. She was very far gone. And so well-fucked, she didn't even care.

He pressed his lips to hers, achingly gentle, then pulled back and whispered, "I like the way you're looking at me right now."

She laughed. "That's funny. I like the way *you're* looking at me."

"Good." He kissed her again, soft and almost reverent. She couldn't ignore the way her heart swelled in response, seeming twice its usual size and inexplicably lighter, all at once.

Then he shifted his weight and pulled out of her, looking down between their bodies…

And his face changed. Was wiped blank. Completely emotionless. Everything about him stiffened, pulled away from her, even though he hadn't moved at all.

"What?" she asked, anxiety skittering along her spine. Suddenly, the air around them felt cool and unwelcoming. She became hyper-conscious of her nakedness, of the vulnerability of her position. "What is it?"

And he said, his gaze still fixed on something she couldn't see, "It broke."

Cherry frowned, confused. "What broke?"

"The condom," he choked out. "It fucking broke." He stood up all at once, as if he couldn't bear to touch her.

Cherry stood too, turning around just in time to catch a glimpse of his face. He looked pale, horrified, as if he were going to be sick. His chest rose and fell as he dragged in air, his breathing becoming a series of heaving pants.

"Ruben," she said, keeping her voice as even as possible. "You need to calm down. Okay? Just breathe."

When he didn't respond, she reached out to touch him, to soothe him. He flinched away as if she were on fire.

The movement, tiny as it was, felt like a punch in the face. Cherry let her hand drop, her heart falling with it. Then she hardened her jaw and lifted her chin and turned away. She needed some clothes. Immediately.

"Wait, Cherry—I'm sorry." His voice sounded like an echo of itself, weak and carried by those anxious, dragged-in breaths. "I'm sorry. I just—"

"What the fuck?" she demanded, whirling around to face him, her temper appearing out of nowhere. "So it broke. Why are you so..." She gestured helplessly at his face, twisted in misery, the sheen of sweat on his brow. "Is there something you're not telling me?"

He frowned as if she'd spoken another language. "What do you mean?"

"Do you... *have* something?"

It took him a second to figure out what she was talking about. "Jesus, no. I would've told you. I mean, I would've—"

"Do you think *I* have something?"

"No," he said, his voice firmer, closer to its usual self. He reached out to grab her wrist, but she jerked away. Because she couldn't erase the look on his face, the way he'd avoided her touch. As if he were disgusted. "Cherry," he said, and now he had the fucking nerve to look upset. "It's nothing to do with you. I just... I can't get you pregnant."

Oh, Christ. Where the fuck were her clothes?

She stormed around the sofa and found her damned Dolly Parton T-shirt lying by a bookshelf. Her underwear was a lost cause, but the T-shirt was just long enough to cover the important parts... if she tugged down the hem and held it there with one hand. Which was *exactly* how she wanted to continue this conversation. Great. Fucking great.

"Cherry," he sighed, as if she were being unreasonable. "You have to understand—I mean, what would we do? If there was a baby? We couldn't just separate. I'd have to—"

"You'd have to marry me," she finished. "God for-fucking-bid." And where the hell had that come from? She didn't want to marry him anyway. This was a business deal. A contractual agreement. But it was her fault for allowing lines to be blurred, for getting carried away. She should've used her new-found riches to invest in a better vibrator instead.

"No," Ruben insisted. "That's not what I meant. I was going to say I'd have to… I don't know. I don't fucking know." His tone became gentle, apologetic, as if he were breaking her goddamn heart when he said, "I can't handle kids, Cherry."

"No-one was asking you to," she snapped. "I'm on the pill, by the way. So don't worry. Nothing will get in the way of you dropping me once our time is up."

"That's not what I meant," he said again, and now he sounded angry. *Him*! Angry! She'd laugh at his fucking audacity if she weren't so bloody furious. "I panicked," he gritted out. "It was a reflex. And I'm sorry. I've never… I've never been in this position before."

"Right," she said, giving him her sweetest smile, her most reasonable tone. "Because I fake engagements with foreign fucking royalty every other week."

"I'm not talking about the engagement. I'm talking about…" He gestured wildly between them, something bright and dangerous and uncontrolled in his eyes. "This! Us!"

"*Us*?" She forced herself to laugh, as if she was truly amused. As if she hadn't a care in the world. "You sound like a child, Ruben. We had sex. That doesn't mean there's an *us*."

His jaw tightened. "Don't fucking do that."

"Oh, is that an order?"

"Cherry."

"Ruben. Let me make something clear: I am not here to trap you. In fact, *you* trapped *me*. And it may be news to you that not every woman on earth wants to carry your royal fucking babies—"

"Cherry—"

"But they don't! Okay? *I* don't! What do you think I am, desperate? Like I'd chase a man who doesn't want me?"

He ran a hand through his hair, his expression almost helpless. "I'm sorry, okay? I'm sorry."

"So am I," she said. "Because I'm not doing this again. Not with you. Clearly we need to keep things as uncomplicated as possible. But it'll be a long fucking year without some dick to pass the time."

He flinched as if she'd hit him. But he didn't stop her as she marched past him and out into the hall.

And Cherry almost convinced herself that she didn't care.

CHAPTER TWENTY-FOUR

S pending hours in a car with a woman who hated him was
painful. Spending hours in a car with a woman he loved to
distraction—a woman he knew from the coils of her hair to
her pink-painted toe nails, a woman who hadn't *always* hated him
but certainly did now—was torture.

Ruben really fucking wished he'd given her the ring before now.
But they couldn't meet his brother without it, and in a few short
minutes, they'd be there. At the palace. The backdrop to all his
nightmares.

"Cherry," he said, cracking the thick slab of silence between them.

She turned her head from the window and looked across the
limo's dark interior to meet his eyes, her movements robotic. She
didn't reply. Just looked, her gaze burning, beautifully furious
and breaking his fucking heart.

His hands clumsier than usual, Ruben fumbled with the pocket
inside his suit jacket for a few heavy seconds before producing the
ring. There was no box; he didn't know where the original one
was, and he didn't particularly care. The ring was all that
mattered, and his mother would want Cherry to have it.

He wanted Cherry to have it.

But Cherry was looking down at the diamond and sapphire ring in his hands as if it were a poisonous snake.

"You need to wear it," he said gently. "For Harald."

"Fucking Harald," she muttered, holding out a hand for the ring. He wanted to smile at the sound of his own personal refrain on her lips. She hadn't even met the king yet, but she already hated him. It almost made Ruben forget that Harald wasn't the only royal she hated right now.

As the car slowed, the sense of panicked urgency that had been choking Ruben all morning—since last night, in fact—swelled to its crescendo. He must've lost his mind for a moment, because instead of handing her the ring, he reached out to take her hand in his.

"Cherry," he said, his voice low. "Listen to me, okay? Just listen."

She glared, tried to tug her hand away, but he couldn't let go. He couldn't.

"Please. *Please* let me explain. Last night—"

"I don't want to talk about last night," she said sharply. Her mouth, so lush and full, was pressed into a hard, thin line. And he caught something vulnerable in her eyes, a wariness he'd put there. The sight threatened to tear his heart in two.

"I wasn't thinking," he said. "It had nothing to do with you. I've always been like that. I can't bear the idea of children—"

"You love children," she said, and for the first time he caught a flash of hurt in her voice. He'd known it was there, but hearing it…

She heard it too, because she looked horrified for a second, and then completely blank. When she spoke again, her voice was hard as steel. "It doesn't matter. It's ridiculous. I just don't think it's wise for us to keep blurring lines like this."

"I hurt you," he said. "I know I did. And that's the last thing I wanted to do, because I don't think of this as blurring lines, Cherry. That's not what we're doing. Being with you is a gift."

The car came to a stop, and she gave him a mutinous glare, tugging at their joined hands. "Stop this. Just give me the fucking ring."

He wanted to blurt out the fact that he loved her, but she'd probably punch him in the face. So he released her with a sigh, and gave her the ring, and she shoved it onto her finger as if it were an afterthought. For all she knew, it was meaningless, something he'd had Demi order for the purpose of this twisted charade. She had no idea how much that ring meant to him, and no idea how much *she* meant to him.

But he'd tell her. He'd make her see. Somehow. And he'd tell her about the thoughts that haunted him, about the anxiety that suffocated him whenever he thought of children, of creating another soul that might one day end up like him: vulnerable. Alone. Abused.

The car door swung open and an anonymous hand reached in to help Cherry out, part of the security team. He heard her greet the man with her usual charm, her sparkling laughter floating into the car within seconds. She was already working her magic. And Ruben was frozen in time, struggling to breathe. Because it had just occurred to him that he might fail. He might not get through to her. He might not prove his feelings or win back her trust.

And then, when the year was up, she'd leave.

RUBEN WAS USED to having Hans at his back. He wasn't used to having Cherry by his side. But there she was, striding down this gilded hall with him, matching him step for step. Though her steps were more of a strut.

The corridor leading towards his brother's receiving room was as splendid as the rest of the palace, which made it fucking abhorrent to Ruben. But he wasn't going to pretend that vaulted ceilings and marble cherubs and velvet tapestries were a hardship on anything other than his taste. No, it wasn't the luxury that sent a bead of sweat crawling down his spine beneath the fancy fucking dress uniform he wore.

It was the memories.

"Good morning, Ruben. Are you ready for your lessons?"

Five year old Magnus blinked up at his older brother. "I already had my lessons, Harald. Who is Ruben?"

"You," his brother said in a voice Magnus didn't recognise. A voice he didn't quite like. It reminded him a little bit of when his daddy would tell him off. But when Daddy told him off, he was never afraid.

"When is Daddy coming back?" he asked.

Harald's face hardened. "He is not coming back, you little idiot. You don't come back from the sky."

Magnus felt tears begin to pool at the corners of his eyes. "Why not? God is nice. God will let Daddy and Mummy come down to see me —"

All at once, Magnus felt his feet lifted from the floor. It made his stomach flip, the way it used to when Mummy picked him up and swung him round. But then the flip went away and was replaced by pain. His back and his head slammed into the wall, and Harald held him tight with hands that felt hard as stone.

Magnus felt his tears stream over his cheeks, but he was too breathless to scream out at the pain. As he gasped for air, he saw his brother sneer.

"Crying like a baby," he spat. "Be a man. Men don't cry."

Magnus couldn't stop himself from sobbing. The pain in his back and his head was searing, burning, the worst thing he'd ever felt, and Harald was scaring him, his face all twisted up and his hands so hard.

"Ruben!" Harald snapped, and shook him, hard.

Magnus cried out, "That is not my name! My name is Magnus! My name is Mag—"

"Harald." The door shut with a sharp click, and light footsteps pattered across the floor. Magnus knew that voice. This was his sister, Sophronia. She would help him. She would fix his head. He held out his arms towards the sound of her voice, his vision blurred by the tears that he still couldn't stop. "Sophy! Sophy!"

"Oh, for goodness sake, Harald. We talked about this."

Magnus didn't know what that meant, but he knew Sophy would help him. She was the one who always played with him and Daddy, whenever she came to visit. She was always smiling and sweet. She would take him away from Harald who had become so mean.

"You can't leave marks on him," Sophy said.

"I didn't. He's crying for no reason. He's spoilt."

"Someone will hear him screaming."

"Let them. He needs to learn. Don't you, Ruben?" Another shake, harder than the first, and Magnus's head rang and rang like a big church bell, pain spreading out like a spider's web.

Still, he cried, his voice halting and choked, "My name is Magnus!"

Then he felt his sister. Her cool, soft touch against his cheeks, wiping away the tears until his vision was clear and his breath was calm. He looked up at her with gladness in his heart. She was so pretty, different to Mummy, but a little the same. Mummy was pretty too.

But she didn't take him away. She glared at Harald, but then she said to Magnus, her voice firm, "You mustn't cry, Ruben."

His face crumpled and the tears returned. "No! No Ruben! My name is Magnus!"

"Shush," she said briskly. "Stop that. Be a big boy. Now, listen: one of your names is Magnus, but that's Daddy's name. We can't call you Daddy's name, now, can we?"

The tears slowed slightly as Magnus thought on this. He looked at Harald. Harald was staring up at the ceiling, his expression bored, like it was when Daddy used to talk to him about school work and things. His grip was still hard, but he wasn't shaking Magnus or shouting anymore.

Warily, Magnus turned his eyes back to Sophy. "Why not?" he asked. "Daddy said—"

"Never mind what Daddy said. Harald is in charge now, and he has decided that you are called Ruben. Ruben is your second name. It would make me very happy if you used it. Alright?"

Magnus nodded slowly. "Okay," he whispered. "I will try."

"Good." She turned away, sweeping from the room in her long dress like a fairy princess. But wait—why was she leaving him?

"Sophy," he called. "Come back. My head hurts."

She paused in the doorway, looking over her shoulder at him. And she said, "Grow up, Ruben."

Then she was gone.

"His Royal Highness Prince Ruben and his fiancée, Miss Cherry Neita."

Ruben didn't recognise the head butler, the tall, gaunt man who introduced them. But that didn't mean he hadn't met the man. It was just, his vision felt slightly blurry and his head ached just a bit.

He hesitated on the threshold of the receiving room, suddenly disorientated. But then he felt a soft hand clasp his. He looked down to see Cherry's sparkly pink nails standing out brightly against the back of his hand. Felt the cool band of his mother's ring on her finger. Then he looked up and locked eyes with the most formidable woman in the world.

His vision cleared. The ringing in his ears faded away. He clutched her hand and set his jaw and walked into the fucking room.

The door shut behind them with a hollow thud, echoing in Ruben's mind like an omen. The room was quiet, its walnut furniture and ice blue walls creating an impression of calmness that Ruben couldn't buy into. In front of the window, through which bright, winter sunlight streamed, the family sat like something out of an old-fashioned photograph.

The children were on the floor, their skirts arranged neatly around them. Girls, both. And didn't Harald hate it. They betrayed a flash of excitement at Ruben's appearance before schooling their expressions, bowing their golden heads over some sort of board game.

Above them, settled into various plush sofas, were the adults. Sophronia, dressed as if ready for a debutante's ball in pink silk, a ransom's worth of diamonds glittering over her chest. Harald, his bored gaze on the ceiling, attired in only a velvet smoking jacket and slippers. A mark of disrespect, of course. Ruben had expected it, but not the sharp fury that cut through him at the sight. He was used to this sort of thing.

But he didn't like the idea that Cherry was being disrespected too.

Lydia sat on Harald's right, the only adult of the bunch who was appropriately dressed. Her airy, navy-blue skirts fluffed out about her knees, her hair in a neat bun. Ruben resisted the urge to smile at her, or at either of his nieces. It would only cause trouble.

"Harald," he said, his tone dancing on the edge of insolence, as always.

Harald tore his eyes from the ceiling and flicked them over Ruben as dismissively as he would a dust mote beneath the bed. Then Ruben waited, holding his breath, to see what treatment Cherry would receive. He realised in an instant that if it was anything less than she deserved, he might do something ill-advised.

But Harald made an attempt to look enthused as he came to Cherry. He stood, as a gentleman ought, and held out his hands in a gesture that belied the pinched, disdainful look on his face.

Ruben wouldn't hold that against him. It was his natural expression.

"Miss Cherry Neita," he said, his voice somewhere between surprise and fascination. "*Taler du dansk?*"

"I'm sorry," Cherry said. "English is my only language, I'm afraid." And then she smiled. It was so fucking beautiful, Ruben thought for a second that he might pass out. Her dimples were deep, her ruby lips were lush and full, and her eyes held that indefinable sparkle that said, *I know. I really am something.* The sparkle that drew people to her like flies.

Harald blinked as if he'd been hit over the head. Sophronia stiffened, sitting up a little straighter. And Lydia, bless her, smiled back, as unaffected as ever.

The children ignored everyone.

Cherry started forward, tugging on Ruben's hand subtly, leading him into the room.

Pull yourself together, man. Good lord.

He kept his eyes on her, as if her brilliance could protect him from the ugliness of this situation. This place. Her outfit was modest, simple—a dress with a low, sweetheart neckline and a skirt shaped like a bell, the ivory bright against her brown skin. And yet, she looked as decadent, as sinful as ever.

She reached the cluster of family and furniture and executed a perfect curtsy, nowhere near low enough to seem outdated, but a little more than the modern head nod. With that same, sunny smile she air-kissed Sophronia's proffered cheek, then Lydia's, then took Harald's hand and lowered her head over it, ever so slightly. Ruben watched, more than a little awe-struck. The rambling, pathetic advice he'd been capable of giving in the car was atrocious. And yet, she had everything right.

"What delightful girls," she trilled, looking down at the golden heads still focused on the floor. "How very beautiful." She sounded utterly convincing, as if she could actually see their faces.

"Thank you," Lydia smiled. Sophronia gave a graceless snort. Clearly, his sister was uncomfortable.

Usually, the title of most beautiful woman in the room went to her.

"Please, sit," Harald said grandly.

Cherry did, sinking into a free sofa with the kind of grace usually found on the stage. Then she looked up at him with the sweetest smile, the kind of smile that old, married couples share, and said, "Sit, love."

He swallowed, and sat.

"How wonderful to meet you," Harald said, turning on the charm as always. "Tea?"

"Yes, please," Cherry said, just as charming. So much pleasant-ness in one room, and all of it false.

Harald didn't ask his wife aloud, or even look at her; Lydia poured the tea automatically, with practiced efficiency. None for Ruben, though. She knew he wouldn't want any.

But then Harald said, "Serve my brother, Lydia."

Ruben frowned. "You know I don't—"

"Lydia," Harald said again, his voice iron. "Pour Ruben some tea."

Ruben could feel Cherry's eyes on him, probably confused, but no doubt hiding it well. He could hardly turn and explain that his brother liked to watch his hands shake. That the older man fed off of any sign of discomfort like a parasite. Ruben had dropped his cup once, scalded himself and stained his trousers, firmly embarrassed himself in polite company after one biting word from Harald, the significance of which no-one else had even understood. Harald rather shamelessly lived for the day that the occurrence might repeat itself. It wouldn't, of course. Ruben had been a young man then, still under his brother's thumb.

And yet, he'd allowed the mental scars his brother had inflicted to push Cherry away. So it seemed Harald still had the power to destroy everything Ruben held dear. Things hadn't changed much at all, had they?

"We're very pleased to be introduced," Lydia said, pouring Ruben's tea. She took care not to fill it too high, because she was kind to a fault, and she knew exactly what her husband wanted.

How Lydia had ended up trapped with a man like Harald, Ruben still wasn't entirely sure.

"How did the two of you meet?" she asked as Cherry sipped her tea.

Ruben cut in. "Cherry works in the educational sector," he said. Hoping that would be enough.

"Still rescuing urchins, brother?" Harald murmured. "It's good to stay in touch with one's roots."

"Yes," Cherry said brightly, lowering her cup. "I agree. Charity is so noble. It's the perfect occupation for the son of a king." Her words stained the air like red wine across white silk. With barely a breath, she moved on. "I met Ruben in a professional capacity, but he pursued me outside of work, of course." She gave him a warm, teasing look, as if they were sharing a secret joke.

With a jolt, he realised that they *were*. The memory of marching into her staffroom and dragging her off for lunch brought a smile to his face. And then, somehow, even with the weight of his brother's presence crushing his lungs, Ruben managed to laugh.

"Something like that," he said, and she grinned, and he felt like himself. He felt like *himself*. What a fucking gift.

As the meeting went on, stilted and awkward and dogged by Harald's jabs, Ruben held that blessing to his chest, and it became his shield.

AFTER A PAINFUL HOUR, they were finally released. Cherry smiled politely as they excused themselves, and she left clinging to his arm as if they were joined at the hip. She stayed that way as an assistant led them through the halls to their private quarters, as they were shown their suite and informed of the dinner hour—like Ruben didn't know it.

But as soon as the door to their quarters swung shut, locking out the outside world, Cherry let go. She stepped away from him. And the laughing intimacy she'd shown him moments before, the smile on her lips and the warmth in her voice, disappeared.

"Fuck," she muttered. "I didn't think we'd have to share."

Ruben tried to hide the way those words hit him, like fists to the gut. They were right back where they'd started. She didn't want to be alone with him.

"We're engaged," he said. "Of course they'd put us together." Then he realised that he'd said precisely the wrong thing.

The glare she gave him could've felled a fucking tree. "How could I forget?" She drawled. "And where the hell is Demi? Or Hans, for that matter?"

Ruben shrugged. "I try to keep my brother unaware of my personal connections."

For a minute, her gaze softened, and she nodded. But then, as if remembering herself, she set her jaw and turned away from him. "I'm taking the bedroom."

He watched her storm off through the suffocatingly luxurious parlour, heading towards the huge bedroom they were *supposed* to share.

He had a feeling that wouldn't go so well this time around.

CHAPTER TWENTY-FIVE

"*Neita.*" Ruben's sister dragged out the name, her accent softening the *T*.

Cherry smiled politely and sliced her sautéed chicken breast into tiny fucking pieces, waiting for the punchline. Beside her, she felt Ruben stiffen. He must have heard that predatory quality in his sister's voice, like a shark sniffing out blood.

"What an *interesting* name," Sophronia continued, her voice dripping with mockery. She was one to talk. "Where *does* it come from?"

"Sophy," Ruben said, his tone warning.

"Calm yourself, little brother. I am speaking with my future sister-in-law."

Sophronia's real sister-in-law, the pale and birdlike Lydia, had spent most of this strained dinner doing everything she could to avoid Sophronia's attention. And her husband's. Cherry rather thought that said it all. Still, she forced herself to smile at Ruben's painfully beautiful sister. She faced off the porcelain skin, the ice-blue eyes and the golden hair, so unassuming on Lydia and so very devastating on Sophronia. "The Caribbean," she said.

"Ah! You're from the West Indies."

Cherry's jaw set. How strange; the colonial name sounded fine coming from the lips of her migrant grandparents, but corrosive from Sophronia.

"I am a British Jamaican," she said slowly. "Third generation."

"Is that what they call it? Fascinating."

"Sophronia," Ruben said calmly. "Shut your fucking mouth."

At the head of the table—which put him a good two metres away from Cherry—the king slammed a hand against the smooth, dark wood.

Silence fell. Sophronia rolled her eyes. Lydia gazed firmly down at her plate, looking even paler than usual.

"I will not have cursing at my table," Harald said.

Ruben sighed, leaning back in his seat. He laced his hands behind his head as if he were lying around in the sun rather than dining with a king. He looked at his brother and said, "Fuck. You."

Cherry tried very hard not to smile.

But then Harald leaned forward with a look on his face that erased all humour. His pale eyes shone with raw fury for a second —just a second—before the disturbing flash of anger was hidden behind a benevolent smile. A smile that looked more like a mask. The monster beneath flickered in and out of view, a twisted merging of the real and the false that sent shivers down her spine.

Harald stared at Ruben for one, long moment. But then his gaze slid to Lydia.

"Get up," he said.

Lydia stood.

So did Ruben. "Harald. What are you doing?"

223

Sophronia sat back in her chair, surveying the scene with obvious satisfaction. She really was beautiful. Cherry wouldn't mind if she died.

Harald smiled blandly at Ruben, as if they were discussing the weather. "You appear to have forgotten how things work here, little brother. Allow me to remind you. Lydia, come here."

The pale woman kept her gaze to the floor as she walked around the table towards her husband. Ruben looked like he was going to be sick. Cherry's heart settled in her throat, threatening to choke her.

Harald stood up and took his wife's hand, but his gaze stayed pinned to Ruben. "You remember the fun we used to have, little brother. You're too big for those games now, but Lydia isn't. I think we'll retire early this evening."

"What the fuck? Harald, no." Ruben shoved back his chair. "Stop it."

"Or what?" The king smiled. "Tell me. What will happen if I don't? What will *you* do?"

A muscle leapt in Ruben's jaw as he clenched his fists, his body coiled tight as a spring. "Don't think I'll allow this. I will tear your head from your fucking body before I let you leave this room with her."

Harald shrugged. "I know how your baser instincts rule you. Always so violent. Enough of my guard are stationed around this room to guarantee my safety. Your threats don't bother me."

Ruben closed his eyes, pain written all over his face. Cherry felt the echoes of his panic, his fury, his helplessness, as if their feelings were connected.

She stood and joined him, her hand coming to rest on his shoulder. And he looked at her, first with shock, then with awe, as if she'd performed a miracle. But Cherry couldn't focus on that. She turned her gaze to the trembling woman on Harald's arm and said, her voice gentle, "Come with us, Lydia. Come with us now, and we'll leave."

"The girls—"

"We'll fetch them," Ruben said. "I'll get them myself. We'll all go now."

Before she could reply, peals of tinkling laughter rent the air. Sophronia watched them all with obvious delight, swirling her wine glass in hand. "Take the king's heirs?" She said. "Ruben, darling. Do be sensible. It pays to know when you're beaten."

At those words, Lydia's face crumpled in on itself. She shook her head. "Your sister is right, Ruben. It's not a good idea."

"I don't give a fuck. Say the word, Lydia."

"It's not so bad. I'm being dramatic. If you'd just..." She smiled, her eyes shimmering with unshed tears. "If you'd just stop provoking him... If we can all be civil, everything will be fine."

Ruben swallowed, hard. "Lydia—"

"*Please,*" she whispered, the word echoing around the grand room.

"Alright," Ruben said, his voice a ghost. "I'm sorry." Then he turned to face his brother and said it again. "I'm sorry."

Harald cocked his head. "I beg your pardon?"

Through gritted teeth, he repeated himself. "I apologise for my behaviour, Your Majesty."

Harald nodded graciously. "I see. I accept your apology." He returned to the table and sat down with easy grace. Across the table, Sophronia sipped at her wine. Lydia sank miserably into her seat and picked up her knife and fork, her hands shaking.

Bile rose in Cherry's throat, but she kept her face carefully blank. "Excuse me," she murmured. "I'm not feeling well."

She turned and headed for the door, not bothering to wait for Harald's permission. If he spoke to her right now, she might lose her mind and stab him with a butter knife. And she was still a British citizen. It would probably cause a political incident.

As she reached the door, she realised that Ruben wasn't following her. She turned back to find him standing there, staring after her with something hopeless in his eyes.

Clearing her throat, Cherry called, "Ruben, I need you to come with me. I don't know how to get back."

He nodded stiffly. Came to join her.

They left together.

THEY STRODE through the halls in silence, and every footstep reverberated through Ruben's mind like the sound of a door slamming shut.

When they were safely in their own quarters, he held his breath, waiting for the blow. For the words, or the complete lack of words, that would tell him it really was over. That she couldn't even look at him, never mind care for him, because what kind of man found himself in this position?

She turned to face him, her skin leached of its usual glow. And she said, "Explain."

Where to fucking start?

"I don't know what just happened," he admitted, his voice shaking. "Harald never—he's never—"

"That's not a common occurrence, then?"

He looked up sharply. "No. I never thought... I thought he loved her. A twisted sort of love, the only kind he's capable of, but—I thought I was the only one he'd..."

Cherry caught his hands in hers. She pulled them, big and rough and clearly fucking useless as they were, to her lips. Kissed his knuckles. "He hurt you. When you were a child."

It felt like freedom to say, "Yes."

"Men like that are never satisfied," she whispered. "They're empty, and the pain of the vulnerable is all that sustains them. We need to do something."

Ruben shoved down the panic that clouded his mind, the memories that suffocated him, and focused on her words. "You're right. God, who knows how fucking long he's been doing this. I should never have left. What was I thinking?"

"You were thinking that this place is hell, and you needed to escape," Cherry said. "That's called survival. Never regret it." She stepped closer to him, her hands cradling his face. In the midst of his horror and confusion and guilt he wished, just for a second, that she was touching him the way she used to. Not out of pity or obligation, but because she cared for him.

He'd ruined that. Add it to the fucking list.

"Listen to me," she said softly. "We're here for a week. You know Lydia well?"

He nodded shakily. "They married when I was a child. She was always nice to me."

"Good. You spend this week convincing her. Reassure her that we can protect her, whatever it takes."

Ruben nodded, her meaning dawning on him slowly but surely. "And if she agrees, we'll take them all. Out of the country. To England, even."

"Exactly."

The tightness in his chest eased slightly. He didn't stop to think about the fact that this plan would cause the collapse of everything he'd ever clung to. He had no doubt Harald would do his utmost to twist this situation, to paint it as some kind of criminal act—kidnapping, probably. Ruben's place in the royal family would disappear, and he'd officially become the shame he'd always been treated as.

But that didn't matter anymore. All of a sudden, he was struggling to understand how it had ever mattered at all.

A thought gripped him. "What if she doesn't agree? What if she doesn't want to risk it?"

Cherry sucked in a breath. "Then we'll stay. We'll make some kind of excuse and stay for as long as it takes."

Ruben looked down at her face, the steely conviction in her eyes. This would work. This would work, because she would make it so, through sheer force of will, through the power that hummed through her like a heartbeat. He wanted to fall at her feet. He wanted to tell her exactly how he felt about her, but he wasn't foolish enough to think that she'd listen.

This didn't change a thing between them. She was just the sort of woman to do what was right, regardless of the circumstances.

So he nodded, and squeezed her hands, and then he let her go. "We should get some sleep," he said softly.

"Yes," she agreed. "We should." She turned away from him without hesitation. It hurt more than ever.

CHERRY SLID FURTHER under the covers of her huge bed, staring into the darkness. She tried her best not to imagine a five-year-old Ruben, orphaned and alone, left in the care of those vipers, but it was hard. Almost impossible.

She hoped more than anything in the world that they'd leave here at the end of the week with Lydia and her children in tow. But she'd seen enough abusive relationships to know that things might not go to plan.

Fuck.

Ruben had gotten ready for bed and laid down on the stiff-looking sofa in the parlour without prompting. Not a single complaint had passed his lips since the horrors that had taken place at dinner.

She didn't like it. She didn't like it at all.

She didn't want him silent and accepting. She wanted him angry, protesting, and pushing his fucking luck.

And of course, at that moment, when she was feeling weak, a memory floated to the surface of her mind. Ruben, explaining why he lived in a normal house on the grounds of his huge bloody mansion.

I don't like big houses. Feels like a palace.

Well, now they were *in* a palace. And she knew he was suffocating.

With a sigh, Cherry pushed the covers aside and got up. She stumbled through the dark, fumbling for the ornate, crystal handle that marked the room's heavy door. Then, once she found it, she pulled it open and whispered through the gap, "Ruben."

For a moment, the silence was as heavy as the darkness. But then she heard a slight creak as the delicate sofa strained under his shifting weight. "Cherry?"

"Come here," she said softly.

He moved faster than was reasonable in the dark, in the middle of the night, when he should have been on the edge of sleep. But she'd known he wouldn't sleep. He probably couldn't.

He banged into something, cursed, and she bit back a smile. She couldn't fall into the trap of laughing with him in the dark, as if they were something other than… associates. Associates who had to maintain a certain level of intimacy, but not an *excessive* level.

When his hands settled on her shoulders, Cherry almost leapt out of her skin.

"Are you okay?" he asked softly. "Do you need me?"

She snorted. "I've never needed anyone, and I don't intend to start now."

"Cherry," he murmured, and his hands slid down her arms, tracing white-hot fire over her skin. "Oh, Cherry. You're perfect."

She jerked back, away from his touch. "Stop that. I thought we could share the bed, since it's so huge, but if you can't keep your hands to yourself—"

"I can," he said immediately. "I can. Whatever you want."

"Hmph." She turned and fumbled her way back towards the bed. "We'll see."

He did keep his hands to himself, in the end. But that didn't stop their bodies from sliding together as they both settled into the mattress. It didn't stop the ghost of his warmth from enveloping her, or the scent of his skin. And it didn't stop memories from drowning her, teasing out her reluctant arousal, even as she gritted her teeth and lay stiffly on her back with her hands by her sides.

This was a bad idea. Terrible. There was no way she could—

He was asleep.

Cherry stayed still and silent for another moment, listening closely to the slow, even cadence of his breathing. He was definitely asleep. Just like that. Jesus Christ, he was irritating.

But still, she found herself reaching for him in the dark, tracing the sweeping contours of his face with gentle fingers. She would happily set this fucking palace alight, with both of his siblings trapped inside. That probably said something about her morals, and definitely said something about her attachment to him.

She couldn't worry about it now though, not with him beside her. Bit by bit, Cherry felt herself relax, felt her mind and her body grow heavy, felt her eyes slide shut.

And somehow, she slept too. Who'd have thought?

CHAPTER TWENTY-SIX

Over the week, a pattern emerged. It was arguably more interesting than the routine she'd fallen into at Ruben's, but it wasn't half as enjoyable.

In fact, it was absolutely awful.

Every morning Cherry would wake up to find her fingers intertwined with Ruben's, no matter how she'd gone to sleep. Every morning she'd open her eyes to see him watching her as if she were something precious. And every morning she'd turn away and pretend it didn't kill her.

Then he'd go about his day, hopefully spending plenty of time with Lydia, while Cherry underwent the complete torture of Magda Jansen's undivided attention.

On her first full day at the palace, Sophronia had pulled Cherry aside at breakfast to discuss Cherry's *introduction*. To *society*. Which was to say, the ball.

Sophronia's soft, pink lips had twisted into a sly little smirk as she murmured, "I understand you're unaccustomed to events of this magnitude, so I have arranged for someone to oversee the preparations."

Cherry had returned the sly smirk with an open scowl. "What preparations?"

"Why, for your presentation, darling. Your appearance. It is truly a *ball*, you understand. You'll need a personal shopper, a stylist—"

"Fine, okay. Whatever."

A flicker of irritation had crossed Sophronia's face, like a snake gliding across still waters. "See that you are available and in your quarters around midday. Magda will arrive to discuss the initial arrangements."

She'd swept away in a swirl of skirts before Cherry could ask who the hell Magda was.

But she found out soon enough.

MAGDA JANSEN HAD KNOCKED on Cherry's door as if she were a giant with fists like dustbin lids. When Cherry went to investigate, she found a diminutive, dark-haired, older woman scowling at her. The woman's hands, Cherry noticed, were a perfectly ordinary size. Smaller than average, even. How she'd managed to make such a racket without bruising her damn knuckles, Cherry had no idea.

"You?" Magda barked. Her accent was more pronounced than Ruben's, or Hans's, or even Agathe's. "*You* are my canvas?"

Cherry arched a brow. "I'm Cherry Neita. Person. Not canvas."

Magda snorted. Then she muttered something in Danish that sounded slightly venomous and pushed her way into the room.

Magda and Cherry, suffice it to say, did not get on.

Over the following days, Cherry became familiar with the sort of misery she'd never experienced before. During the day, Magda picked her apart piece by piece, all in the name of putting her back together again, somehow better than before. Demi and Hans's absence continued—though, every so often, she *thought* she caught sight of a familiar, huge, scowling man marching along the corridors like a giant toy soldier.

But the worst part was Ruben.

She and Ruben shared a space. They shared a room. They shared a bed. They shared a plan.

And absolutely nothing else.

She had done this. She'd wanted a wall between them; she'd wanted to regain control of a situation that had been spiralling beyond her understanding, beyond her power. And every time she thought back to the way he'd looked at her, the panic in his voice on that fateful night, the fact that he couldn't even bear her touch, she felt the hurt all over again.

But now her time spent in this gilded house of fucking horrors had added another dimension to her perspective.

She remembered what he'd said to her—*I can't bear the idea of children*. And she started to think about why that might be.

She wanted to ask him about it. She wanted to hear his explanations, now that the sting of rejection and her own damned pride weren't ruling her thoughts. She wanted, more than anything, to forgive him. But clearly pride still played a part in her emotions, because she couldn't bring herself to start that conversation. She couldn't bring herself to make the first move. And he, respecting her wishes, did exactly as she'd asked.

He kept his distance. Even when they lay together in the dark with nothing between them but her own damn stubbornness.

THE DAY BEFORE THE BALL, Cherry's worry was almost suffocating. Somewhere in this palace was a woman trapped in an impossible situation, afraid for herself and her children...

And Cherry sat in a chair, in front of a thousand bright lights, having her makeup done and her hair pulled at by a group of strangers.

Magda hovered around the transformed parlour, rifling through racks of elaborate gowns, all of which seemed to be in shades of grey or lavender. A tall, slender man stood beside Magda, towering over her tiny frame, and the two chattered away in Danish, gesturing wildly between the dresses and Cherry.

They were probably discussing the fact that the gown she was currently wearing—or rather, had been stuffed into—wouldn't zip up. At all. Not even close.

Cherry didn't mind. It was pretty fucking ugly.

She flinched as the girl doing her makeup jabbed at her eye with a mascara wand. "Ow!"

"Stop looking all over the place. Eyes over here, over there, bah. Look up," the girl said sharply. "*Up.*"

This was the fourth makeup trial they'd done that week. If Cherry was told to *look up* one more fucking time, she'd throw herself out the damn window. Especially since she knew that, just like the last three times, her foundation would be caked on and ashy as hell. Apparently, Helgmøre didn't produce foundation darker than a paper bag.

Well. Either that, or the makeup artist—whose name Cherry still couldn't remember—was absolutely awful at her job.

"Alright," announced a strident voice from behind her. The hair stylist. Ana, her name might be. "I know what we will do. We will, make it, ah... *glatte.*"

Magda broke off from her conversation to nod approvingly. "*Ja, ja.* Good. And then a nice, ah…" She waved her hand around the back of her head. "Like this?"

"Oh, yes," Ana said. "Beautiful, yes."

Well. Cherry was glad that Ana and Magda were on the same page, but it would help if she had some idea what fucking book they were reading.

"What do you mean *glatte*? What does that mean?" She twisted around in her seat, looking back at the hair stylist.

The makeup artist tsked in irritation. "Come here! Look *up!*"

Cherry ignored her. It was either that, or say something very impolite.

Ana was bent over her little trolley, filled with mysterious hair products. She looked up at Cherry with a smile as she produced a straightening iron. "With this," she said helpfully. "*Stijltang.*"

Cherry recoiled.

The makeup girl threw up her hands and spat, "*For fanden!* Come here!"

"No." Cherry stood up, clutching the bodice of her unzipped dress. "Nooo way. You're not straightening my hair."

Ana looked at her with obvious alarm. "It's okay. It does not, ah… hurt?"

"I know it doesn't bloody hurt!" Cherry snapped. "I haven't straightened my hair since I was a damn teenager and I don't intend to now. Do you know how long it took to grow out all that heat damage? Good Lord." She clutched at her curls as if to check they were still there, springy and coarse and bouncing against her hand. "No. *Hard* no. Jesus Christ, what am I even doing here?"

It felt like someone had dashed a glass of ice water into her face. She turned to look at Magda, the little woman staring at her with a lingering distaste that, just five minutes ago, Cherry had been content to ignore. She didn't want to make a fuss. She didn't want to make any of this harder than it already was.

But she'd be damned if she was going to let some rude, tiny tyrant send her to a ball looking like a caricature of herself.

"Magda," she said, drawing herself up to her full height. Being tall really came in handy at times like these. "I don't like the direction we're taking. I want to try something new." Magda's face was pinched and sour. Clearly, this speech was not going down well. But really, a woman had to draw the line somewhere. "I want to try a new stylist. And a new makeup artist. A new everything, really."

Magda squinted up at her. "No."

"No?" Cherry frowned. "What the hell do you mean *no*?"

"I mean what I said, Miss Neita. You have no idea what is expected of you in terms of appearance, and I do."

Cherry cast a speaking glance at the racks of subdued, too-small dresses. "I'm expected to show up looking like a Victorian widow? Without the corset?"

Magda swept a look over Cherry's body. "I thought it best if we drew attention *away* from your body type."

Cherry stiffened. Her patience, already worn thin by the events of the week, was in serious danger of snapping. The consequences, at this stage, could be fatal. If shoving Ana's straightening iron up Magda's arse constituted *fatal*.

"You know what?" she said tightly, forcing herself to remain calm. "I don't have to listen to you. You effectively work for me."

Magda arched a brow. "I work for the crown," she clipped out. "And I don't think your future husband wants you to embarrass him at the ball. Do you?"

Her *future husband*?! Cherry opened her mouth to ask who the fuck cared what Ruben thought—but then she realised the implication of the other woman's tone, the mistaken belief she was clearly labouring under. And she felt herself smile. "Alright," she said. "Why don't we ask him, then?"

Magda's nostrils flared, her jaw set. "Fine. We will."

And so Cherry stormed out of her private quarters, holding an ugly, grey dress up over her chest, with a tiny harridan bringing up the rear. She had no idea where Ruben was, but thankfully asking a nearby footman—yes, they really had bloody *footmen*—yielded quick results.

Five minutes later, they arrived at Ruben's makeshift office in a swirl of too-short skirts and competing outrage. Ruben looked up from his desk, his face drawn and tired. For a second, Cherry forgot the reason she'd sought him out. She wanted to go over and massage his shoulders or kiss his forehead or something equally sickening.

Then he rubbed a hand over his face and blinked his tired frown away, looking handsome as always, if a bit subdued. "Cherry. Magda. Is everything alright?"

"Certainly not, Your Highness," Magda said, before Cherry could get a word in edgeways. "Your betrothed is being *most* difficult—"

Cherry bristled. *"I'm* being difficult? I sat through your bullshit for days—"

"Your Highness, you know I have extensive experience with—"

"She wants to straighten my hair!"

Ruben held up a hand, cutting them both off. "Hold on. Who's straightening whose hair?"

Cherry folded her arms. "She wants. To straighten. My hair. So I told her to piss off."

Magda sucked in an outraged breath. Ruben's lips twitched, just for a second, before they flattened out into a bland line.

He picked up one of the papers strewn across his desk and said, "I fail to see the problem."

Cherry's heart dropped. Then her temper rose. That fucking—

"It's Cherry's hair. If she doesn't want it straightened, that's that."

Oh. Cherry unfolded her arms, then grabbed at the front of her dress as it threatened to slide down. She resisted the immature urge to stick her tongue out at Magda. "And another thing! I want different dresses to choose from."

Ruben shrugged. "Why are you asking me? You know you can have whatever you want."

"*Magda* apparently doesn't trust my judgement."

Ruben's dark gaze pinned Magda with such ferocity, she was surprised the other woman didn't flinch. "You don't need to micro-manage my fiancée, Magda. I assure you. Cherry knows how to look good."

Well. Though it galled her to be there at all, asking Ruben about her damn dresses as if he were her keeper, Cherry decided to press her advantage. "I want a black makeup artist."

"What?!" Magda shrieked. "How am I supposed to find a new makeup artist in a day? Never mind a…"

Ruben looked up. "They're not unicorns, Magda. You're usually very good at your job. Don't disappoint me now."

Magda's tiny nostrils flared like a panting horse's. But she stretched her thin lips into a smile and said, "Of course, Your Highness. I apologise."

Ruben gave her a bland look. "I don't think you need to apologise to me."

Cherry could almost feel Magda's fury, radiating from her body in waves. But still, the little woman turned stiffly to Cherry and bowed her head. "I am very sorry if I made you at all uncomfortable with my behaviour, Miss Neita. I will endeavour to meet your needs more fully from now on."

Cherry blinked. At least the woman knew how to apologise. "That's okay," she said. "Perhaps we could start over."

Magda nodded sharply. "I would appreciate that. With your permission, Your Highness, I will see about making the necessary rearrangements…"

"Of course," Ruben nodded.

Magda left, but Cherry trailed behind, because she was pathetic. Because she was hoping that he'd do something or say something to cross the growing distance between them. But the silence stretched out as she walked away, and he didn't call her back. Cherry stood on the threshold, forced herself to grab the ridiculous crystal doorknob—

"Shut the door."

CHAPTER TWENTY-SEVEN

She sucked in a breath as the words sank into her skin, like fresh rain after a drought. And then she did as Ruben had asked and shut the damn door.

She heard his chair slide against the thick carpet as he stood. He walked over to her, and then his hands settled on her waist, and he turned her around and pushed her against the cool wood.

"God," he said, a little smile curving his lips. "They really made a mess of your face."

She huffed out a laugh, as if her heart wasn't beating a mile a minute. "I look half-dead."

"The prettiest zombie I ever saw," he murmured wryly.

She smiled. And he closed his eyes, frowning as if he were in pain. "It's been days since you smiled at me. For real, not for someone else's benefit." He opened his eyes and studied her, his face more serious than she'd ever seen it. "I've been thinking a lot, since we got here. About... the things I've valued in my life. And the things I've allowed to define me."

Cherry swallowed down the lump in her throat, forced back all the things she wanted to say, and let him talk. His hand tightened on her waist—and then he pulled back as his fingers brushed her skin through the open zipper.

"You're not dressed," he said, his voice hoarse.

"Of course I am. Just doesn't fit."

He shook his head, his gaze latching on to the slice of bare skin exposed by the gaping fabric. She wanted him to touch her again, but he moved his hand away.

"Cherry," he said softly. "I know I messed things up. Twice. Probably more than twice, but I'm too clueless to keep track of these things effectively."

She laughed. "You're not clueless. Okay?"

"You don't have to feel sorry for me, you know. I'm sure it doesn't seem like it, but I'm not a victim. Not anymore." She wasn't sure what Ruben was talking about until he went on. "I made a choice to stay in this twisted situation, and I'm starting to realise it was a bad one. I give Harald power over me and feel like *I'm* holding power over *him* because... Because it kills him that I'm even here. But it's a pointless cycle. It's childish. It's not me."

Cherry rolled her lips in as she tried to sort her thoughts, tried to put this in a way he'd understand. "I don't pity you, first of all. I mean, aside from being literal royalty, you're very gorgeous and very rich and you have a loving family—"

He snorted. "No I don't."

"Yes, you do. Agathe is your family. And so is Demi, and so is Hans. So no, I don't pity you. I would like to kill everyone who has ever hurt you, but I don't pity you." He smiled slightly at those words, and Cherry felt like she'd done something right. It gave her the confidence to keep going.

"When all of this started, I didn't understand why you were so caught up in what the media thought, in your family name and your brother. I understand now. I do. But I also think that you're strong enough to let that go. Your brother is so desperate to convince you that you're unworthy, because he knows you're a better man than he will ever be. And I never met either of your parents, but if five years with them turned you into the kind of child who could survive Harald, and still care about people and… *feel* things, then they must have been amazing. And they must have loved you really fucking hard."

Ruben wrapped his arms around her, pulling her into the safety of his broad chest, burying her face against his shirt. Her eyes closed as she drowned in the familiar, soothing scent of him, as she felt his hand come to rest against her hair.

"The other night," he whispered, "I freaked out because I decided a long time ago that I couldn't have a family. Especially not children. I see all the ways children are vulnerable, even children who are loved, whose families *want* to protect them. And I've never been able to handle it. I just couldn't. But when I was with you, and I thought there was a chance that I could get you pregnant, I thought—I thought, 'There's no need to panic. She might be on the pill, or something.' But I didn't want you to be. I had this idea, for all of half a second—I must have lost my fucking mind. But I had this idea that you'd be pregnant and then you'd be stuck with me." He laughed. "Ridiculous, I know. And then I panicked. I didn't understand what was going on in my own head."

He shrugged, and Cherry pulled back, just enough to see his face. He looked rueful and more than a little embarrassed. "Oh, so you're saying you want to knock me up?" she teased.

He rolled his eyes. "Stop that. You brat."

"You said it, not me."

"It was just…" He waved a hand. "Instinct. A reflex. I don't know. Forget about that. I'm trying to apologise, here."

"You're doing very well," she smiled. And she meant it. "But, seriously, Ruben. I like you." *Understatement*. "A lot. And even though

243

I understand, I really don't know if this is a good idea. I don't think I can keep my feelings separate from whatever this is."

He slid a hand under her chin, tilting her head back until she couldn't avoid his eyes. "I don't think you should keep them separate," he said. "I'm not. I can't."

She bit down on the inside of her cheek, pushing away the hope that was desperate to run rampant. "What does that mean?"

"It means I have feelings for you. It means that after tomorrow, if Harald doesn't somehow take my title, I'll give it up. And no-one will care about who I sleep with or who I'm engaged to, but... I'll still want to be with you." He found her left hand, raised it to his lips. And then he kissed the ring he'd given her with such reverence that she knew it wasn't the trinket she'd assumed.

"What is this?" she asked, nodding towards the arrangement of sapphire and diamond.

"It was my mother's," he said softly. "My father gave it to her, and she left it to me."

She forced herself to ask. "Why did you give me this?"

And he said, completely calm: "Because I love you."

Cherry bit down on the inside of her cheek so hard, she was surprised it didn't bleed. "You can't—"

"Stop," he said. "Don't. I love you. Okay? You can do whatever you want with that information, but you can't change it."

She smiled, even as she felt tears trailing down her cheeks. "Okay."

He tutted, sweeping his thumb across her cheekbone. "Even I know you're supposed to use waterproof mascara. What kind of makeup artist did Magda bring you, anyway?"

"Oh, God. I look a mess." She swiped uselessly at her cheeks. "I don't know much about balls, but I have to warn you, this one will probably be a disaster."

"Oh, I know," he said cheerfully. And then he pressed his lips to her ear and whispered, "If Lydia agrees, we'll leave that night. Everything is in place."

She nodded. She'd seen the fire in his eyes when he realised that Lydia was facing what he'd once been through. She didn't doubt that he would pull this off.

As long as Lydia felt safe enough to agree. Would she? Suddenly, Cherry's chest was a storm of anxiety. "I should go," she said. "I have a lot to do."

He released her waist and stepped back, out of her space. She felt oddly bereft. Still, she forced herself to leave, because there was a ball tomorrow night, and that should be her greatest concern. It had to *appear* to be her greatest concern, at least.

But as she stepped out of the room, Cherry gave in to the urge to look back. He was watching her, something soft and warm in his gaze, and that gave her the courage to speak. "I have feelings for you, too." She sounded stilted, robotic, but she wasn't used to this. Not at all. She was used to being adored and feeling no inclination whatsoever to return that sentiment. She wasn't used to *caring*, to craving a man's affection.

To grappling with huge, impossible concepts like love.

From the smile on his face, though, you'd think she'd confessed her undying devotion. "Good," he said, and for the first time since they'd met, his barely-there accent thickened. "Good. You will keep it?" He nodded down at her hand. At the ring. She heard the rest of his sentence, the words he'd left unsaid. *After? When all this is over and the pretence falls apart?*

She tried to hide her smile, but it fought free. Just a little. She murmured, "I'll look after it for you."

His face lit up like the sunrise.

RUBEN SAT beside his youngest niece's bed, studying her sweet little face in the glow of her nightlight. Hilde was nine, but still afraid of the dark. He didn't blame her. He'd been afraid of the dark as a child.

He hoped that was the only similarity between them.

The bedroom door creaked as it was pushed open by gentle hands. He looked up to find Lydia in the doorway, her face resigned.

"You're here," she said.

He smiled. "Don't say you're surprised to see me."

"How could I be? You've been chasing me all week."

Ruben stood, holding up his hands. "You know I want to help, Lydia. You used to help me. Remember?"

She swallowed. "Of course I remember."

"Then you understand why I can't leave you here. I never should have left in the first place."

She shook her head. But she approached without fear, walking past him to look down at her daughter. That was something. The first time he'd gotten her alone, she'd been afraid of him.

And he'd understood.

"It didn't start right away," she said softly. "Things were fine for the first few years."

"Fine?"

"Well." She shrugged. "As fine as things can be with a man such as my husband. But eventually he turned on me. I expected it, in the end."

"Lydia," he whispered. "I don't understand why you won't let me help you."

She smiled up at him, tired but gentle as ever. Hopeless, and yet so kind. "You've always been reckless, Ruben. Fearless. I admire that about you, but I cannot become you. I am a mother. I will not have my children running from their own father, their king, without protection or safety—"

"*I* will keep you safe," he insisted.

But still, she shook her head. "Safety lies in certainty. If I go along with this plan you have devised, is the outcome certain? Certain enough that I should stake the safety of my family on your word? This is one small island, ruled by corrupt officials, easily swayed by Harald's money and influence. You have—what? A private jet, a loyal faction of the royal guard on your side? I'm sorry, Ruben. It's not enough."

He swallowed. He understood, and yet...

"I can't give up on this," he said.

She smiled. "I know. I know you, little brother."

It was the first time anyone had ever called him that with love in their voice. For a second, he could barely breathe.

Then she turned her back on him, ghosting a hand over her daughter's golden head. "Leave us, now. The nurse might come."

"Tomorrow," he said. "Any time. Say the word, any time."

She didn't reply. He left.

HE ARRIVED at the room he and Cherry had shared uneasily for so many nights, and found her waiting for him.

She was curled up in bed with the lamp on, wearing that damned Dolly Parton T-shirt, the blankets pulled up over her lap.

"You're turning me into a Dolly Parton fan," he said.

"Good," she replied. "I have at least four of these T-shirts."

He moved towards the bed as if it might disappear at any moment. A small part of him worried that it could. That the sight of Cherry waiting for him, smiling at him, as if this was normal and natural and forever, must be a fucking mirage. He felt like a beast in comparison to her beauty as she sat there, utterly composed, watching him with a gleam in her endless eyes. This was nothing but a fairytale. A fantasy. It had to be.

But he sat down, and it was real.

She pushed the blankets aside and crawled over to him, and sat on his lap. She helped him fumble with his tie, laughing when he lost patience with the buttons of his shirt and tore the whole thing off over his head. Then she kissed him. Soft and slow and sweet, like a blessing. A blessing that set his blood alight, left him both satisfied and insatiable.

He pulled back, cradled her face in his hands, looked her in the eye. "Do you think there's something wrong with me?"

She frowned. "What do you mean?"

"The way I want you. The things I need from you. Do you think I'm fucked up because of—"

"No," she interrupted sharply. "No. I don't. My childhood was fine. Perfect, really. And I want this just as much as you do. It's just the way you are. There's nothing wrong with it."

He didn't need convincing. He already knew that, had decided long ago. But the idea that she might think otherwise had hit him like a truck, and he'd needed to know.

"Good," he said. He kissed her again. "Good."

Then *she* kissed *him*. She appeared to be enjoying herself. He let her take control for a while, but eventually, the need became too great.

He lifted her up, turned and threw her down against the bed. If they'd been in darkness, he'd have focused on the tiny exhalation she made—almost a gasp, but not quite. Only they weren't in darkness, so instead he drank in the way her full lips parted, the wideness of her doe eyes.

"Spread your legs for me, sweetheart."

She smiled, flashing those damn dimples at him, looking so sweet and so sexy all at once. And then she did as she was told.

He couldn't play games tonight. He couldn't bring himself to do anything but sink into her—into her arms, into her body, into the sense of fulfilment that only she could provide. Kissing her felt like a rebirth. Every touch was fresh and light and clean; even when he slid between her thighs and whispered filthy things into her ear.

When she came, he whispered, "I love you." And then he couldn't stop saying it. Not when she came a second time, not when she bit his shoulder and clawed at his back, and definitely not when *he* came, so hard he saw stars.

He loved her. He *loved* her.

Nothing could go wrong.

CHAPTER TWENTY-EIGHT

Ruben smiled tightly at aristocracy, foreign dignitaries, the odd multi-billionaire of common birth—whoever was put in front of him got the same treatment. His best effort at charm.

It was probably atrocious, considering the mass of nerves this evening had turned him into.

The ballroom was alight, sparkling with jewels and laughter and champagne glasses, gowns swirling a rainbow of colours across the marble dance floor. Ruben floated above the glamour and gaiety as if watching from another place. He kept an eye on Lydia at all times, but his brother stuck to her like a fucking limpet—all smiles and courteousness in public, of course. Ever the benevolent king.

Part of Ruben's mind was occupied with running over the plan, the contingency plan, the last-ditch emergency fuck-it plan, and the many things that could go wrong with them all. Hans and Demetria were ready, working behind the scenes to slide everything into place, but he'd failed at his only task.

He hadn't made Lydia feel safe.

And goddamnit, where the fuck was Cherry? He spent another ten minutes working the room, hoping his anxiety came off as some kind of brooding charisma, before she arrived.

And when she arrived, Lord did she *arrive*.

There was no sudden hush to alert him to her presence, no awed whisperings as the orchestra came to a stop. No; it was a swell in the racket around him, a sharp spike in the excited voices filling the ballroom, that made Ruben turn towards the grand staircase.

"Is that her?"

"It must be."

"Well, I wasn't expecting that."

"But she's quite beautiful, isn't she?"

Ruben stared up at the figure descending the sweeping staircase. Yes, she fucking was.

Cherry's hair was piled high atop her head in a riot of curls, a few sweet, coiled strands escaping. Her eyes were wide and dark and her lips were red. Red as they'd been the day he met her. And just as tempting.

She wore a gown of crushed silk, red as her lips, that swept low across her cleavage, leaving her shoulders bare, and flared out from her waist like something out of a fairytale. With every step, the fabric flashed in the light, black-cherry here and bright scarlet there, a riot of shades from claret to poppy.

Ruben's feet carried him through the crowd as if by habit, but he'd never done this, felt this, loved like this, in his whole fucking life. He reached the foot of the staircase and she took the last few steps with a smile on her face, holding out a hand. He took it, just as he had the day they'd met, bending low to press a kiss to her skin. And when he rose, she was looking at him as if he were the only person in the room.

Someone had announced her, but he'd barely heard it. Now, he noticed that same voice saying something else about them, the affianced couple—but he didn't bother to listen. He just followed the sound of the orchestra as it swelled into a waltz.

"Dance with me?" he whispered.

She smiled, her cheeks plumping and her dimples doing funny things to his insides. "If I must," she murmured.

He grinned, forgetting his worry, forgetting his nerves, and pulled her onto the floor.

"You're very good at this," she said, as they settled into the familiar rhythm, his hand a little too tight at her waist. He couldn't bring himself to let go, though. If he did, she might disappear.

"So are you," he replied truthfully. "Magda's doing, I assume?"

"Yep. She's quite a useful woman. She just has terrible taste."

He laughed. "Fair enough. At least she listened in the end. You look absolutely stunning."

She smiled, her eyes sliding away from his. As if she were shy. But Cherry was never shy. "Thank you," she said softly.

"Thank *you*. I was ready to fall apart tonight before I saw you."

She arched a brow. "And now?"

"Now I'm incredibly hard and slightly less nervous."

"You're absolutely awful," she laughed. "I can't *stand* you."

"Yeah, you keep saying that. But you didn't seem to mind when I—"

"Do not finish that sentence!" Her eyes danced, and her lips tugged up into a reluctant smile. "We're in public, Ruben."

"Fine," he sighed. "I'll have to save my seduction techniques for later."

"Yes," she said crisply. "I suppose you will."

God, he loved this woman.

CHERRY NODDED POLITELY at the Archduke of Something or Other. He was very old, his voice was very reedy, and he was speaking entirely in Danish. But she decided to pretend that he was being utterly charming and completely complimentary. She tended to assume the best of the elderly. And there was a positive to the language barrier; it allowed her mind to wander freely.

Her eyes followed.

Ruben was just a few metres away, captured in conversation with a couple who looked rather intimidatingly wealthy—diamonds everywhere. Frankly, it was a bit much. Cherry rubbed an absent thumb over the diamonds and sapphires decorating her ring finger. She never had been one for jewellery, but she thought she might wear these particular diamonds for a rather long time.

At that moment, Ruben turned his head slightly and met her eye. His serious expression flickered, something light and happy taking over. He'd caught her staring. She'd never hear the end of it. He'd be full of utter rubbish about how *infatuated* she was. Oddly enough, she couldn't wait for a point far in the future, past this knife-edge of an evening, when everyone was safe and happy and Ruben had nothing better to do than try his best to make her blush.

She wanted that. She wanted that formless, endless future in her mind, the one where the only certainty was his presence. The rest, she was starting to realise, didn't really matter.

"Wow," she said out loud. "I'm… in love."

The Archduke nodded agreeably and said something in Danish.

"With Ruben," she told him. "I'm in love with Ruben."

The Archduke became very excited at the sound of Ruben's name, and the pace of his Danish increased exponentially.

"I'm sorry," Cherry said, grasping the old man's hand. "It's been lovely talking to you, but I think I need some air." She bowed her head over his knobbly knuckles, hoping that was clear enough.

It seemed to work; he nodded back, and his Danish slowed down. She caught a single word: *prinsesse*.

No, she thought as she wound her way through the crowd. She was something greater than that. She was loved.

CHERRY WENT LOOKING for a private little room to settle in, just for a while. She needed to catch her breath, control her rampaging thoughts, perhaps order some tea. The realisation that she was in love with her fiancée had left her in need of fortification.

But she took one wrong turn, and then another, and the looming shadows of the palace, emptier than usual with all the staff focused on the ball, began to feel like a threat. Cherry walked very quickly, trying to remind herself that no-one here would hurt her. And that if they did, she had two perfectly good high-heels on her feet, whose stilettos could be shoved up a man's nose with ease.

Or a woman's, she thought darkly, her mind settling on Sophronia.

She was almost ready to start tearing scraps of silk from her dress and leaving a trail behind her when she heard... something. Something that sounded promisingly human-like. Cherry followed the sound, hoping to come across a search party armed with a map of the palace and a cake or two. Instead she found what appeared to be a music room, the door slightly ajar, moonlight flooding the instruments scattered within its narrow walls.

Well, narrow for a palace. Pretty decent for anywhere else.

Cherry frowned and held perfectly still, straining to catch the snatch of sound she thought she'd heard. She couldn't see anyone in here, and after a moment, she decided she couldn't really hear anyone either.

But then the sound came again, softer this time. A sort of subdued, choked sound, small and high-pitched.

Cherry stepped fully into the room and said, "Is someone in here?"

Silence. But her eyes caught on something she'd missed the first time around. Beneath the piano, a huddled little figure sat on the floor, half-hidden in shadow.

She moved closer. "I'm a little bit lost. Do you think you could help me?"

The figure sniffed. It looked up, revealing a familiar pair of wide blue eyes. One of Lydia's daughters, the eldest. What was her name...?

"Ella," Cherry finally recalled. "Hello. Do you know who I am?"

The girl sniffed loudly, tossing Cherry a disdainful look. "Of course I do. I am not a child."

Right. This was the teenage one. Cherry bit back a smile as she moved closer, sinking down to peer beneath the grand piano.

"What are you doing under there, Ella? Shouldn't you be in bed?"

"This is my piano," the child said glumly, her accent thick as syrup. "This is my special room. I come here."

"Right," Cherry murmured. "Okay. Fair enough. Well—"

Outside, the clouds shifted slightly, and the moonlight pouring through the windows grew even stronger. Strong enough for Cherry to see the child's face. And the imprint of a palm against her cheek.

Cherry swallowed down the curse she wanted to spit out and kept her smile in place. "Ella," she said gently. "What happened to your face?"

The girl turned away. "Nothing," she sniffed.

"You can tell me," Cherry said, trying to sound reassuring. Jesus, where was Ruben when she needed him? "I promise you can trust me. I'm engaged to your uncle, and you know you can trust him, right?"

Ella looked back at Cherry, seeming to mull this over. "Uncle Ruben is kind to my mother."

"That's because he loves her. He loves all of you. And if someone has hurt you, he'd like to know."

The girl shook her head. "I am not telling you."

Before Cherry could reply, she heard the heavy tread of footsteps along the hall outside. Low voices murmured words she couldn't understand, but they made Ella's eyes widen, made her huddle deeper into the shadows.

Cherry straightened up and pulled out the plush little seat in front of the piano, angling it *just* so. When she sat, arranging her huge skirts around her, the space under the piano was hidden completely from view.

CHAPTER TWENTY-NINE

nd just in time. The door opened, revealing a pair of men in the same all-black suit that Hans favoured, clear earpieces curling about their ears.

They both blinked at the sight of her, clearly confused. The taller man collected himself first, and stepped forward.

"Miss Neita," he said, inclining his head. "We are sorry to disturb you." He didn't mention how odd it was for her to be sitting in front of a piano with her back to the keys, in the dark, during a ball held in her honour. "We are looking for Princess Ella. She is not in her room, and the king was concerned about her roaming the halls when we have guests."

Roaming the halls with the reddened outline of his hand on her face. Yes, he would be concerned about that, wouldn't he?

"I haven't seen any rogue children," Cherry said sweetly. "But I am glad you found me. I was looking for my fiancé, and I got lost." She let out a sparkling laugh. "Do you think you could have him come here and get me? Put those little earpieces to use?"

The man shifted slightly. "Miss Neita, we would be happy to accompany you—"

"Oh, no," she said blithely. "That's not necessary. I'd *really* like to see my fiancé." She rested her hands against her knees and leant forward, smiling as both men's eyes flew to her cleavage. "Please?"

The taller man cleared his throat. "Ah, yes. Of course. I'll—we'll pass that message on right away. Good evening, Miss Neita."

"Good evening, gentlemen." She smiled sunnily after them. They rushed out of the room as if it were on fire.

When the door clicked shut behind them, Cherry slid off the little stool and sank onto the floor. She met Ella's eyes, still glistening with unshed tears, and said, "Was it your father, or was it your aunt?"

Ella sniffed, swiping a hand over her nose. "Aunt Sophy likes to make trouble," the child said. "She does not like to feel trouble."

Hm. Surprisingly apt.

"Alright," Cherry said. "Your father. Would you like to come out from under there?"

The child shook her head.

"Has he done this before?"

Ella hesitated. But then she said, the words tumbling out, "Not like this. But he hurts me sometimes, and worse now. Tonight I asked him, too many times, why I cannot go to the ball. And he lost his temper. So..." She waved helplessly at her cheek.

Cherry nodded. "I see."

They were interrupted by more footsteps, and yet again, Cherry swirled into position before the piano.

But in the end, the subterfuge wasn't necessary. The door opened to reveal Ruben, his face tight with worry. He fiddled with the light, bathing the room in a low, golden glow. "Cherry? Is something wrong?"

"Well," she began, trying to keep her voice calm. Before she could go any further, Ella shot out from under the piano and ran across the room, throwing her arms around Ruben's waist.

He looked down at her with a frown. "Ella? What are you doing out of bed?"

Cherry saw the exact moment that Ruben caught sight of his niece's face. Everything about him hardened in an instant. Even as he tried to smooth out his expression, to keep his voice steady and calm, she saw.

He tipped Ella's head back with shaking hands and stared at the mark on her cheek. It was even worse in the light. It would almost certainly bruise. Then he spoke curtly in Danish, which was still incomprehensible to Cherry. She really needed to learn.

He finished in English, "Go and sit with Cherry. Stay here. I will come back soon."

The child obeyed, and Ruben turned and stalked from the room without another word.

Cherry stared after him. "What did he say?"

She wasn't expecting an answer. But Ella replied with satisfaction in her voice. "He said we're leaving and we're never coming back."

———

RUBEN SHOULDERED his way through the crowds, all of his focus on the couple at the centre of the room.

Lydia and Harald might as well be joined at the hip; he hadn't let her go all night, and he clearly didn't intend to. Now Ruben knew why. Harald didn't want his wife to catch wind of the fact that Ella was running around the palace—or, more importantly, why.

Wouldn't want a scene in front of all these people, now, would he?

Ruben relied upon that fact to get him what he needed. He approached his brother with the biggest smile he could muster, dredging up what he imagined a brotherly greeting might sound like. "Harald! If I could borrow my lovely sister-in-law for a moment…"

Lydia gave him a mutinous glare, shaking her head infinitesimally.

But Harald didn't betray even a second of surprise. He grinned back at Ruben as naturally as if they were old friends, as if they really were family instead of just blood. "Of course, little brother! Don't keep her too long, will you?" He bent to kiss Lydia's cheek, lingering for a few endless seconds. Then he looked up and met Ruben's eyes, his own cold, the threat there clear. "You know I hate to be without her."

The assembled crowd cooed as if this were the most adorable thing they'd ever heard. Ruben tried not to look as sickened as he felt and swept an arm around Lydia's shoulders, steering her away.

"What are you doing?" She muttered under her breath, a smile pinned to her face. "I told you, I cannot—"

"You will," Ruben said. "You will."

HE PULLED out his phone as he and Lydia hurried through the halls, sending a quick text to Hans. A signal.

The reply was swift.

We're ready.

Ruben slid his phone into his pocket as they approached the door to the music room. He turned to Lydia and said, "I can't take you in here without warning you. Harald—"

She held up a hand. Sometime over the last few minutes, she'd become cold and remote. Now her gaze was flinty, her jaw hard as stone. She said, "Which one of my daughters is in this room?"

He met her eyes as he said, "Ella."

She swallowed. Nodded. Took a deep breath, and opened the door.

Cherry and Ella had been sitting side by side on the little piano stool. At the sight of her mother, Ella disentangled herself from Cherry's voluminous skirts and ran across the room, her tears starting all over again. "I wasn't supposed to tell," she sobbed.

"Shh." Lydia swept her daughter into her arms, her tiny figure suddenly seeming ten feet tall. "It is good. You must always tell. We talked about this, remember? No matter what anyone says, you must always tell."

Ruben left mother and child for a moment, turning to Cherry. Letting her see every inch of his gratitude for the things she'd done tonight.

She stood, and he pulled her into a hug, giving himself a few blissful seconds to melt into her softness, her sweet, cinnamon scent. She rubbed a soothing hand across his shoulder, and only then did he notice the tension in his own muscles, the pounding in his head. Only then did he realise how drained his fury had left him.

She whispered into his ear, "Everything will be fine. This is the darkest moment. From this point on, everything will be fine."

He wished he could believe that. But just hearing the words from her lips gave him strength.

He pressed a kiss to her forehead before turning back to Lydia. She was watching him over Ella's head, her gaze hard.

"Tonight," he said.

She nodded. "I should've listened to you."

"No. Your priority was your daughters, just as it is now. Things have changed. We change with them. Put Ella to bed, and go back to the ballroom."

She stiffened. "I can't—"

"You have to. Go to him. Smile at him. We will too. Retire early, tonight, and ready the children. Hans will come to get you."

She nodded slowly. But then she asked, as if she couldn't help herself: "Are you *sure*? Are you sure this will work?"

"No," Ruben said. "But I am sure that one way or another, you're getting out of here tonight. No matter what I have to do."

CHAPTER THIRTY

Cherry's dress was gorgeous, but in hindsight, she should've chosen something slightly less... dramatic.

She watched Lydia settle her children into the back of the waiting Hummer. First Ella, then Hilde, who had been carried from the palace asleep in Hans's arms.

"Don't worry," Demi said, placing a hand on Cherry's shoulder. She had to reach up to do it, but she still managed to sound like a parent comforting her child. "We've planned everything. Nothing will go wrong, *inshallah*."

Cherry exhaled, her breath condensing in the midnight air. "I'd feel a lot better about this if I'd seen you at some point in the last week."

"Oh, I was around," Demi smiled. Her gaze trailed to Hans, as if by habit.

Cherry managed to spare a smile of her own. "I don't doubt it."

The children already settled, Lydia climbed into the car. Ruben appeared, a few familiar members of his guard trailing behind him.

"We're ready," he said. "We'll go round to the front entrance and slide in with all the cars leaving tonight. He shouldn't notice we're gone until we reach the airport."

With a nod, Demi stepped forward and slid into the passenger seat. Hans walked round to the other side of the car, leaving Cherry alone with her prince.

Prince no longer, after tonight.

Ruben reached out to her. "Let's go."

She put her hand in his. And that was when it all fell apart.

"HOW *SWEET*," Harald said.

His voice rang out through the darkness. And then the floodlights drowned Ruben in their bright, white glow, blinding him for a second. He squeezed Cherry's hand, and felt her squeeze back.

Then he turned around to face his brother.

Harald stood at the entrance to the basement garage they'd parked in front of. He was flanked by a dozen members of the royal guard, dressed in Hans's all-black uniform. They shared his intimidatingly blank expressions too, but theirs were made truly terrifying by the dead look in their eyes.

"You have your boys, little brother." Harald held up his hands, indicating the men behind him. "And I have mine."

Ruben steeled himself. Calculated all the possibilities in his mind. His brother's men were armed, but they couldn't get away with any real damage, could they? Harald wouldn't risk the complications. Of course, if he did, Lydia and the girls would be safe. They were already in the car, an official royal vehicle, bulletproof.

But Cherry was right here.

"Harald," Ruben said, his voice low. "We can discuss this sensibly, can't we?"

"Discuss *what*?" Harald hissed. "You kidnapping my wife? My heirs?"

"I'm just taking the girls on a trip. They don't want to see you right now." Ruben gentled his tone. "You understand, Ella's in shock. Lydia's—"

"Do you think I'm an idiot?" Harald's eyes bulged as he spat out the words, fury blooming red beneath his pale skin. He stepped forwards, across the tarmac, his hand's fisted at his sides. He was still wearing the gold-braided dress uniform he preferred for formal engagements, military medals pinned to his chest. None of which he'd earned.

But then, he hadn't had the chance to. By the time he came of age, the throne was essentially his.

"If you take her," Harald said, "she'll never come back." For a moment, Ruben thought that his brother might actually miss his wife. But then Harald cried out, his voice ragged with panic, "What will people think of me?"

Cherry's voice rang out before Ruben could even open his mouth. "They'll suspect what we already know. That you are a weak, pathetic man who hits his own *children*—"

Ruben pulled her closer to him, cutting off her words, angling his own body in front of hers. "Stop," he whispered tightly. "You don't know what he's going to do."

"I don't care," she hissed. "The girls are in the car. Tell Hans to leave. He won't follow them with all those witnesses." Even now, from behind the palace's jutting East Wing, they could hear the chatter and laughter of guests, the engines starting as people piled into their cars and limousines. It would take seconds to reach the safety of the crowd, if Hans put his foot down.

Which would leave Cherry here to face his brother's wrath, and Ruben with nothing but his bare hands to protect them both. All his life he had stormed into situations based on nothing but instinct, passion, sheer bloody-mindedness. He couldn't do that anymore.

"Harald," he shouted across the tarmac. "You must realise you've gone too far. This is ridiculous. I'll take the girls home with me, just for a while, and it'll all blow over. Be reasonable, will you?"

His brother scowled at that, as Ruben had expected. "You presume to dictate to *me*? You, the son of a gutter-born whore!" He spat out the familiar words, his voice rising as he got into the swing of things. Ruben didn't bother to listen. He knew the gist. *Your very existence is a stain on the great history of this proud nation, your mother, the seductress,* destroyed *our lives, blah blah fucking blah.*

As his brother ranted and raved, throwing out the words that had once torn Ruben apart, Ruben turned his head slightly to catch Cherry's eye. He kept his lips as still as he could, and murmured under his breath, "Phone in my pocket."

Cherry looked at him as if he'd lost his mind. But evidently she decided to trust him anyway, because her hand slid into his left pocket and then his right, her movements hidden by her skirts. She found the phone and looked up at him, widening her eyes in question. *What now?*

"Are you *listening to me*?" Harald roared, tearing at the sash across his waist, his neatly slicked-back hair falling over his sweaty brow.

Ruben said, "Kathryn."

"*What*?" Harald hissed.

"I said, yes. I'm listening." He squeezed Cherry's hand. Hard. Hoped she got the message. "But I think it's time you listened, Harald." He took a deep breath. Prayed to every god he could think of that somehow, this would work. And then he began.

"When our parents died, you and Sophronia and I, we were all alone together. We should have been a comfort to each other. I realise that you hated my mother, that you were angry with Father for throwing everything away for a love you couldn't understand. I get it. I really fucking do. But you didn't have to take that out on me, Harald. I was just a child, and you did your best to break me. Do you know how fucked up I was, the day I left this place? How long it took me to stop hating myself? Too long.

"But I got better. I figured out how to be myself, instead of someone else's punching bag. And I swore that no matter what you did, no matter how much I despised you, I would never give up the one thing you swore I didn't deserve. I would never let you push me out of this family.

"But you know what? This place is poison. The family fucking name, the royal fucking household, is poison. I keep waiting for you to change the way I have, for you to become a better person, but that's never going to happen, is it? Because this isn't about our parents, and this isn't about who I am or anything I've done. This is about you. You're the problem. You can't stop hurting people. You hurt Lydia, who loves you—I have no idea why, but she does. Or at least, she did. But you couldn't stop with her. You hit your own fucking kid, Harald. Ella is thirteen years old. She's your *daughter*.

"What kind of so-called king preys on his own family that way? You're so obsessed with titles and power, and what everybody thinks... What if the man you *really* are was exposed to the world? What would you do?"

Harald stood before them, his face twisted into a sneer. "Very philosophical, Ruben. I'm utterly shamed. *So* embarrassed. Now get my wife out of that fucking car, before one of my boys loses control of his weapon and shoots your darling fiancée."

Cherry brought a hand down on Ruben's shoulder even as he started to react, his vision blurring, his world a haze of red. She dug her nails into his flesh, hard. "Stop," she whispered. And then she pushed the phone into his hand.

He looked down at the screen, and relief flooded through him.

There was a little red light blinking in the left corner, next to the words: **LIVE STREAM.**

Ruben faced the king with a smile, holding the phone up between them.

"Well, would you look at that," he called. "It seems everyone does know."

"Know what?" Harald demanded.

"Who you really are." Ruben tossed the phone across the tarmac, watching as his brother snatched it out of the air and looked at the screen.

The way his eyes widened, frantic and afraid, was almost the sweetest sight of Ruben's life.

Almost.

"Tell me," Ruben said. "Can you see how many people are listening right now?"

Harald looked up, his face slack. "The number... the number keeps changing."

"Ah, that means people are still watching. I'm not great with social media, but I think that video stays up for the next 24 hours. Plus, you know, it's still—"

Harald threw the phone against the tarmac. He released an unearthly scream, stamping on the device again and again, his movements vicious and brutal. The men standing behind him began to mutter amongst themselves, watching him warily, as if wondering whether they should take action. When he threw himself to his knees and began punching the phone, smashing his fists against the ground, Ruben backed away, towards the waiting car.

"Go," he said to Cherry, keeping his eyes on Harald.

"But—"

"I'm coming. But I'm not about to turn my back on him. *Go.*"

To his relief she went. He heard the swish of her skirts as she stuffed them through the car door. And then, with halting, backwards steps, he reached the car himself.

Cherry's hands guided him in. He didn't tear his eyes from his brother, a ragged mess screaming at shards of glass and plastic on the ground.

Not until Cherry shut the door and shouted, "Hans!"

The engine roared. And just like that, they were away.

CHAPTER THIRTY-ONE

"**A**gathe!" Cherry couldn't hold back her grin as she caught sight of the old woman, sitting patiently at the back of Ruben's jet. There was a familiar, plastic pet carrier in her lap. "You brought Whiskey!"

"Hello, *min kære*. Of course I did! And look at you, so beautiful this evening."

Cherry patted awkwardly at her hair. The ton of enormous hair grips that had been used to pin it into place were mostly gone. It sprang out around her head like a cloud. "Thanks, Agathe."

"You are welcome." The old woman's tired face lit up as Lydia appeared, leading Ella onto the plane. Ruben followed behind, Hilde in his arms. That child could truly sleep through anything. Cherry was rather impressed. "Children," Agathe whispered happily. "How wonderful! We will have an excellent time."

"Right..." It occurred to Cherry that she had no idea where they were going. A private jet and a hell of a lot of money were one thing, but she didn't even know if Agathe had a passport. Unless Helgmøre was part of the European Union. How did that work, again? Free movement, or something like that?

Demi would know, for sure. Cherry scouted the narrow space for her friend's reassuring presence and found... nothing. There was Lydia, strapping the sleeping Hilde into a seat, and Ruben having a very intense talk with Ella, but no sign of Demi.

Well, there weren't many places to hide on a plane. "One second, Agathe," she murmured. "I just need to ask Demetria something..." With a smile, Cherry headed for the front of the jet.

When she pushed aside the flight deck's thick, cream curtain, the first thing she saw was Demi, head bowed, standing before the cockpit's myriad controls. Then she looked down and saw Hans kneeling at Demi's feet.

The bodyguard's massive arms were wrapped around Demi's waist, his face buried against her stomach. Demetria ran a soothing hand over his golden hair. "It's okay," she was whispering. "I'm fine. Everyone's fine. Hans, you have to get up."

Cherry slowly slid the curtain back into place.

"What are you grinning at?"

She nearly jumped out of her skin at the sound of Ruben's voice. "Quiet," she hissed, tugging him away from the cockpit. Usually, when she tried to move him around, he had the grace to pretend it was working. This time, though, he wouldn't budge. Cherry watched in horror as, with a teasing smile on his face, he reached for the curtain.

"Ruben, don't—"

Too late. *Oops.*

Hans and Demi leapt apart, and Cherry stifled a sigh. Oh, dear.

Ruben was staring at the pair as if he'd caught them practicing a satanic ritual. He spluttered uselessly for a second before choking out, "What on earth is going on?"

"Nothing," said Demi.

At precisely the same time, Hans said, "We're getting married."

Even Cherry coughed at that, but it was a pleased sort of cough. She'd been worried that the pair might never pull their heads out of their arses and get on with things. Clearly, she'd worried needlessly.

Demi kicked Hans in the shin with a gasp of outrage. "You are the bane of my existence."

"I love you too."

"Will you shut *up*?"

"Quiet!" Ruben demanded. Apparently, he'd regained his senses. The look of utter astonishment he'd worn just seconds ago was nowhere to be seen. He pinned a hard look on his best friend. "Are you marrying her or not?"

"Yes," Hans insisted.

Ruben looked to Demetria. "Did he ask you?"

She nodded mutely.

"Properly?"

"Um... Yes?"

"And you agreed."

Demi slapped her hands to her cheeks. "Will you stop? This is very embarrassing."

Ruben's face softened slightly. "I'm sorry," he said. "I just want to make sure you're okay."

Hans snorted. "Charming."

"Shut up. I wasn't talking to you."

Demi intervened before a real argument could break out. "Yes, I agreed," she said firmly. "I'm fine. Everything's fine. We're all fine! Now if you could just *go away*, Ruben, that would be wonderful." With those words, she strode towards the entryway and tugged the curtain back into place. Right in front of her boss's face.

Ruben blinked. For a moment, he looked slightly shell-shocked. But then his lips spread into a grin. He turned to Cherry with a look of elation of his face. "They're getting married!"

"Yes," she replied, biting back a smile. "It would appear so."

"I had no idea," he said. "God, he's my best friend and I had no idea. I can't believe he didn't tell me! I'm going to wring his bloody neck..." He trailed off with a frown. "You don't seem surprised. Why aren't you surprised?"

Cherry rolled her eyes. "I don't know. Put it down to my razor-sharp instincts, or something."

Ruben shook his head. His face softened, and suddenly, the narrow space between the cockpit and the rest of the jet seemed even smaller than before. His hands settled at her waist, his eyes raking over her face as if he'd never seen her before. "Cherry," he whispered.

She looked up at him, hypnotised. "Yes?"

He kissed her. Hard.

There was no delicacy, just desperation. And yet, it was still tender. Still loving. Still everything she needed.

By the time he let her go, they were both panting. He grinned at her, looking impossibly, painfully young. He said, "I love you so fucking much." Then he cupped her face in his hands and kissed her again.

Cherry forgot herself for a moment. It was quite difficult to concentrate when his tongue was caressing hers, his lips achingly gentle. But eventually, she pulled herself away, her cheeks burning.

"Stop that," she murmured. "Agathe's looking!"

"I highly doubt she's looking."

"She's in the room!"

"We're not in a room, sweetheart."

"Oh, bugger off. I love you too. Where are we going, by the way?"

A smile spread over his face, slow and sure and utterly gorgeous. "What did you just say?"

"Where are we going? Also, who's flying the plane? Because, no offence, but—"

He slid a hand into her hair. "You said you loved me."

"Well…" She rolled her eyes. "Yeah. Don't make a big thing of it."

"You, Cherry Neita, are the most baffling person I've ever met," he laughed. But he pulled her in for yet another kiss, and this time, she didn't stop him.

CHAPTER THIRTY-TWO

Magz: Can you hear anything?

Cherry looked warily towards the living room door. Her father's study was just down the hall. Certainly close enough to hear him cussing Ruben out. And yet…

Cherry: Nothing. Quiet as a mouse.

Magz: What's Mum doing?

Petra Neita was sitting in the corner of the living room on her favourite sofa, crocheting. *What* she was crocheting, Cherry had no idea, but the fact that she was doing it at all seemed… vaguely ominous.

Cherry: She's crocheting

Magz: Since when does Mum crochet?

Cherry: Apparently Ms. Jeanne from next door has started a club. They all choose something to crochet and spend a month putting it together. And then they go to Ms. Jeanne's house and get wasted and try on each other's shitty hats. Or something.

Magz: Okay, but is she talking to you?

Cherry: No. She's crocheting.

Magz: I'm not sure if that's good or bad.

Cherry wasn't either. She'd never brought a boy home. Her sister had never brought a girl home. They had no point of reference for this sort of thing.

Magz: I hope Dad doesn't bite his head off.

Magz: But, all things considered, I think he might.

Because the video they'd recorded in icy terror had turned into a scandal that shook the world—or at least most of western Europe. When the recording of Ruben's speech and Harald's guilt reached her parent's living room via BBC news, Cherry had received a rather concerned phone call from dear old Mum and Dad.

If *concerned* meant *suspicious, furious,* and *demanding an explanation.*

So she'd come clean. About everything. It had just come pouring out, really.

But that was—what, three months ago, now? Things had settled down a little since then.

Ruben was learning to cope with the media speculation, along with the lasting effects of his upbringing. And this time, he was doing so with professional help. Apparently he, Ella and Lydia had made a pact: if they talked to a nice doctor about their feelings, he would too.

Cherry thought it was going rather well.

Cherry herself had spent the past months organising Hans and Demi's upcoming wedding, and that was going well too. Although, Demi was being *very* uncooperative about the dress. What she had against silk trains, Cherry would never know.

And, in between all that, Cherry had made regular visits home. Just to reassure her parents that she was A-okay and not... you know, trapped in a false engagement with a foreign prince to pay for her sister's degree, or anything like that.

But this was the first time Ruben had joined her on one of those visits. Not that he hadn't *wanted* to come. Only, after the things her father had said about him over the phone, Cherry was slightly hesitant to put them in a room together.

Magz: Where are you? What's happening? Did Dad kill your boyfriend? Cuz if so RIP, he was cute or whateva.

Cherry: Has anyone ever told you that you're really annoying?

Magz: You, every day since my birth. Jealousy is a disease, sis.

Cherry was hunting down the appropriate emojis for her response when her mother spoke over the soft hum of the TV.

"So," Petra said, her eyes still on her crochet hook. "That's your gentleman friend, then?"

This was Petra's first mention of Ruben since he'd arrived at the house with Cherry almost an hour before. Cherry took the odd timing in stride. Her mother liked to unnerve people.

"Yes. That's him." She swiped her palms against the front of her jeans. They felt suddenly clammy.

"*Mm.*" Petra said. She imbued that single syllable with a wealth of meaning that Cherry could not begin to decipher, but was slightly worried by. "He sort out his family problem?"

"Yes," Cherry said, for what felt like the thousandth time. "He and his family have been granted indefinite leave to remain."

Petra looked over the top of her silver reading glasses. "His poor sister all good?"

Cherry didn't bother to say that Lydia was Ruben's sister-in-law, or that soon she wouldn't even be that, once her divorce went through. It didn't seem pertinent. "Yes. She's doing quite well. So are the children."

Petra nodded, her lips pursed. She had dimples rather like Cherry's, but they were no indication of good will.

"Mum, could you stop being all mysterious and just tell me if you like him or not?"

Petra looked up at her daughter in apparent surprise. "Why wouldn't I like him?"

"Um..." Cherry floundered. "I don't know. You weren't very happy when you found out about... the engagement."

"The *fake* engagement," Petra corrected with a sniff. "*He* isn't my own blood who lied to me and disappeared out the country without warning! Why wouldn't I like *him*?"

Cherry sighed. "Would you like me to apologise again?"

Petra snipped off the end of her yarn. "It couldn't hurt, Cherry Pop. Keep going 'til I tell you to stop." She flicked her gaze over to her daughter, a slight smile tugging at the corners of her lips. "And come over here. Sit by me. I want another look at that ring."

Just as Cherry settled down beside her mother, the door to the study finally opened.

It took her a moment to realise that the voices floating down the hall were raised in friendly exuberance rather than disagreement. Cherry pressed a hand to her chest and breathed out a sigh of relief.

"We must cycle. Do you cycle, Ruben?"

"Not really, Sir, but I can. I'd like that."

"Excellent, excellent. I cycle every morning. Good for my blood pressure, doctor says." As always, David Neita's voice entered the room before he did. Ruben stepped in first, meeting Cherry's eyes with a grin. She knew by the look on his face that things had gone well. Then she looked at her dad's face and realised things had gone *really* well. As soft-hearted as he was on the inside, his expression tended to hover somewhere between vague displeasure and pained annoyance, unless he was in an extremely good mood.

Right now, he was looking positively joyful. What on earth had Ruben said to him?

Petra set her crocheting aside and clapped her hands. "Well! Now you two are done, I'll set the table. Come, Cherry, pour the drinks for me."

"Coming." Before she followed her mother into the kitchen, Cherry pulled out her phone and replied to Maggie.

Cherry: All good. Dad seems to like him???

Magz: This one's a real prince charming ;-)

RUBEN WAS no stranger to high-pressure situations, but meeting Cherry's parents had taken at least five years off his life.

Still, it was over now. And nothing had gone wrong. In fact, he thought, as he slid into the driver's seat of his new BMW, things had gone pretty damn right.

Cherry was in the passenger seat, fussing with her hair in the visor mirror. It was late, but there was still some light in the sky. Enough to cast shadows over the soft planes of her face, the curves of her lips, her cheeks.

"You're so beautiful," he whispered.

She turned to face him with a smile. Her lips were bubblegum pink. He'd spent the whole day wanting to find out if she tasted as good as she looked. But he wasn't about to give in to that temptation. Not now. He had something important to say, and if he didn't get the words out while he was still on a high, who knew when he'd find the courage.

"You're quite pretty yourself," she said. "You clean up well, Mr. Ambjørn."

He'd never get tired of hearing that name. It really was his now, and it suited him better than his title ever had. Especially because it was who he'd been when they'd first met—or who he'd been trying to be. It had taken Cherry for him to finally become that man. A man who was truly free.

He took her hand in his. Her left hand, where his mother's ring gleamed on her fourth finger. Neither of them had mentioned it over the last few months, in the chaos of adjusting to a new life, weathering the media attention. But every morning, when they woke up in Cherry's flat holding hands, he felt the stones pressing against his fingers.

"When I gave you this," he said, "I was in love with you." He brought her hand up to his lips, kissed it softly. "I'd never been in love before. I thought the way I felt then was impossible to beat. That my heart couldn't bear anything more intense. But I was wrong.

"Every day I spend with you, my love grows. I go to sleep thinking I can't possibly need you more than I do in that moment. But every morning, without fail, I wake up and see you and fall all over again, harder every time. I love it. I love you. And I never want to be without you, Cherry. Not ever. I've given you the ring, I've paraded you in front of family and strangers as my fiancée, but I've never really asked you this before. So I'm asking now."

He took a breath, and it felt like the first one he'd taken since starting this speech. His eyes were focused on the ring, *his* ring, on her finger. She hadn't taken it off, and that meant something. It had to.

"Cherry Neita," he said, and wondered if she could hear his voice shaking, or if it was all in his head. "I have waited my whole life for you." He forced himself to look up, to meet her gaze as he asked, "Will you marry me?"

Her face broke into a smile. Of all the smiles he'd seen on this brilliant woman's face, *his* woman's face, this was the sweetest. Tears swam in her deep brown eyes, but she grinned helplessly, without restraint, joyous as the sun.

"Yes," she said, and her voice was shaking too. "Oh, my God, yes." She grabbed the back of his head and pulled him forward, kissing him with reckless passion, still smiling. It was probably the most awkward kiss they'd ever had, teary and laughing with teeth catching teeth, and he'd never been happier.

"Oh, Lord," she giggled. "Did you tell my dad about this?"

Ruben shrugged, biting back a smirk. "I may have begged his daughter's hand in marriage..."

"No wonder he likes you so much! Jesus, Ruben, what year is it?"

He pressed a kiss to her nose. "The year I marry the love of my life without her father scowling at me through the service."

She snorted. "You're impossible."

"That's why you like me so much."

Cherry cupped a hand against his jaw. "No," she said, her voice soft. "That's why I love you."

EPILOGUE

Ruben was halfway through an email to the Tackle It Foundation when he heard the front door slam. Since this sound *wasn't* followed by panicked footsteps racing toward the living room, he assumed it wasn't Demi or Hans using their emergency key. Which meant it was Cherry.

Ruben checked his watch. She'd been gone for less than two hours. Bad sign.

"Sweetheart?" he called, setting aside his laptop and standing up in the cool shadows of the living room. It was hot—hotter than it had any right to be in May—and he'd closed all the shutters and turned on the aircon, even though his lovely wife insisted no-one in the UK had air-conditioning and called him feckless Eurotrash for destroying the planet.

Usually, he might listen to her. But right now, 'keeping the house perfect for Cherry' came marginally higher than 'always listening to Cherry' on his list of priorities.

His wife appeared in the living room doorway, one hand supporting her back, the other cradling the pregnant belly that had caused Ruben's recent shift in mindset. There was a scowl on her pretty face, her curls were pulled back into a no-nonsense bun, and for once, she'd gone without her usual flawless makeup. He tried, for dignity's sake, not to go on and on about how beautiful Cherry was. It seemed excessive, when he'd already waxed lyrical over her this morning.

"Remind me," she said as Ruben rushed over to her.

"Remind you that…?"

"That murder is wrong."

He swallowed a laugh as he took her in his arms. "You're very beautiful when you're feeling violent." Oops. Oh, well. Ruben was starting to suspect that dignity had no place in a marriage anyway. Love, he'd learned over these last few years, was quite alarmingly silly. "I take it shopping didn't go well?"

Cherry's sister was home for the summer. Maggie, along with their mother, had whisked Cherry away that morning to shop for pushchairs and prams. Because, apparently, the two things were not the same.

"They *talked*," Cherry said gloomily.

"Oh no," Ruben said dutifully, tugging her as subtly as possible in the direction of the staircase. If he kept this conversation going, he could have her in bed before she even noticed they'd moved. That way, there'd be no arguments about how she wasn't tired at all—false—and how pregnancy didn't make her a china doll—technically true, and yet, it wasn't a walk in the park, either.

"You usually enjoy talking," he went on, "so I assume that, in this case, they talked *too* much?"

She huffed as they meandered up the stairs. "*Yes*. It was baby this and baby that, and did I have a breast pump yet, and did we have an emergency hospital bag—I mean, really. I'm barely 37 weeks."

"Indeed," said Ruben, who had made up three emergency bags and hidden one in the bedroom, one in the coat cupboard, and one in the pantry by the back door.

"I just can't think when they get going, I really can't. I had a list, you know, of pushchairs I wanted to look at. And did they respect the list? Did they fuck. We puttered all over the place with no regard for order. Mum called me uptight. Can you believe that? *Me*?"

"Hmm," Ruben murmured. It was as noncommittal a sound as he could muster. They entered the master bedroom and he lowered Cherry onto the bed, propping her comfortably against the small mountain of pillows she required these days.

"What does that mean?" she demanded. "*Hmm*?"

He offered his most charming smile. "Nothing, my dearest, sweetest, loveliest one."

"Oh, cut the shit, Ambjørn. *What*?"

Avoiding his wife's narrowed gaze, Ruben pressed a hand to her stomach—not because he held any illusions about his ability to distract her, but because he loved doing it. Beneath the soft cotton of her sundress, her belly was round and firm. Back when they'd realised Cherry was pregnant, she hadn't been showing at all. He'd sunk to his knees and pressed his forehead to her unchanged stomach, awed and terrified.

It seemed like, with every month she grew, the terror faded just a little bit. Now, he was barely scared at all.

"Ruben?" she asked softly, and he realised he'd drifted off, eyes on her bump and mind elsewhere. "Are you okay?" Cherry's irritation had vanished, her dark eyes careful and concerned as she laid a hand over his.

It hurt him—hurt him almost physically—to remember the first time they'd ever discussed children. How his own pain had caused hers in turn. But she understood, now, that he'd only ever feared fucking things up.

And he'd decided, with all the confidence this woman inspired in him, that he *would not* fuck up. He simply wouldn't. The choice, the determination, was enough to calm his pounding heart.

"I'm fine, sweetheart," Ruben murmured, squeezing her hand. "I promise." He'd always be fine with Cherry. He could face anything with her.

"Good," she said, a smile curving her gorgeous lips. "Now. What's all this *hmm* business about?"

Ruben rolled his eyes and went about the very important business of pulling up his wife's dress. "Well, your mother isn't entirely wrong. You *are* a bit… touchy, at the minute."

She gasped. "I can't believe you just said that!"

"Well," he winked, "you did ask." Cherry's clingy, grey dress rose from her ankles to her knees, then from her knees to her thighs, as he pulled. Another tug brought the hem up past her hips, revealing her plain, white underwear. How did plain, white underwear have the ability to make him hard in seconds?

It wasn't the underwear at all, he decided. Just her.

"Get off me, you horrible man. I cannot believe you're taking her side."

Ruben let go of the dress and rested his hands on her belly again. "Sorry. Ignore me. Your mother is wrong; you are the most laid-back woman I know, and the list should have been closely followed."

Cherry settled back against the pillows, looking pleased. "Quite right. Continue."

"Continue?"

"With the…" She waved a hand in the direction of her underwear.

Satisfaction shot through him, closely followed by arousal. He ran a finger along the elastic waistline and watched her shiver. "Don't think you can tell me what to do," he said, "just because you're in a delicate condition."

She smirked. "Delicate, am I? I suppose that means you should stop taking off my knickers and leave me alone."

Funny; Ruben had barely even noticed his hands tugging off the fabric. "Or," he said, as he slid them off completely and left her bare to him, "it means I should be extra, extra gentle when I suck on that pretty clit."

Cherry's eyes darkened with desire as she arched her back, sinking deeper into the pillows. "Oh," she said softly. "Yes. That."

"Good girl," he murmured, running slow hands over the rippled, velvet surface of her inner thighs. "God, you look so fucking perfect." Her dress shoved up over her swollen belly, her legs spread for him, her pussy plump and parted and glossy with arousal. Cherry was extra horny these days, and Ruben had decided worshipping her cunt every morning, afternoon and night was the very least he could do.

He pushed her thighs wider as he bent his head. "Hold your knees for me, baby." He wanted full access to his favourite fucking meal.

The breath rushed out of her as she complied, her heavy tits rising and falling as she panted. She was completely open to him now, her clit a fat little bead, her needy pussy begging for him. Ruben inhaled the sweet, sharp scent of her as he pressed his face against her sex.

"Oh, God," she gasped.

He groaned, hearing the raw, animal edge in his voice and unable to stop it. His cock was so hard it felt almost dangerous, like he could snap in two at any moment if he didn't get a taste of this woman. *His* woman. He nuzzled her softness for a second before sliding out his tongue to lick through her folds. Cherry's hips jerked when he made contact, pressing her wetness against his mouth. Fucking incredible. He grabbed handfuls of her arse to keep her there, completely exposed to him, and licked her again.

"*Ruben*—"

"What, baby?" As if he didn't know. He rubbed his tongue, slow and wet, over her clit, then sucked gently until she sobbed. "Tell me, Cherry. Good girls ask, or they don't get."

"I need—can you—" She broke off as he sucked her again. Her hips rolled as she moaned. Ruben felt the flood of her honey against his chin and growled. Released her clit so he could tongue her soft little hole, taste her arousal from the source. She was so sweet he almost passed out. He found himself humping the mattress, desperate for pressure against his aching cock.

"You want something inside you?" he murmured, when she still couldn't speak for gasping.

"Yes. God, yes."

He eased two fingers into the tight, wet heat of her cunt, arousal zipping up his spine at the way her channel tightened and released around him. "You going to come for me, sweetheart? Already? Greedy girl."

All she managed was a breathless sob in response.

"Come, then. Come all over my fucking face," he gritted out, and then he was sucking her clit again, swirling his tongue around that sweet little nub and fucking her with his fingers. Everything around him was Cherry—the soft, gasping sounds she made, the intoxicating scent of her, the taste. And the feel of her coming on his fingers, gushing into his palm, her clit pulsing under his tongue. Fuck yes, fuck yes, *fuck* yes, he loved this. He loved her. He loved his goddamn life, and he'd never thought he could. Not like this.

Cherry grabbed his hair as she rode out her orgasm, writhing and moaning like a goddess. When she was done, she lay limp, her eyes heavy-lidded and her smile lazy and perfect.

"Hmm…" she murmured dreamily.

Ruben arched a brow. "Hmm?"

"Kiss me."

"Always," he said softly, and crawled up the bed to lie down behind her, cradling her body against his. He kissed her throat, her jaw, and then, as she turned her head toward him, he took her mouth. The kiss was slow and deep and filthy. It went on for long, lazy minutes, until Cherry was wound-up and moaning again, until Ruben couldn't hold off any longer.

They had something of a routine going, these days. He used one hand to undo his belt and shove down his trousers, and then Cherry was there, grasping his hard cock and raising one leg. Guiding him inside her from behind. He felt the hot kiss of her cunt against his sensitive head—

And then she stiffened.

He pulled back slightly, his eyes opening. "Cherry?"

"Fuck," she breathed. But this wasn't a good *fuck*. It was a tight little release of air, a panicked wheeze that had Ruben's blood pressure spiking.

"Cherry," he repeated, sitting up and pushing her on to her back. "What's wrong? Talk to me."

"Fuck," she repeated, squeezing her eyes shut. Then she pressed a hand to her abdomen and choked out, "I think…"

"What?"

"Pretty sure I'm having a contraction. God, I *hope* it's a contraction. Wait." Her eyes shot open. "Aren't these supposed to get *worse*? Good Christ."

Ruben stared at her in silence, his brain frozen like an old Windows desktop. Contraction. Con…trac…tion… He knew that word. Sammentrækning. *Lort.* Åh, Gud i himlen.

"Baby." He said. "Baby. Is. Having. You are—"

"Ruben, darling," she said, her breaths evening out, her frown fading away. "If you're feeling up to it, now would be an excellent time for you to jump into action."

Yes. Yes. "Yes!" Ruben said, and jumped into action. Or rather, he jumped up from the bed. His brain kicked into gear again, faster than ever before. Contractions. Labour. Emergency bags. He was ready. "Okay," he said, sounding vaguely authoritative and impressively coherent. "Don't panic. Everything's under control. Let's just find your knickers, shall we?"

Also, he should probably put his dick away.

TWO WEEKS Later

Cherry forced herself to breathe slow and deep. She relaxed her face and snuggled into her pillow, careful to keep her movements languid and drowsy.

It didn't work.

"I know you're up." The quiet rasp of Ruben's voice sliced through the silence. "You don't have to pretend you're asleep."

With a rueful smile, Cherry opened her eyes.

Her husband was slouching in an armchair just a few feet away, illuminated by the orange glow of a nightlight. His eyes seemed darker in the weak light, shadows dancing along the muscled planes of his body. He was wearing nothing but his briefs, and a tired smile played across his full lips. He was beautiful. He was worn out. They both were. But she'd hoped to convince him she was getting *some* rest, at least.

No such luck. She never could fool him.

Cherry sat up, taking care not to disturb the healing stitches in her abdomen. Though she was careful, Ruben followed her movement with anxious eyes.

"Can't sleep?" he asked softly.

"It's okay. I don't want to miss the fun, anyway."

He shook his head ruefully. "We woke you up, didn't we?" He looked down at the baby cradled in his muscular arms, love suffusing his features. "Tell Mummy to go back to sleep. She needs her rest. She'll listen to you."

Cherry laughed softly. The man was absolutely silly for his daughter. And Cherry, knowing all the tender love hidden in her husband's reckless heart, wasn't remotely surprised.

But she was grateful. Grateful to have him, and to have their child. Grateful that he'd worked through the pain of his own past to take this leap with her. Grateful that he was brave and true and good.

"Come over here," she whispered. "Let me."

Ruben stood, easing the bottle of pre-pumped milk from their daughter's mouth. The newborn whimpered immediately, but she wasn't bereft for long. As he sat down on the bed, Ruben handed baby Freja to her mother. Cherry accepted the snuffling bundle with the same surreal feeling she'd had for the past two weeks. Freja latched on to her breast, and Cherry ran a finger along the plump curve of the baby's cheek.

"She's so soft," Cherry whispered, moving a hand to her daughter's sparse curls. She'd said it at least a hundred times since Freja's birth. But she was still in shock.

"And tiny," Ruben said, his voice achingly gentle. Cherry hadn't thought she could love him more than she already did. Then Freja had been born, and Ruben had turned into a worshipper at his own daughter's temple. He looked at the baby now with the kind of adoration some people waited a lifetime to see.

And her child would have it forever.

Cherry blinked the tears from her eyes, but it was too late. Ruben reached up to cup her cheek, his thumb smoothing back and forth over her skin.

"You okay?" he murmured.

She nodded. "I'm fine. I'm just... I'm so glad I married you."

His face lit up. The grin she'd fallen in love with danced into view, and he leaned forward to kiss her forehead. "I'm glad you married me, too. Because until I had it in writing, I wasn't sure I could hold on to you forever."

"Stop," she laughed, slapping his shoulder lightly. But then she looked up into his eyes, her tone serious. "You're stuck with me, Ruben Ambjørn. And you know it."

"Yeah," he admitted with a wink. "I do." He pressed his lips lightly against hers, his touch gentle. In his kiss she felt pure devotion. And she'd never get enough of it.

He pulled back slightly, rubbing his nose against hers until she giggled. Between them, Freja suckled away, burbling sleepily.

"I love you, Cherry," Ruben whispered, brushing his lips over her temple. His arm settled around her shoulders, warm and strong. "I love you so much."

She relaxed into him. Freja's soft, snuffling sounds became a lullaby, dragging her into drowsiness. "I love you, too," she murmured, the last word stretched into a yawn. "My very own Prince Charming." She closed her eyes, smiling at her own joke as sleep crept over her.

She almost didn't hear his reply. "Goodnight, Princess."

AUTHOR'S NOTE

I was supposed to be writing my dissertation when I dreamt up a character named Cherry Neita.

For every 1000 words of research I wrote, Cherry dragged 1000 words of prose from me. And she kept going until I'd finished her story. I did manage to finish the dissertation, too, but it took a lot longer than it should have.

I can't say I mind, though.

Some people might say that this story is about a black princess, but Cherry never actually becomes a princess. This is entirely due to my own bias; as much as I love Disney films, the reality of the monarchy has always made me uncomfortable. Probably because, y'know, colonialism and classism and all that good stuff.

Plus, as the characters of Harald and Sophronia show... all that glitters is not gold.

There are many domestic violence charities in the U.K., but there's one I've found especially helpful: https://www.womensaid.org.uk

If you or anyone you know is experiencing or has experienced domestic violence, or intimate partner violence, remember

Women's Aid. They have a free, 24 hour helpline, too: 0808 2000 247.

Stay safe.

Talia x

WANNA BET?

ANOTHER STEAMY ROMANCE FROM TALIA, OUT NOW.

Seven Years Ago

He saw her on a Monday.

He'd gone home for the weekend, to reassure Mum that he was still alive and hadn't lost any weight, or contracted any life-threatening illnesses, since last month.

But on Monday he returned to university, and went to his usual spot in the library—second floor for accounts and finance, at the back, by the windows that wouldn't open, just to *feel* like he was getting fresh air.

And there she was. In his seat, actually.

But of course, no-one owned library seats. Rahul just liked to stick to his routine.

He sat a few rows away and wasted an hour staring at her. At first, he told himself he was actually staring in longing at his seat, which she'd stolen, but that was a terrible lie. He knew from the start that he was staring at her.

And she was staring out of the window, her hair a dark cloud around her face. It was a pretty face. That wasn't why he stared, though.

He stared because she was sexy. Sexy like Marilyn Monroe or Sridevi. When she raised her arms in a languid, lazy stretch, it was sexy. When she wrapped a springy curl around her finger, it was sexy. Fuck, when she stared blankly out of the damn window, it was sexy. He'd never seen raw sex appeal in person. He told himself that studying it closely was academic.

The rest of the accounting floor seemed to agree. They were staring, too. But she didn't notice, or if she did, she must not care. Because she kept staring, kept shamelessly *not* studying, and kept being sexy. He suspected she couldn't help the last part.

"Jasmine Allen."

Rahul turned at the whisper, delivered with the kind of smug bite that suggested bad news was forthcoming. Luke Schnaigl, from his Financial Management seminar, had come to sit beside Rahul at some point in the last hour. He hadn't even bloody noticed.

Rahul raised his brows, leaned in close and whispered, "What?"

Whispering in a library was an Olympic sport. Trying to out-silence silence while *not* being silent took practice and dedication. Rahul was shit at it.

But Luke was okay. "The girl," he murmured. "That's Jasmine Allen."

Rahul's gaze slid back, inevitably, to her. *Jasmine*. Yes, he decided. It suited her. But Allen? He wasn't sure. Jasmine Khan would sound much better.

Not because Khan was his last name. He was just spitballing.

Since Luke seemed to expect a response, Rahul whispered, "She's pretty."

Jasmine Allen looked away from the window. She looked right at him. She smirked.

Rahul felt his cheeks heat. He raised a hand self-consciously to his hair, stopped himself, and pulled off his glasses instead. Now she was just a blur, and he couldn't see the sharp amusement in those dark, dancing eyes. But he could still feel her gaze. Fuck.

Beside him, Luke released a little huff of laughter. "Careful, mate. If you give her a reason, she'll eat you alive."

Rahul snorted, cleaning his glasses needlessly on the hem of his T-shirt. "What are you, the student body's fucking tour guide?"

"Just looking out for you. Everyone knows Jasmine Allen. But I know you don't get out much. Thought I should warn you."

Rahul's lips compressed. "Warn me about what?"

"She's a look-but-don't-touch kind of girl. For guys like us, anyway."

"And what does that mean?" Rahul put his glasses on again and was relieved to find that Jasmine had returned to the window. Relieved, and yet a little deflated. In the instant he'd had her gaze, he'd been as alive as he was embarrassed.

There was something powerful in her attention. He supposed that was part of the sex appeal.

"It means she's out of our league," Luke said dryly. "She's a genius. Her family's loaded. You know she's secretary of the law committee? You know she's a *cheerleader*? And," he added darkly, "she looks like *that*. I don't know what she's doing here. I bet it's part of an elaborate plot to get one of us to make a fool of ourselves."

Rahul raised his brows. "Why would she do that?"

"It's what they do," Luke said. "Those kinda girls."

Rahul stared at his friend—well, *acquaintance*—for a moment as he turned that logic over in his head. He made sure he was quite positive of his conclusion before he spoke. "You're a fucking twat."

Luke scowled, holding up his hands. "Piss off."

"Alright." Luke hadn't meant it literally, but Rahul gathered up his things. It wasn't hard; he'd barely unpacked anyway. Certainly hadn't got a head start on the term's assignments, as he'd intended. He shoved his stuff into his rucksack with no concern for order—for once—and made his way towards Jasmine Allen.

He had no idea what he was doing.

But she was looking at him again. Watching him. In fact, everyone in the vicinity was watching him, most with looks of dawning horror. He didn't care. He came to the table where she sat and took the end seat, leaving space between them. She studied him with a little smile.

"Hi," he said awkwardly.

She nodded. "Hello." She sounded like Joanna fucking Lumley. Posh, but like she'd just finished screaming someone's name.

What the fuck is wrong with you right now?

"I usually sit here," he said, words tripping over themselves. "And I... didn't like that table."

The tables were all identical.

But she murmured some sound of vague understanding and turned back to the window.

Rahul pulled out his work and tried to focus on his research assignment. For almost another hour, he failed. Then she left. It should've been a blessed occurrence, should've improved his concentration at least—but of course, it didn't.

He was surrounded by the ghost of some tropical scent that might belong to her. Why had she been on this floor, if she was a law student? And why had she stayed so long and only looked out of the window? And why the hell had he come to sit next to her?

He left the library woefully early. When he came back the next day, she was in his fucking seat.

On Tuesday, he sat beside her like a fool, imagining a taut string stretched between them. A thread of glittering tension that connected his furtive gaze and his pounding heart and her raw beauty. He knew he was the only one who felt it.

On Wednesday, he finally got some work done. Not as much as he'd like, but more than he'd managed over the last few days. He must be getting used to her. Growing immune to her magnetic pull. He'd just started on the second part of his assignment when the rain began.

"Ah, fuck," she said. "I didn't bring a jacket."

She was still staring out of the window, but she didn't sound as if she was talking to herself. So Rahul looked out of the window with her, at the insistent drizzle, and said, "You can have mine."

She looked at him, finally, a little smile teasing her lips. "You'd give me your coat?"

Rahul shrugged. He couldn't speak. Turned out, he wasn't used to her at all.

"What a gentleman," she murmured, her smile growing into a full-blown grin. Her cheeks plumped up and little lines fanned from her almond-shaped eyes. She had an adorable smile. That was unexpected.

Rahul smiled back. "I don't mind a bit of rain."

"That's good to know, but I can't take your coat." She said it with authority, in a tone that brooked no argument.

Still, Rahul hesitated to give in. His father had raised him to be a gentleman, whatever the hell that meant. So he said, "Look, I really don't mind—"

"But I can win it."

He blinked at the interruption. "Win it?"

"Yes." She turned back to the window and said, "Choose a raindrop."

"A raindrop?"

He watched as Jasmine leant forward. She put her finger over a fat drop dribbling on the outside of the glass. As it moved, her finger followed it. She had a dark, raised scar on the inside of her forearm, long and narrow. "Go on," she said. "Choose."

Feeling self-conscious, Rahul ignored the stares from the people around them. He got up to stand beside her and chose a drop at random.

She clucked her tongue. "That's higher than mine. Choose one about the same."

"For what purpose?"

She smiled up at him. "I like the way you talk. You should talk more."

He didn't point out that he'd had no reason or opportunity to talk to her before now. He didn't point out that they didn't know each other, so for all she knew, he might be the most talkative person in the world.

Instead he repeated, "For what purpose?"

"Your raindrop is your horse. The windowsill is the finish line. I bet your coat on my raindrop."

Gambling. Dad would smack him upside the head for even considering it. But it wasn't *really* gambling, because he intended to give her his coat no matter what. It was a game, a game that brought a smile to a pretty girl's face. He wanted that smile to stay. He wanted a reason to stand beside her. He chose a raindrop.

"So we start like this?" he asked, frowning slightly.

"Yes," she said. "This is how we begin."

WANNA BET?: IS AVAILABLE NOW

ABOUT THE AUTHOR

Talia Hibbert is a *USA Today* and *Wall Street Journal* bestselling author who lives in a bedroom full of books. Supposedly, there is a world beyond that room, but she has yet to drum up enough interest to investigate.

She writes steamy, diverse romance because she believes that people of marginalised identities need honest and positive representation. Her interests include makeup, junk food, and unnecessary sarcasm. Talia and her many books reside in the English Midlands.

And, as Talia would say... that's all, folks. Love and biscuits!

https://www.taliahibbert.com

CPSIA information can be obtained
at www.ICGtesting.com
Printed in the USA
LVHW031044200322
713908LV00006B/893

9 781913 651053